A WIFE
for
MR. DARCY

MARY LYDON SIMONSEN

sourcebooks
landmark

Published by Sourcebooks Landmark, an imprint of Sourcebooks, Inc.
P.O. Box 4410, Naperville, Illinois 60567-4410
(630) 961-3900
FAX: (630) 961-2168
www.sourcebooks.com

Library of Congress Cataloging-in-Publication Data

Simonsen, Mary Lydon.
A wife for Mr. Darcy / by Mary Lydon Simonsen.
   p. cm.
1. Darcy, Fitzwilliam (Fictitious character)—Fiction. 2. Bennet, Elizabeth (Fictitious character)—Fiction. 3. Social classes—England—Fiction. 4. Courtship—Fiction. 5. England—Fiction. I. Austen, Jane, 1775-1817. Pride and prejudice. II. Title. III. Title: Wife for Mister Darcy.
   PS3619.I56287W54 2011
   813'.6--dc22

                              2011004638

Printed and bound in the United States of America
SB 10 9 8 7 6 5 4 3 2 1

To my fellow Jane Austen fans at A Happy Assembly
who encouraged me to write this story

Chapter 1

WITH ALL PATHS TO Meryton muddied from recent rains, it was impossible for anyone at Longbourn to venture into the village without risking ruining shoes or soiling frocks, so all of the Bennets were at home. While Mrs. Bennet was in her bedchamber resting, Mr. Bennet kept to his library, successfully ignoring Mary's attempt to master a new piece on the pianoforte. In the parlor, Lydia and Kitty perused a magazine obtained from the circulating library showing the latest London fashions, and Lizzy was upstairs pinning up the hem on Jane's new dress. It was then that Mrs. Hill came to announce that Mr. Darcy was in the parlor and wished to speak to Miss Elizabeth.

"Mr. Darcy! Here to see me?" Lizzy looked at Jane with a puzzled expression. After their awful meeting at the assembly, she was hoping the gentleman would return to London and that she would never have to be in his company again.

"Yes, miss. The gentleman asked your father if he could have a word with you, and Mr. Bennet said he had no objection."

"What can he possibly want?" Jane asked.

"Perhaps he thinks I did not hear his insults regarding my beauty, or lack of it, and has come to tell me in person." Both sisters giggled, and when Jane offered to go downstairs with her sister, Lizzy said that she was not afraid of him and would go into the lion's den alone.

When Lizzy entered the parlor, she found Mr. Darcy lost in thought and staring out the window, so much so that he had not heard her come in.

"Mr. Darcy, I understand you wish to speak to me," she said, interrupting his reverie.

"Yes, I do, and I thank you for receiving me." He declined an offer of tea, explaining that his visit would be brief, but then said nothing. If it was to be a short visit, then why did he not begin? He obviously had a purpose in mind but was having difficulty finding the right words with which to express it.

"Miss Elizabeth, at the assembly, you overhead a remark I made in which I stated that I chose not to dance with you because you were tolerable but not handsome enough to tempt me. Even if the statement had been true, it was incredibly rude to have uttered it, and I have come to apologize."

Mr. Darcy's confession came as a complete surprise to Lizzy, but she now understood the reason for his struggle. He was not in the habit of admitting he had erred.

"Your apology is accepted, Mr. Darcy. I appreciate that you took the trouble to come to tell me in person that I am more than tolerable," Lizzy said, half laughing at his clumsy effort to repair any damage resulting from his comment.

Darcy winced at her response. "I can assure you that I find you to be much more than tolerable, Miss Elizabeth. You are a very handsome woman, and I might have had an opportunity to express such a sentiment if I had sought an introduction. However, I do not have the talent of conversing easily with those whom I have never seen before. I cannot appear to be interested in their concerns as others do, and I find I have little patience for the type of discourse one hears at these dances."

"What type of discourse is that, Mr. Darcy?"

"The usual banter about weather and roads and other such things that are of little interest to me," and leaning forward in his chair, he continued, "Whether it be Meryton or London, I hear the same conversations. A lady will comment on the number of couples in attendance at a dance, and the gentleman will respond by mentioning the size of the ballroom. And what, pray tell, do we learn from that exchange? One party is good with measurements, and the other can count."

Now Lizzy laughed openly. "Sir, you mistake the purpose of such an exchange. It is certainly not about the dimensions of the room or the number of couples. The parties are merely trying to sketch each other's character so that they might discover if this is a person they would like to get to know better. If that is the case, one can hope that another conversation about some weightier matter might follow in a quieter venue."

"But you are an intelligent woman. Do you not find the whole exercise to be tedious?"

"No, I do not, and may I add that you puzzle me. You tell me you are uncomfortable conversing with those with whom you are not acquainted, but then you complain about a lack of conversation. This puts me in mind of a gentleman I met at a card party. He said that he did not like the food and then grumbled that there was not enough of it."

"I realize that is a contradiction," he said, crossing and uncrossing his legs, indicating his discomfort.

"It is indeed. I take it that what you really want to do is to begin in the middle. Somehow, without benefit of introductions or the casual conversation that follows, you may come to know your party well enough to discuss what? The war with France? No matter how well acquainted you are with your party, you will have little success with such a topic in a ballroom or assembly hall. Those are subjects best reserved for dinner parties where you are not trying to speak above the dancers and musicians."

"I see," Darcy said, nodding his head in understanding. "You are recommending that if I wish to have a substantive conversation at some future date, then I must become better acquainted with my neighbors so that I might be invited to these more intimate venues. I must lay the foundation for weightier discussions by talking to Mr. Long about his purchase of a breeding pair of Border Leicester sheep, or I must give ear to Mrs. Long, who is unhappy with the quality of fabric being sold in the village. I am quite capable of conversing about sheep, as it is a frequent topic of discussion with my steward and tenants, but I am less sure about my ability to wax eloquent on the quality of calico and muslin."

Lizzy smiled. It was a pleasant surprise to know that the dour Mr. Darcy had a sense of humor.

"Mrs. Long has a daughter who lives in Kensington," Lizzy responded, "and has been complaining about the inferiority of goods in the village shops for as long as I can remember, so no one would think you rude if you did not engage her. Instead, may I suggest Sir William Lucas, a kind gentleman, who has recently been knighted at St. James's Palace? He would be happy to share his experience with you."

"I shall seek him out at the first opportunity."

"There *is* another difficulty, sir. By virtue of your rank, it is *you* who must initiate the conversation. No one will approach Mr. Darcy of Pemberley without being properly introduced."

"You know the name of my estate?"

"Such information is widely circulated as is the case whenever any single man comes into the neighborhood. Ladies must have dance partners, Mr. Darcy."

"I see. May I ask what else is said about me?"

Lizzy hesitated. Did Mr. Darcy really want to hear about the discussions in the village regarding the size of his fortune or, worse, that he was considered to be a most disagreeable man, completely lacking in the charm of his friend, Mr. Bingley?

"Your silence speaks for you, Miss Elizabeth, and it is not undeserved. But do you think it is possible to overcome a bad first impression?"

"Most definitely. A more satisfactory performance will replace the previous image, and it would reflect well on you in that you recognized where you fell short and..."

"...and that I was willing to make corrections," Darcy said, finishing her sentence. At that point he stood up. "The Bingleys and I have been invited to the home of Sir William Lucas. Will you be there, Miss Elizabeth?"

"Most definitely. Charlotte Lucas is my dearest friend."

"Then I shall look forward to having a conversation with you on a topic somewhere between the number of couples in the room and the wars on the Continent," and then he smiled, thanked Lizzy for receiving him, and took his leave.

After watching the gentleman ride down the lane, Jane asked her sister, "What are we to think about Mr. Darcy?"

Lizzy shook her head, confused by the whole visit. But some things *were* clearer. Mr. Darcy was more handsome than she had remembered and had eyes that were more green than gray, attractive legs, and a voice that was very pleasing to the ear, especially when he used it to say that she was handsome and intelligent. Because of these things, she found that her determination never to think well of him was faltering and that might not be a bad thing at all.

Chapter 2

IT WAS DURING THE ride from the assembly to Netherfield that Darcy had recognized the need to apologize to Miss Elizabeth Bennet. The carriage was barely out of sight of the assembly hall when Bingley had begun a litany of praise for all that he had experienced that evening. The food was delicious, the music lively, the men agreeable, and the ladies handsome, and of all those attractive ladies, the most beautiful was Miss Jane Bennet. Although Darcy found little to admire at the assembly, he had refrained from commenting as he had no wish to dampen his friend's recollections. His sisters were less generous and had used Darcy's comment that Miss Elizabeth was "not tolerable enough to tempt him to dance" to support their low opinion of their neighbors.

Darcy had been in ill humor the whole of the evening, and his unhappiness had been reflected in that thoughtless statement. He realized that if Bingley's sisters had overheard his remark, then others may have as well.

On the ride to Longbourn, Darcy had planned out exactly

what he would say. He would acknowledge that the remark may have given offense. He would make an apology, which she would accept, and he would leave. But that was not what had happened. Having never been in such an awkward situation before, he had been uncomfortable, so much so that he had actually repeated the offending remark. After laughing at his ineptitude, Miss Elizabeth had taken him to task for his contradictory statements regarding what conversations were appropriate in a ballroom.

Sitting across from her, he had noted a playfulness in her manner that indicated she was not in the least bit in awe of his rank, wealth, or connections. This interlude also provided an opportunity to truly and honestly appraise her beauty. Although her face lacked symmetry, she was quite pretty with expressive dark eyes that reflected her intelligence and curiosity, and her smile was a reward in itself. By the end of their visit, he found that he wished to know her better, and despite plans to return to London, Darcy decided to accept Sir William's invitation to come to his home.

Because Bingley was so eager to see Miss Bennet again, their party was one of the first to arrive at Lucas Lodge. In an attempt to soften the harsh impression he had left on those who had attended the assembly, Darcy joined Bingley in circulating about the room. In doing so, he learned that the Robinsons' best milk cow had mastitis, Mrs. Long was still unhappy with just about everything, a certain Miss Conyers was visiting relations in London, and on and on. But there was only so much goodwill he was willing to impart, and he had sought refuge in a corner of the room where Sir William lay in wait.

"Mr. Darcy, I noticed at the Meryton assembly that you are a fine dancer, and you and Miss Bingley gave a polished exhibition earlier this evening." Darcy acknowledged the compliment, but here was another of those pointless discussions for which he had so little patience. He would rather talk about Mr. Robinson's cow. But not wishing to offend anew, he appeared to be listening with great interest when Sir William announced that the Bennet family had arrived.

Once Bingley saw the Bennets, he nearly tripped over his feet in his efforts to cross a crowded room so that he might greet Miss Bennet. With her sister thus engaged, Miss Elizabeth walked toward Sir William and the gentleman from Derbyshire.

"Miss Elizabeth, we were just speaking of dancing. Mr. Darcy was commenting that it is an amusement appreciated by many cultures around the world, and with his quick wit, he noted that 'every savage can dance,'" a remark that caused Sir William to laugh heartily. He was clearly delighted to have such an august personage as Mr. Darcy as a guest in his home and thought that with his elevation to the knighthood, the presence of people of rank might be a less rare occurrence at Lucas Lodge.

"What did Mr. Darcy have to say, Sir William? Was he knowledgeable on the subject?" Lizzy asked. "I would not be surprised if he was as it is my experience that those who observe an activity have more to say about it than those actually performing it." Turning her attention to Mr. Darcy, she continued, "Although we do not have the grand settings of the London balls nor the finest musicians in the land, I believe you will not find us lacking in skill or enthusiasm."

"Once again you are correct, Miss Elizabeth, and as an observer rather than a participant at the assembly, I can testify that there was no lack of enthusiasm in the hall. In fact, the room could barely contain all the energy given off by the dancers."

Unsure if that was praise or censure, she looked at him with a quizzical expression that seemed to amuse him, and she was preparing to question him about his comment when Sir William suggested that they dance. "Mr. Darcy, considering the inducement, you cannot refuse when so much beauty is before you."

"I would be honored, Miss Elizabeth."

Lizzy would have accepted him, but at that moment, Mary had given in to Lydia and Kitty's pleas to play a jig, and after the first chords were struck, numerous guests flocked to the small dance floor.

"That is very kind, sir, but as you can see there is little room for another couple, but hopefully you will ask again."

With Sir William believing he had brought the pair together, he departed in search of the few guests who might not have heard his story of being knighted at St. James's Palace, leaving the couple to make their own way. And then there was the silence Mr. Darcy dreaded. These pregnant pauses were a particular irritant to him because he was ill-equipped to fill them.

"I was beginning to think you might not come, Miss Elizabeth."

"Yes, I can imagine. Since you are new to the neighborhood, you do not know our family's history. We are *always* late. You have no idea of the complexities of having five daughters and their mother leave a house all at the same time."

"I may have some idea of your situation as my sister recently came out into society. I must say armies have marched with fewer provisions and less fanfare than that required of a young lady making her debut."

And then he smiled, and Lizzy felt her heart flutter. Alas,

Mr. Darcy was someone who was far beyond her reach. She would have to be grateful for just the one dance. Unfortunately, he did not ask again.

Although Mr. Darcy did not claim his dance, the evening passed agreeably. Lizzy had found partners in John Lucas, Colonel Forster, and Captain Denny, and after dancing with Mrs. Hurst and Miss Long, Mr. Darcy had joined Charlotte and Lizzy, who were urging the colonel to host a ball in Meryton. When Lizzy noticed that Mr. Darcy was listening to their conversation, she asked, "Will you add your support to my efforts, Mr. Darcy?"

"That is unnecessary as you expressed yourself with great energy. The subject of dancing always renders a lady eloquent."

"That is because there are few things I enjoy as much as dancing, sir."

"Would teasing be among the few?" he asked.

"Only when the person being teased has little experience with it."

Sensing the levity in their exchange, Charlotte took Lizzy's hand and explained that she was leading her friend to the pianoforte so that she might exhibit her talents. "It is her turn to be teased, Mr. Darcy."

"If that is the case, then I shall not move from this spot."

Lizzy was not a proficient, but the delight she experienced in playing was evident, and her performance merited a request for another. While she performed her second piece, Miss Bingley came and stood next to Mr. Darcy, and he felt as if a sinister shadow had darkened his path.

"Is it not insupportable that we must pass an evening in such society because my brother insists on having a house in the country?" The whine continued at length. She complained of the noise, the heat, the lack of fashion, and the self-importance of the guests.

"My mind was more agreeably engaged, Miss Bingley. I was reflecting on the pleasure a pair of fine eyes in the face of a pretty woman can bestow, as is the case with Miss Elizabeth Bennet."

Miss Elizabeth Bennet! He could not be serious! If she had fine eyes, then that was the only thing that was attractive about her. Her clothes were out of fashion, and who did her hair? And what of her family?

"I agree with you, Mr. Darcy. Other than Miss Jane Bennet, Miss Elizabeth is certainly the most attractive of the Bennet daughters, and I am sure you were entertained by Miss Mary Bennet's exhibition on the pianoforte. I do not recall if you were introduced at the assembly to the younger sisters, but they are certainly enthusiastic in dancing with all of the young officers. Then there is their mother, Mrs. Bennet, who has so much to say and is so easily heard saying it."

"None of which affects my admiration of Miss Elizabeth's eyes," he answered. Nevertheless, he found it unfortunate that the lady had such a family, especially in light of Bingley's attentions to her sister. Caroline might be right. This may not be the best place for a young man, such as Charles, whose heart was easily touched, and because of that, their continued stay in Hertfordshire would require more thought.

Chapter 3

SHORTLY AFTER THE GATHERING at Lucas Lodge, Mr. Darcy left Hertfordshire for London to visit with his sister. He was glad to be away from Netherfield Park. Although he enjoyed Bingley's company, he could not say the same for his sisters and brother-in-law. With the exception of Jane Bennet, whom they were damning with faint praise, they found nothing to admire and considered the local society to be inferior in every way. Darcy could not agree to such a general statement, but as a rule, society in the country varied little from one month to another, which was to be expected. Anything new was immediately seized upon and shared, including what had happened at Lucas Lodge. While he was listening to Miss Elizabeth play on the pianoforte, Lady Lucas had made a remark to Mrs. Long concerning how much attention he had paid Elizabeth. As a result, he had decided not to fuel the fire by dancing with her, which was unfortunate because she was a skilled dancer and pleasant company. In addition to visiting with his sister, Darcy had another purpose in going to London, and that was to begin a courtship with Miss Letitia Montford, an attractive lady of twenty-two years, and a granddaughter of an earl and, thus, his equal in rank. Because the Darcy estate was entailed away from the female line and Georgiana could not inherit, Darcy must have an heir, and for that he needed a wife.

As soon as his carriage pulled up in the front of the Darcy townhouse, Georgiana was out the door. She had not seen her brother in weeks. While he was in Hertfordshire with Bingley, she had been in the country staying with friends. Georgiana quickly brought Will up to date on what was happening in London. Some of the families who had spent the summer at their country estates had returned to town, among them Sir John Montford and his daughter.

"Miss Montford is truly lovely and has a most pleasant disposition," Georgiana began. "I twice invited her here for tea, and in return, I was invited to dinner. She is very accomplished. Her sketches are so well executed that they are prominently displayed in their drawing room, and she has a gift for painting tables which to my mind is unmatched. And did you know she speaks French *and* Italian?"

"I see you have decided that Miss Montford is to become my wife."

"I would never be so presumptuous as to tell you whom you should marry, but of all the ladies who earned your notice during the season, Miss Montford was clearly superior to all of them. If you were to ask my opinion on the subject, I would not hesitate to name Letitia."

"We shall see," Darcy said in an attempt to tamp down her enthusiasm. If he gave any indication that he agreed with her choice, Letitia Montford would be their only topic of conversation. "I will be in town for at least a week seeing to my business affairs before returning to the country to go shooting with Bingley, and I most certainly will call on Miss Montford. I assume your plans are unchanged and that your preference is to remain in town?"

"I have no wish to speak ill of anyone, but if you and Mr. Bingley are to spend all of your time shooting, that would mean I would have to spend all of my time with his sisters."

"I understand. You need say no more."

In the week that followed, Darcy spent a fair amount of time with Miss Montford and her family and friends. He found Letitia to be a lovely woman, who deserved the high praise she received for her many accomplishments. Her only flaw was that she was rather dull, and he was sure he would not have noticed just how lacking she was in any sense of irony or wit if it had not been for Elizabeth Bennet.

Elizabeth was unique to his experience. She liberally voiced her opinions but seemed unaware of the accompanying hazards, or maybe she didn't care. No matter. There was an excellent chance he would not see her again as he was determined to spend most of his time shooting and riding and had no intention of attending social events in the neighborhood. In ten days' time, he would return to London and begin a courtship with Miss Montford in earnest.

Fortunately, the approach to Netherfield did not require that he pass through the village of Meryton as he was sure its inhabitants would assign some romantic reason for his return. As he turned down the lane, his only thoughts were about Bingley and if he had made the necessary arrangements with the gamekeeper for the shoot, but he noticed that at the bend in the drive, a woman was walking toward the manor. Much to his surprise, it was Elizabeth Bennet.

After dismounting, he took his horse by the reins and walked toward her, wondering all the while what on earth she was doing. Elizabeth turned around and greeted him, giving the appearance that there was nothing unusual about a young lady, miles from home, walking down a muddy lane.

"Miss Elizabeth, what are you doing here?"

"I have come to visit my sister. Have you just come from town, Mr. Darcy?" she asked, after looking at the amount of mud on the horse's hooves.

"I have."

"Then you do not know my sister, Jane, was taken ill during dinner yesterday, and I have come to visit her."

"On foot?"

"As you see," she answered, looking down at her dirty hem. "Because we have had so much rain, chores on the farm have been neglected, and I did not wish to ask my father for one of the horses. Besides, after dancing and teasing, walking is one of my favorite things to do."

Although his eyes were drawn to her muddied hem and soaked boots, Darcy had also noticed her rosy complexion and that her eyes were brightened by the walk, and because of the humidity, her beautiful dark, curly hair was trying to escape from beneath her bonnet.

"I can see you are looking at my boots, Mr. Darcy. I successfully avoided every puddle, except one," she said, laughing. "However, you need not be concerned; I promise to stay off the rugs."

"Please allow me to go ahead and secure dry shoes for you. I believe you are about the same size as Mrs. Hurst."

"Please do, and warn them that I am coming."

"I am sure they will be pleased to see you again," Darcy said, knowing that Louisa and Caroline would be anything but pleased.

Lizzy thought that Jane would definitely be happy to see her. Mr. Bingley, highly likely. Mr. Bingley's sisters, not very likely at all.

In the foyer, Lizzy was greeted by Mr. Bingley, Mrs. Hurst, Miss Bingley, Mr. Darcy, and Mrs. Hurst's maid, who handed her clean hose and shoes. After removing to an anteroom where she changed her footwear, Mr. Bingley escorted Lizzy to her sister's suite. Although Jane had asked that he not send for the apothecary, Mr. Bingley, in exercising an abundance of caution, had done so. The diagnosis was that she had a bad head cold and needed to rest and recommended some draughts specific to her complaint.

Lizzy spent the whole of the afternoon seeing to the care of her sister. The Bingley sisters visited several times to ask after Jane's health, and on their last visit offered to send for a carriage to take Lizzy home. But Jane gave out a cry imploring her to stay, and Caroline and Louisa, with great reluctance, sent a servant to Longbourn for a change of clothes for Elizabeth.

"They do not want me here, Jane."

"Lizzy, you have frequently said that you do not care what they think about you, so why give in to them now when I am in need of you, if not to nurse me back to health, then at the very least to cheer me up."

"You are right. How dare they not like me? I shall punish them by staying."

Jane took her sister's hand and smiled. "I feel better already, but you must go downstairs for dinner as you have not eaten a morsel all day."

Lizzy did join her hosts for dinner but immediately returned to Jane's room to find that the apothecary's potions had done their work. Even though Jane was sound asleep, Lizzy remained in the bedchamber as she had no wish to spend an evening with Louisa and Caroline, who had stared at her through the whole of dinner as if she was a specimen from a distant land. Mr. Bingley was all charm as usual, but Mr. Darcy had very little to say, except to share some news of his sister.

The following day, Lizzy spent most of the morning reading to her sister, but she could have read the same chapter over and over as Jane was so sleepy that she could not keep her eyes open. The prescribed rest was doing her a world of good, and hopefully, they would be able to leave the day after tomorrow as her color had definitely improved.

After supper, all adjourned to the drawing room. Louisa, Caroline, and Mr. Hurst were in favor of playing cards, while Mr. Darcy chose to write a letter to Georgiana Darcy. But Miss Bingley could not be kept from commenting on anything to do with Mr. Darcy.

"How I long to see Miss Darcy again. She is so elegant and represents the very best in polished society." She proceeded to wax rhapsodic on all of her many accomplishments.

Lizzy thought how silly all of this was. Caroline's purpose was to show that the Bingleys and Darcys moved in a society inaccessible to the Bennets, but her monologue was wasted on Lizzy as she had no pretensions to be anything other than what she was—a gentleman's daughter.

"It is amazing to me how young ladies have the patience to be so very accomplished as they all are," Charles said.

This statement brought an immediate challenge from Caroline, who listed the requirements for such praise. She must play an instrument, sing, draw, dance, know the modern languages, and improve one's mind through extensive reading for the word to be half-deserved.

Mr. Darcy nodded in agreement. "I do not know more than half a dozen ladies who are truly accomplished."

Unable to remain silent any longer, Lizzy said, "I am no longer surprised at your knowing only six accomplished women, Mr. Darcy. I rather wonder at you knowing any."

"You are severe upon your sex, Miss Elizabeth," Mr. Darcy said with that quizzical expression that Lizzy found to be adorable.

"Not at all, sir. My idea of an accomplished woman is someone who has mastered some discipline to a level that is beyond the ability of most of us. For everyone else, we do the best we can. In my family, my grandmother saw to our education. We all learned to net purses, cover screens, paint tables, sketch, and play the piano. You can imagine in a family with five daughters that there are boxes in the attic filled with aging purses, painted canvases, and samplers. My forte is needlework, and I will compare my letter *E* to anyone's."

Lizzy had meant this last comment as a means of lightening the mood, but there was hardly a moment's pause before Caroline added, "And you are also an excellent walker, Miss Elizabeth."

"I do enjoy walking as there is so much to observe in Nature, and I make no apology for it. In fact, it is my intention to take the air tomorrow morning as soon as my sister has had her breakfast." Rising, she bid them all a good night.

As soon as she left the room, Miss Bingley started to complain about Miss Elizabeth. "I am fond of Jane Bennet, but with such a father and mother, no connections, and an uncle who lives in Cheapside…"

"Their lack of connections and an uncle in Cheapside do

not make the Bennet sisters one jot less agreeable," Bingley said, interrupting his sister.

"But it lessens their chance of marrying any men of consideration in the world," Darcy added.

"That would be true if I were a Darcy, but I am not. And although the Bingleys are rising, we do not have ancient ties to Norman kings, nor am I the grandson of an earl. In fact, I lack any pedigree whatsoever, and as such, I may marry where I choose without the pillars of society collapsing all around me."

Darcy said nothing, but Bingley's sisters made up for his lack of response with howls of protest. After a heated exchange, Bingley left, only adding that he would not be joining them for breakfast as it was his intention to go riding. He had deliberately not asked Darcy to join him as he had no wish to be lectured about choosing a suitable marriage partner by his friend.

Later, in the quiet of his room, Darcy thought about what Bingley had said. It was true the Bingleys were moving up in society, but if he did not marry into a prestigious family or one with excellent connections, he would find his progress checked. But Bingley did not seem to care about such things, and because of that, Darcy envied him. For all of his advantages over his friend, there was one thing he could not do. He could not marry where he wished. That was a luxury even a Darcy could not afford.

Chapter 4

In the morning, Jane was feeling so much better that she told Lizzy that she anticipated joining the others for supper. "I am not sure if I will eat, but I would enjoy being out of this room."

"And seeing Mr. Bingley, perhaps?"

"He is all that a man should be, and we are of such like temperaments," Jane freely admitted.

"It is as if the two of you were made for each, and I believe you were. I think you may safely depend upon an offer in the very near future."

This was not idle conjecture. After leaving the drawing room, Lizzy had stopped in the library to retrieve the second volume of a book she had been reading and had heard the heated debate between Bingley and his sisters regarding Jane. However, Charles had prevailed, and Lizzy did not think it necessary to mention it to her sister.

Looking out the window, Jane said, "When you walk this morning, you may have company as Mr. Darcy is in the lane."

Lizzy joined her sister at the window. "Well, I shall not

disturb him as it is easy enough to go out through the breakfast room onto the terrace." But when she went downstairs, she found that the maids were in the room cleaning. *Well, he does not bite*, Lizzy thought and went out the front door. She walked quietly and as closely as possible to the house to avoid his notice.

"Miss Elizabeth, are you trying to escape?" Darcy asked as she emerged from behind a bush.

"I was trying to avoid intruding upon your privacy, Mr. Darcy," an embarrassed Lizzy answered.

"If that is your goal, I would suggest you stay off the gravel," and then he smiled. It was an infrequent event, but when it did happen, it was a reminder of how truly handsome he was. It seemed rather unfair. If you were rich, you should not be handsome, and if you were poor, you should be blessed with good looks. One person should not have it all.

"I am not in need of solitude this morning. Quite the contrary, I would enjoy your company."

Lizzy was used to walking at a brisk pace, but Mr. Darcy preferred to amble along. But the pace did lend itself to conversation, and he shared with her his visit with Miss Darcy.

"When Bingley and I first planned to come to Netherfield, I had hoped my sister would join me, but instead she chose to be with friends in Hampshire. It is very strange. I have spent five years moving her toward adulthood, and now that she has reached it, I find I want to pull her back."

"As her guardian, I think that is a natural inclination as you wish to protect her. Up to this point, you have been more father than brother, but you may now look forward to a mature relationship. It may take some time for you to get used to it as she will probably wish to make her opinions known."

"Oh, it is too late for that. Her powers of observation are amazing, and there is nothing that does not merit some comment."

"Since you are of a taciturn nature, Mr. Darcy, surely the pleasure she derives from talking takes some of the burden of conversing off of you. And since you do not like the preliminaries necessary for friendship, she may catch you up, and you can jump right in without enduring the tedious parts you so dislike."

"I would most definitely have benefited from such assistance before being formally introduced to you. I would have been warned of your penetrating wit and ability to strip a person of all pretenses."

"Would you have avoided me, sir, if you had known?"

"No, but I would have asked you to dance at the assembly, thereby avoiding your censure."

"But you had an opportunity to dance with me at Lucas Lodge, but chose not to. Did you not risk the same result?"

"I think not. You now know me better and understand that my comments at the assembly were not malicious, merely thoughtless and inaccurate."

"And the dance?"

"A lost opportunity, not to be repeated."

"Does Mr. Bingley plan to have a ball at Netherfield? He spoke of it when he first arrived. If so, you may yet claim your dance."

"Yes, there will be a ball, and the date has been set for the first night of the full moon. Bingley will soon be sending his cards around, and after the ball, his sisters will return to London." Looking at her to make sure she understood the importance of what he was about to say, he added, "but Bingley will remain at Netherfield. Unlike his sisters, who have tired of the country, Bingley has found much to admire here."

Lizzy's assessment had been correct. Mr. Bingley would not yield to his sisters on the matter of whom he should marry, and because of that, she smiled, letting Mr. Darcy know that she had understood his meaning.

"Who will keep house for Mr. Bingley if both of his sisters leave?" Lizzy asked.

"Most likely it will be his eldest sister, Diana Crenshaw. If she comes to Netherfield, you will know of it. She has a large family, actually more like a tribe, on the order of the Red Indians of America. Her two eldest are twin boys, impossible to tell apart and equally inclined to mischief. Mrs. Crenshaw was greatly influenced by Rousseau's concept of the noble savage in rearing her children. The savage part of the equation has been achieved. However, I have seen no evidence of anything noble in their behavior."

"Do you mean to frighten me, Mr. Darcy?"

"No, but I do mean to warn you as one of their favorite entertainments is to dig up repulsive creatures from stream beds and share them with the ladies. And they are fearless. Do not be surprised if you find them in the top branches of your apple trees throwing fruit at your servants and laborers."

"When I hear of the Crenshaws' arrival, I shall send up a hue and cry to alert the population. And your plans, Mr. Darcy? Will you stay at Netherfield and provide the neighborhood with some protection?"

"No," he answered looking away from her. "After the ball, I shall return to London as I have important business to attend to, and it is likely that I will not come back to Netherfield at all."

"Lizzy, Mr. Darcy likes you," Jane said to her sister upon her return from her walk.

"And I like him."

Although she was sorry that he would be leaving the country for good, she had enjoyed their short time together. But someone of Mr. Darcy's elevated rank would have no interest in the daughter of a gentleman farmer, so that was that.

"What I mean is that he admires you."

"Jane, if you are inferring that Mr. Darcy has a romantic interest in me, let me disabuse you of such a notion. Mr. Bingley will have his ball, and immediately afterward, Mr. Darcy will permanently return to town. However, I confess that I will miss him as Mr. Darcy possesses a fine wit, although he definitely uses it in moderation. But I do not wish to speak of Mr. Darcy, but of Mr. Bingley, and I have news to share."

Jane was elated when she heard that Mr. Bingley would definitely remain in the country, especially since, by his own admission, he frequently succumbed to his need for movement and would abandon the city for the country, and vice versa, at the spur of the moment. So this was very good news indeed.

With the exception of Jane and Bingley, who were clearly enjoying each other's company, supper proved to be a somber event. The sisters were still upset at Charles's announced intention of marrying whomever he pleased as they knew full well that it would please him to marry Miss Bennet. Mr. Hurst, as usual, had nothing to add as his only interests were in food, wine, and cards, and the engaging Mr. Darcy of the morning was missing. He was distracted and made no effort to converse with anyone. After removing to the drawing room, he once again chose to write letters, but even so, Lizzy found that he was often glancing in her direction, but in an abstracted manner, as if he were looking past her to things he must do when free of Netherfield.

Mr. Darcy *was* thinking of Elizabeth. During their walk in the grove, he had found himself so attracted to her that he had decided that it would be best if he left Netherfield immediately and not to wait for the ball. What purpose would be served by remaining? He was enchanted with a lady whose position in life was so beneath his own that any possible alliance was out of the question. Besides, he was not of a nature to toy with a woman's affections, and he had already made overtures to Letitia Montford. It would indicate a deficiency in his character if he were to alter his course now. He just wished that Elizabeth had not chosen to wear her hair down for supper as he could think of no other sight that brought him more pleasure.

Chapter 5

ALTHOUGH JANE BENNET HAD been gone from Netherfield for only one day, Charles informed his sisters that he intended to ride over to Longbourn to see her. Unsurprisingly, Louisa and Caroline were unhappy with his plans and launched a two-pronged attack.

"You are being ridiculous," Caroline began. "There cannot possibly be a change in her health in such a short time."

"You do not want to give the appearance of being a love-struck adolescent, now do you, Charles?" Louisa added.

"I do not care if it was only an hour ago that Miss Bennet left. I am going to Longbourn, and since I am in love with the lady, if people wish to call me a love-struck adolescent, so be it."

"And what of Mr. Darcy, who came here to shoot?" Caroline asked. "You have neglected your duties as host as he has done no shooting at all because you have been distracted with other matters."

"Do not trouble yourself on my account, Miss Bingley," Darcy said, quickly jumping in. "I think it may work to our advantage. The birds will be lulled into a false sense of security thinking that there will be no shoot this year, and they will get careless and expose themselves." Seeing the look of bewilderment on their faces, he continued, "Or we may find ourselves with too many birds as the pheasants will flock to Netherfield from adjacent properties seeking sanctuary from the shooting going on all around them."

Louisa and Caroline stared at Mr. Darcy. Was it even possible for birds to understand the concept of a sanctuary?

"Darcy, what a cutup you are!" Charles said, laughing. "I am glad you are willing to find humor in the situation because you have come from London to shoot, and despite the fine weather, we have not had the guns out."

"You have had other things on your mind, and speaking of the weather, since it is such a beautiful day, may I accompany you to Longbourn?"

"Of course. I was just about to ask you to join me."

"Then I shall go change my clothes and meet you at the stables."

Caroline waited for the servant to close the door behind Mr. Darcy before lashing into her brother. "If you persist in continuing with this ill-advised courtship, Louisa and I shall return to London."

"Caroline, you have already said that you were going back to town after the ball," Charles answered, refusing to back down.

"Then it is settled, and I shall write to our sister, Diana."

"I thought you already had."

On the ride to Longbourn, Charles thanked Darcy for lending him his support. "I saw Caroline and Louisa looking to you for assistance, but since you did not express any objections to the match, they may yet change their minds, especially Caroline, who looks at you as if you were the Delphic oracle. They truly mean well. It is just that they have become obsessed with status and ignore everything else."

"You have no need to thank me," Darcy answered, ignoring the comment about Caroline. He tried to say as little as possible about the lady because he would be hard-pressed to find anything positive to say about someone so petty and mean. "It was impertinent of me to attempt to impose my views on you. Like your sisters, I, too, was eager for you to make a good match, but since I have observed how greatly Miss Bennet and you complement each other, I can comfortably say that you are, in fact, marrying well."

Darcy realized his withdrawal of any objections to the match was a complete about-face from his earlier position that such a marriage would greatly harm his friend's chances to advance in society. But then Darcy thought back to the most recent season. Although he never missed a ball, his friend had avoided the more intimate card parties and dinners because most of the conversations were laced with spiteful comments from those ladies who were not yet married and replete with sexual innuendo from those who were, and Bingley had shared with Darcy that he had found London's closed society to be repressive, almost suffocating.

As Bingley had said, he was not a Darcy, the grandson of an earl, and as such, he was not shackled with preserving a line that went back to those who fought with the Conqueror. His obligation to all of those Darcys who had preceded him required that he produce a male heir or Pemberley would pass to his cousin,

David Ashton, and it would no longer be Georgiana's home. So Bingley would marry Miss Jane Bennet, and they would remain in the country at Netherfield and have a house filled with laughing children while Darcy would return to London and Miss Montford. If he could not marry for love, then why not Letitia?

"Do you have a particular date in mind when you will make Miss Bennet an offer?" Darcy asked.

"Oh, it will be very soon. Very soon indeed," Bingley answered, grinning from ear to ear.

"Bingley, are you saying that you are on your way to Longbourn for that very purpose? If so, I shall turn back immediately and not interfere with such important business."

"Yes, I am going to Longbourn to propose, but I wanted you there because you are my closest friend and because it is a house full of women. I need more than Mr. Bennet's presence to balance the equation. And speaking of engagements, how do things go between Miss Montford and you?"

"Slow but steady."

"I only met her the one time, but she seems to be quite pleasant. She even meets Caroline's definition of an accomplished lady."

"She is very pleasant, truly accomplished, and according to my sister, paints tables like no other."

"Will there be an announcement soon?" Bingley asked, but found his friend lost in thought, and his question went unanswered for many minutes.

"If only she was less serious. If she had more… If she was able to…" Darcy finally gave up searching for words to cushion Miss Montford's defect: She wasn't very funny. "It is the humerus that is supposedly responsible for our sense of humor, and like Adam and his missing rib, Miss Montford lacks a funny bone.

"You would think with all the ladies out in society," Darcy continued, "I could find one woman of marriageable age who is attractive, accomplished, and witty. Is that too much to ask? Apparently, it is. And I absolutely refuse to consider the eighteen-year-old girls who have recently debuted."

Most of those young ladies were friends of his sister, and Darcy shook his head at the memory of a procession of debutantes, all dressed in white, who were being paraded before London's eligible bachelors for the purpose of marrying them off as quickly as possible.

"Georgiana, who protested when I enrolled her in Mrs. Bryan's Academy because of its arduous curriculum, thanked me for doing that very thing after listening to the conversations of her peers. Unlike my sister, these ladies were coached by their governesses on the few topics that they might safely engage in while talking to a prospective suitor: the weather, the number of couples in attendance, the splendor of their surroundings, et cetera, et cetera."

"Darcy, is it necessary that you look for a wife exclusively from among the aristocracy?"

"Yes, of course. Every decision must now be made with my sister in mind. If I do not marry well, it may adversely affect her prospects."

"Are you saying that someone as lovely, intelligent, accomplished, engaging, and, I might add, wealthy as Georgiana will be ostracized if her brother marries, say, a gentleman's daughter?"

"Again, yes. The women, the select few, who rule during the London season are unforgiving of those who deviate from their rules. Besides, I paid Miss Montford sufficient attention so that she is entitled to think that an offer will be made, and once I return to London, I will get about the business of making it. And no more about me, Bingley. You are about to become betrothed, so let us pick up the pace so that we might arrive at Longbourn before dark."

Chapter 6

SHORTLY AFTER BREAKFAST, LYDIA and Kitty announced they would be going into Meryton to buy ribbon to trim their bonnets. Mary indicated she would like to visit the circulating library, and the idea proved attractive to her two older sisters. The sun was shining, and even some of the deepest puddles were finally drying up after weeks of rain and gray clouds. Because of the break in the weather, the streets were crowded with people from the village as well as many of the militia officers and their families.

When Mary, Lizzy, and Jane emerged from the library, they found their younger sisters talking to Captain Denny and his friend, Lieutenant George Wickham, who had recently joined the regiment. In a few minutes of conversation, the handsome Mr. Wickham had succeeded in impressing upon his company that he was well educated, self-assured, and quite charming. His arrival in Meryton would definitely make Lydia and Kitty happy as they were becoming bored with seeing the same faces at the dances and dinners and had expressed a desire for some new blood to be added to the mix.

It was Lizzy who first sighted Mr. Bingley and gently tapped Jane on the arm. When Jane saw him, she broke out into a broad smile, prompting everyone to turn around to see what she was looking at. Lydia, who was only interested in men in a smart, well-tailored uniform, announced the obvious: The two men, Mr. Bingley and Mr. Darcy, were not officers.

Both gentlemen had dismounted before they recognized the man who was with Captain Denny. After bowing to the ladies, Darcy excused himself and quickly retreated into the bootmaker's shop. It was an uncomfortable few minutes before Wickham and Denny departed, and although it seemed as if an explanation was in order, Mr. Bingley said nothing. When Mr. Darcy returned, he too made no comment.

"Miss Bennet," Charles finally said, ending the impasse, "Mr. Darcy and I were coming to Longbourn to inquire after your health."

"I am well, sir. My sister's excellent care and your attentions resulted in a quick recovery, and I am free of all complaints."

With the two lovers staring at each other, Lizzy turned to Mr. Darcy. "Sir, we were just making our way home after visiting the library. Will you join us for tea?"

This offer was met by protests from Kitty and Lydia, who declared that they were not ready to return to Longbourn.

"Lydia, it would be helpful if you went ahead to tell Mrs. Hill that we will be having two visitors for tea," Lizzy said in a voice that made it clear it was not a request. Kitty, who was somewhat more mature than her sister, tugged on Lydia's sleeve, indicating they needed to return home, and together with Mary, they made their way toward Longbourn.

As they had done at Netherfield, Mr. Darcy walked beside

Lizzy leading his horse by his reins. Unlike their previous encounter, the gentleman was not in the mood for conversation, and they walked side by side in silence. When they finally reached the house, Lizzy let out a sigh of relief.

With Mr. Darcy accompanying his friend, no one had guessed the purpose of Mr. Bingley's visit, but after tea and cake, Charles could wait no longer and asked Mrs. Bennet if he could have a word in private with Miss Bennet. The question catapulted Mrs. Bennet out of her seat. She had been running about the room, urging everyone to leave as quickly as possible, when Lizzy suggested that the couple should go across the hall to the parlor, and everyone again sat down. Mr. Darcy continued to say nothing, but the chaotic scene had caused his mood to lighten, and it appeared to Lizzy that he was struggling not to laugh.

Everything played out as expected. Jane and Charles returned to the parlor to announce their engagement, with Charles quickly leaving to ask his future father-in-law for his daughter's hand. Mrs. Bennet was beside herself with joy at Jane making such an advantageous marriage and ordered Mr. Hill to open a bottle to toast the occasion, and a spontaneous celebration ensued.

"I believe, Mr. Darcy, it will prove to be an excellent match as they are well suited to each other," Lizzy said. "Is life not full of surprises? A gentleman from London signs a lease on a property in Hertfordshire, and the result is my sister will shortly be married."

"Everyone seemed to be surprised by Mr. Bingley's sudden proposal, except you. I attribute that to your keen powers of observation."

"You give me too much credit, Mr. Darcy. Mr. Bingley's joyful countenance revealed his purpose in coming to Netherfield. Most people are more difficult to read than Mr. Bingley."

"Am I one of them?"

"Yes, on most occasions, you show very little."

"You say 'on most occasions.' I imagine I was less difficult to read today in Meryton."

"I believe you are referring to Mr. Wickham. Do you know the gentleman?"

"Yes. When Wickham was about six years old, both of his parents died, and the steward at Pemberley and his wife adopted him. He is blessed with such happy manners as may ensure his making many friends here in Meryton, but I would caution you to be wary of anything he says."

"With regard to you, Mr. Darcy?" Elizabeth asked, puzzled by his ambiguous statement.

Darcy hesitated, unsure of how much should be said. The previous autumn Wickham had tried to arrange an elopement with Georgiana, and even with the passage of a year's time, it was a subject that caused his blood to boil.

"Miss Elizabeth, you have had sufficient time to sketch my character, and since I shall soon depart for London, I shall leave you to judge the truth of any assertions he may make regarding me. I believe I can safely rely on your justice."

Lizzy, sensing his distress and not knowing how to respond, changed the conversation and asked if he would be attending the Netherfield ball.

"I have important business to see to in London, and I am not sure if I will be able to return."

"I hope you will, Mr. Darcy, as I owe you a dance."

"Which I would very much like to claim, but everything turns on events in London."

Chapter 7

DARCY WAS SITTING WITH Miss Montford in the parlor of the family's Mayfair townhouse. They had already discussed the weather and had talked about the families who had returned to London from their country estates, and with all the easy topics got out of the way, Darcy was staring off into the distance, hoping for divine intervention to assist him in finding something else to say.

"While you were in the country, did you shoot many birds, Mr. Darcy?" Miss Montford asked, and he silently thanked Providence for intervening.

"Actually, not a one. Mr. Bingley's time was quite taken up with Miss Jane Bennet, a most agreeable lady and the daughter of a gentleman farmer. Shortly before I left Hertfordshire, he made her an offer of marriage, and she has accepted him. Understandably, he could think of little else."

"That is very good news for Mr. Bingley that he is marrying well."

Did he hear her correctly? Did she just say that Bingley was marrying well and not the other way around?

"Knowing Miss Bennet, I agree that Mr. Bingley is marrying well, but considering his fortune, it is also a good match for the lady."

"What I meant is that Mr. Bingley is not a gentleman, but will be marrying a gentleman's daughter."

"You don't consider Mr. Bingley to be a gentleman?"

This seemed to make Mr. Darcy unhappy, and so she demurred. "Who am I to say who is or who is not a gentleman? I was only basing my opinion on my understanding that his father was in trade."

"Have you met his sisters, Miss Bingley and Mrs. Hurst?" If she had, then she would know they were well educated, accomplished, and elegantly attired.

Miss Montford tilted her head to the side, which was something she did when she was puzzled. "How would I know them, Mr. Darcy, as we do not have the same friends? We may have attended some of the same events, but I have never been introduced to them. Do you think that I might be introduced to them?"

Darcy could not tell from her tone if she considered that to be a good thing. But surely if they were to marry, she would understand that the family of his closest friend would be invited to their home.

"Mr. Bingley tells me they will marry around Christmastime," he said, ignoring her question. "He has a large family, so it will be quite an affair if all can attend the wedding celebration."

"How nice for them," she responded, and then the silence returned for what seemed an eternity. "Shall I play something, Mr. Darcy?"

"Yes, please," he answered eagerly, and then sank back into

the chair with a sigh of relief. They would not have to talk as long as she was playing.

"Do you have a request, sir?"

"Surprise me," and then he thought of something Elizabeth Bennet had said about what constituted an accomplished woman: *"You see, Mr. Darcy, we are of necessity more practical in the country. Jane and I have painted many screens, but when every fireplace has one, we stop. Even the largest house can only hold so many tables, no matter how beautifully painted, and when it comes to the matter of music, many of our friends are talented on the pianoforte. But if the truth be known, most people prefer an air or a jig to a concerto as we love to dance."*

After thinking about Miss Elizabeth's comments, he asked, "Miss Montford, something lively, if you will," and she searched among the music sheets before finally settling on a Scottish air, and while she was playing, he could not help but notice how many painted tables there were in the room.

While Letitia played, Darcy's mind was flooded with visions of Elizabeth. How he would love to wrap his fingers around her dark curls while gazing into her coal black eyes and to trace the outline of her face with his fingers. His thoughts of the lady spurred him to action.

"Miss Montford, I do not recall if I mentioned that Mr. Bingley is hosting a ball at his home in Hertfordshire, and I have promised that I will attend."

She showed no sign of unhappiness at his news, and after deciding that the visit had lasted long enough, he rose, bowed, and beat a hasty retreat, and when he got into the hackney, he loosened his neckcloth as he felt as if he was being strangled.

At supper, after interrogating her brother about his visit with Miss Montford, Georgiana pronounced it to be satisfactory.

"Since you are gone so frequently, perhaps you might consider writing a poem or love letter."

"Please, Georgiana, I am not a romantic."

"Flowers?"

"May we have this conversation after I return from Hertfordshire?"

"Yes, and I have a surprise for you, Will. I have been feeling guilty about not going to the country with you, so I have changed my mind. I *shall* attend the ball at Netherfield."

Instead of the expected response, her brother put his head back and rubbed his temples as if fighting a headache.

"Georgie, would you pour a glass of Madeira for me? I have something unpleasant to tell you," and he advised her of Wickham's presence in Meryton.

It had been several weeks after Wickham's attempted elopement before Darcy could speak to his sister about the events in Ramsgate, and he had only relented because Anne de Bourgh had written, encouraging him to listen to what his sister had to say. Georgiana had successfully convinced her brother that she would never have married without his permission and that she was ashamed of the romantic notions she had harbored.

"Will, surely, you do not think I would have anything to do with Wickham. I have learned so much from that unfortunate affair, and it has stood me in good stead this past season when I was able to recognize insincere flattery for what it is: an attempt to secure my fortune."

"No, it is not that at all. I know he will not come to the ball as he is a coward and will not face me. It is just that the militia is always about in the village, and there is the possibility you might encounter him."

Georgiana, whose clothes were made by the finest dress-makers in London, laughed. "I am going to Netherfield for the purpose of attending a ball, not to shop in Meryton."

"Forgive me. I am tired. As an aside, you may be interested to know that after the ball, Louisa and Caroline will return to town, and Mrs. Crenshaw will come to keep house for Bingley."

"Mrs. Crenshaw and her little band of ruffians! The same ones who put mud in my riding boots? I am convinced that it was Athena who actually did the deed, but she was put up to it by those monster brothers of hers."

"I can easily believe it. When Bingley leased the house in Surrey, I saw Athena throwing rocks at the ducks. For such a little girl, she was remarkably accurate."

"Why does Charles put up with their obnoxious behavior?"

"He finds them spirited."

"Spirited! If they were in my care, I would spirit them away to the nearest woodshed for a proper whipping."

Darcy reached out his hand, and his sister came and sat beside him. "I know you are eager for me to begin a courtship with Miss Montford, and I will do so upon my return from Hertfordshire. Since it is now certain the Crenshaws will take up residence with Bingley, I can assure you I will not be at Netherfield nor in Meryton nor in Hertfordshire when the Crenshaws arrive. I think I can safely remain in England. However, it is a good thing to know where they are at any given time," and brother and sister shared a good laugh.

Chapter 8

George Wickham was the talk of the village. Within three days of his arrival, everyone knew the basics of his biography. He had been brought up on a great estate in Derbyshire. After attending Cambridge, he had planned a living in the church, but his dreams went unrealized because the money that should have been available for such a purpose had been denied him. However, being a gentleman, he would not name the person who had caused him so much personal suffering, and the Darcy name went unmentioned. Fortunately, he explained, he had many friends, among them Captain Denny, who had assisted him in securing a commission in the militia.

Because he was so handsome in his regimentals, gracious in his manners, and possessing a fine baritone voice, Wickham had been inundated with invitations to dinners and card parties. As a result, he had appeared almost nightly at some social event in the Meryton neighborhood, including a card party hosted by Mrs. Philips, the wife of the local solicitor, and the sister of Mrs. Bennet. Out of curiosity, Lizzy decided to attend.

As Elizabeth watched the gentleman move about the room, it was easy to see why he had the village all abuzz. He showed a genuine interest in his company, and with his deep, resonating voice, he had a way of conversing that created an intimacy that had some of the girls, as well as their mothers, all aflutter. Lizzy made no attempt to engage him. She was there to observe, not to be charmed, but as soon as she had stopped playing cards, Mr. Wickham sought her out.

"I did not think you would ever quit the whist table, so that I might seek an introduction," Wickham said, after sitting on the sofa next to Lizzy.

"But you did not seek an introduction, sir."

For a brief second, Lizzy saw a flash of displeasure before he stood up and asked Mrs. Pritchard to do the honors.

"So, Miss Bennet, now that we have been officially introduced, I am no longer at risk of being denied the pleasure of your company."

They chatted about topics that Mr. Darcy would have found to be tedious: the weather, Meryton, the next assembly, the vicar and the important role the church played in the lives of its parishioners, and other such drawing-room topics. After those subjects were exhausted, Mr. Wickham mentioned Mr. Darcy.

"I believe we have an acquaintance in common, Miss Bennet: Fitzwilliam Darcy of Pemberley."

"Other than that he has an estate in Derbyshire and a house in town, I do not know very much about him. He is of a taciturn nature and says but little."

"I know Mr. Darcy very well, as I was brought up on the Darcy estate. My father was the steward at Pemberley, a truly wonderful man, as was the elder Mr. Darcy," and as he said this,

his tone softened to great effect. "I wish I could say the same for the son."

With Mr. Darcy's warning echoing in her mind, she sat quietly, giving him no encouragement, but Mr. Wickham was determined to have his say.

"You might ask why I do not hold the son in the same regard as the father." Fearing that Lizzy might not ask, he continued, "It was my greatest desire to study for the church, and the elder Mr. Darcy, recognizing my calling, left me a bequest sufficient to purchase a living. However, his son gave the living to another."

"That is a truly shocking statement, Mr. Wickham," Lizzy said in genuine amazement. "For Mr. Darcy to go against his father's wishes, I assume you and the son had quarreled."

"I wish that were the case. Then I could understand his actions." Mr. Wickham went quiet and a look of sadness came over him, and Lizzy had the impression she was watching a performance. "We were friends all through our childhood. Although it was true we did not see each other much while at Cambridge, when we were in each other's company, I sensed no rancor."

"If you remained friends while you were at university together, how do you account for his subsequent actions?"

"Many a night I have lain awake trying to come up with a reason, but with little success. Possibly because of his superior rank and being free of his father's guidance and supervision, he became conceited and arrogant. There might also have been some jealousy involved as his father made no attempt to hide his affection for me. When Mr. Darcy died, his son sought to diminish my importance by denying me the living I so ardently desired."

"As I said, Mr. Wickham, I know little of the gentleman."

"From what I have heard in the time I have been in Meryton, Mr. Darcy made a very poor first impression."

"That is true," Lizzy said, and her remark made Mr. Wickham smile. Wickham, who was used to women hanging on his every word, was unhappy with Lizzy's reaction to his comments. Why was she not asking for more details about the injustices he had suffered? "However," she added, "realizing he had slighted many, he made a real effort to begin anew."

"That is typical of Mr. Darcy. He offends and gives the appearance of amendment. But I can assure you it does not last, and his true nature eventually emerges."

"As to his true nature, at the moment he has succeeded in hiding it. He has been our guest at Longbourn on several occasions because his friend, Mr. Charles Bingley, is engaged to my sister Jane."

This information startled Wickham, and he quickly looked about the room to see if Mr. Bingley was present.

"Mr. Bingley is not here, Mr. Wickham. He is at Longbourn visiting with my sister, and Mr. Darcy is in London with his sister. The two men are very close friends, and considering your description, I am surprised to find Mr. Darcy developed a friendship with someone not of his sphere. Do you know Mr. Bingley?"

"I do not. But do not be surprised by his friendship with someone who is his social inferior, as he is most comfortable when surrounded by subordinates and sycophants."

"In light of all that you have told me, you will be happy to know that Mr. Darcy will be returning to London following a ball being hosted by Mr. Bingley at Netherfield. All of the officers have been invited. Will you be attending?"

"No, Miss Bennet, I will not. My temperament is such that

I do not seek confrontation. If Mr. Darcy was to see me in his friend's home, it might put him in a foul mood, and that would ruin the evening for others." And that was his final word, as he stood up, bowed, and moved on in search of a friendlier audience.

When Lizzy returned home, she related the whole of the conversation to Jane and asked for her thoughts.

"I do not see how Mr. Bingley and Mr. Darcy could be friends if Mr. Darcy is so very bad, but Mr. Wickham's recollections are so detailed."

"I thought about that, and to my mind, he supplied too many details, especially in light of Mr. Darcy supplying none. Instead, Mr. Darcy relied on my knowledge of his character to make up my own mind."

"But do you think there is any truth in what Mr. Wickham said?"

Lizzy quickly ran the events of the evening through her mind, as well as her last conversation with Mr. Darcy, and shook her head. "No, I do not. In fact, I suspect the injury was to Mr. Darcy and that is why Mr. Wickham is so eager to have us all think ill of him. In that way, we will be distracted from an examination of his character."

"When I next see Charles, I will ask him what he knows about it."

"Please do. Although Mr. Darcy has his faults, I do not think he is in any way dishonest or vengeful."

"Lizzy, think of how much your opinion about Mr. Darcy has changed since that first meeting at the assembly."

"Yes, my opinion of him altered when he came to Longbourn to apologize for his unkind words, especially since I would have thought I would have been beneath his notice."

"You certainly are no longer beneath Mr. Darcy's notice. All during the celebration of my engagement to Charles, Mr. Darcy was looking at you."

"Jane, I like him very much, but you know very well that I am of a practical nature. I know that the Mr. Darcys of the world do not court the daughters of gentlemen farmers."

"But by that measure, a man such as Charles, who could marry practically anyone because of his wealth, should not be interested in *me*."

"I wish to take nothing away from Mr. Bingley, but he is not a Darcy and that may be a good thing. Unlike Mr. Darcy, Mr. Bingley is not burdened with a legacy that extends back to the Conquest and who must marry a lady of a rank. It is sad to think that with all of his money, his name, and his elevated position in society that happiness might elude him because he may have to marry a woman he does not love. On the other hand, it would be difficult to truly be miserable when you take into consideration the enormity of his wealth, his large estate in Derbyshire, and a house in town."

"Elegant carriages and paintings by the Masters," Jane said, adding to Lizzy's list.

"An invitation to Almack's."

"Tickets to the opera."

"A stable full of horses…"

Chapter 9

WITH MR. BINGLEY COMING to Longbourn every afternoon, it wasn't but a day or two before the subject of Mr. Wickham arose, and Jane was able to share with Lizzy what she had learned.

"Charles said that in all the time he has known Mr. Darcy, the name 'Wickham' has come up only once. It was when they were discussing how powerful people attract enemies. Mr. Darcy said he knew of his having only one enemy, the son of his late steward, and that Wickham had 'injured his family.'"

"He said 'his family,' not just himself? Then this must have something to do with his sister."

"When Charles realized Mr. Wickham was included in the invitation to all of the officers," Jane continued, "he offered to speak to Colonel Forster. But Darcy told him that it was unnecessary, saying, 'He will not come. He is a liar, and you cannot lie about a fellow if he is in the same room with you.'"

"Charles was all praise for Mr. Darcy, and although it is never discussed, he is aware that there were some in London who criticized Mr. Darcy for his friendship with a man whose fortune was made in trade. Charles emphasized that the most important person in Mr. Darcy's life is his sister, which is the main reason he travels so frequently to town, but there is another reason for his visits. Because the heir to the Darcy estate must be a male, Georgiana Darcy cannot inherit. Therefore, Mr. Darcy must take a wife and have a son. During this past season, he seemed to settle on Miss Letitia Montford, the daughter of Sir John Montford, and the granddaughter of the Earl of Darent."

"If he intends to make Miss Montford his wife, why did Mr. Darcy come to Hertfordshire for such a lengthy visit?"

"Because Mr. Darcy has little enthusiasm for the match, and Charles said it is getting worse, not better. Although he honored Miss Montford with his attentions during the season, when everyone went back to their country estates, Mr. Darcy went to Derbyshire with his sister. For the whole month of August, while Miss Montford was in the country with her family, he never visited her.

"I also learned Mr. Darcy's name was once linked to Mrs. Conway, the widow of a Whig Member of Parliament. She is a few years older than he is, but because there was no issue from her marriage to Mr. Conway, Charles believes marriage was never a consideration. He added that Mr. Darcy would not even consider what he calls 'the latest crop' of eighteen-year-olds, as he craves mature conversation and debate. He likes to be challenged."

"And Miss Montford is lacking in that area?"

"Apparently. But even so, after the ball, he is to return to London to begin the courtship in earnest or he risks hearing from Sir John that he is playing loose with his daughter's affections by his inconstant attentions."

"To a man like Mr. Darcy, such a charge would be insupportable, so there is little doubt he will marry Miss Montford."

Jane looked at her sister and thought what Lizzy could not say. She was in love with Mr. Darcy, and in all likelihood, Mr. Darcy was falling in love with her. But they were destined to be separated because of class differences.

"Do not look at me like that, Jane. I already have a plan. I shall ask Mr. Bingley to introduce me to some of his wealthy friends, but from a less lofty position in society than Mr. Darcy. However, if I do not find a husband, I shall live in an attic room at Netherfield and become the governess to your many children."

Jane took her sister's hand in hers and smiled. "Lizzy, I would never make you live in the attic, and you have my permission to teach the children how to play the pianoforte but, please, no French. Your accent is worse than mine."

Although the two sisters laughed, Jane could not continue to appear cheerful when she was not. The thought that there would be no Mr. Bingley in her sister's life made her profoundly sad.

"Please do not trouble yourself on my account," Lizzy said. "I shall go to the ball and position myself in such a way that Mr. Darcy will be forced to ask me to dance. I shall write at length about it in my diary, and then I shall turn the page and write of other things. As I have repeatedly told you, I am of a practical nature, and I never imagined that it would end in any other way."

Georgiana wished she could fall asleep in a carriage the way her lady's maid, Mrs. Brotherton, and her brother's man-servant, Mercer, did. But the rocking of the carriage that lulled them to sleep kept her awake as she could not block out the sound of the grinding of the wheels or the sound of the whip. With her companion in a deep sleep, she looked to her brother for conversation.

"Will, when you visited Miss Montford, did you notice her new coiffure?"

Darcy shook his head. This disappointed Georgiana because it was she who had encouraged Letitia to adopt a softer look. "Because her face is so angular, I suggested she not wear it so high and to have curls around her face to make it look rounder."

"You know I do not pay attention to such things, but I promise to take notice when I next see her," and he turned his attention to the passing countryside.

"May I ask when that will be?"

"As I have said, after the ball at Netherfield." Looking at his sister with a quizzical expression, he asked, "Is that why you have come along—to drag me back to London to court Miss Montford as soon as the ball is over?"

"Of course not," she answered quickly. "I would *never* try to force you to do anything."

Darcy could see he had hurt his sister's feelings, and so he gave her his full attention. "We have already established that Miss Montford is all that a young lady of twenty-two years should be, so why are you so concerned?"

"Caroline Bingley."

"Surely, you do not think I am in danger of being ensnared by Miss Bingley."

"Not Miss Bingley in particular, but someone like her. For example, Augusta Selridge, who is very beautiful…"

"…and a viper. You look surprised that I know her true

nature. That is why I move slowly and methodically, so I am not taken in by someone like Miss Selridge."

"You are my darling brother, and all I want is for you to marry someone who is sweet and kind and who will be a good wife to you."

"Then you will be comforted to know that when I placed the advertisement for a wife in *The Times* those were my exact specifications."

Her brother's good humor seemed to reassure Georgiana, and despite claims that she never slept while on the road, she dozed off, leaving Will to his thoughts. He suspected that returning to Hertfordshire was probably a bad idea, as any hope of his coming together with Elizabeth Bennet collided with the reality of their situations. But he had to see her one more time. In that way, it might be possible to banish her from his dreams.

When Georgiana awoke, her brother informed her that they were within a few miles of Netherfield, and his sister, who loved meeting new people and visiting new places, asked about the neighborhood. After hearing Will's description, she decided it was little different from the village of Lambton near Pemberley.

"It is a market town, Georgiana, so if you need ribbon or hose, you will be able to find it easily."

"But what of the ladies? Are there many pretty girls here to tempt a gentleman?"

"A few. There is a Miss King, who has pretty red hair, a Miss Long, who has lovely hands, and a Miss Robinson, who is attractive in profile," and Will tapped his teeth to indicate her defect.

"And what of Miss Bennet's sisters?"

"They are an attractive family. The eldest and the three younger sisters are light of hair and comely. Only the second eldest has dark hair, which is very curly and difficult to restrain, and she is always putting it back in place. She has luminous dark eyes, almost like onyx, that reflect the light, and a very pretty smile."

Unrestrained curls? Onyx eyes? For a man who said he did not notice such things about a lady, that was a very detailed description, Georgiana thought.

"What is her name?"

"Did I not say? Miss Elizabeth Bennet. But you will have an opportunity to meet all of them at the ball. We are very near to Longbourn, so you might gently nudge Mrs. Brotherton."

"Longbourn? I thought the name of the estate was Netherfield Park?"

"I meant to say Netherfield Park. Longbourn is the Bennet estate."

"I am looking forward to meeting all of the Bennet sisters," Georgiana told her brother, and she was most especially interested in meeting Miss Elizabeth Bennet.

Chapter 10

MRS. BENNET WAS AS excited as her five daughters were about attending the ball at Netherfield. Mr. Bennet and she had had their first dance in its ballroom more than two decades earlier, and she fondly remembered the pale blue *robe a l'anglaise* with matching petticoat she had worn that evening and which had greatly complemented her blond hair, blue eyes, and tiny waist. But after only a few moments of remembrance of things past, she returned to the business of the day. Now that Jane was to marry Mr. Bingley, she needed to concentrate her efforts on seeing that her four unwed daughters made advantageous marriages.

Mrs. Bennet was disappointed when she learned that Mr. Bingley chose not to invite any of his friends from town to the ball. Because he had settled comfortably into the neighborhood, he was often seen riding into the village on his way to Longbourn, waving to the merchants and their families as if he had grown up in Meryton. As a result, he felt no need to seek company outside of Hertfordshire. Occasionally, he was accompanied by his friend, Mr. Darcy, but because someone of such an exalted rank would not be interested in any of her girls, the gentleman from Derbyshire served no useful purpose and was, therefore, of little interest to her.

Mrs. Bennet decided that Kitty, whom she considered to be second in beauty only to Jane, would have no difficulty finding a suitor, possibly from amongst the officers who would be in attendance at the ball. And although Lydia was only sixteen, her effervescence always attracted attention, and her mother would not say "no" to a good offer for her youngest daughter. Mary, of course, was hopeless. If only she would do something about her looks. A little rouge, a nice pair of earrings, a less severe style to her hair would do wonders for her, but any suggestion about improving her appearance brought on endless sermonizing about the fleeting nature of beauty versus the enduring benefits of integrity and character.

Then there was Lizzy with her dark hair and eyes, so unlike her fair sisters. In the privacy of their bedchamber, Mr. Bennet occasionally teased his wife about their second daughter, accusing her of having had an assignation with a Spanish wine merchant that had resulted in their dark-eyed daughter.

Lizzy was certainly pretty enough to attract a suitor, but it was her habit of expressing her own opinions that would prove to be her downfall, and there was no hope of improvement in that area as no one seemed to intimidate her—not even Mr. Darcy. Lizzy's conversation, in which she had teased that gentleman about his knowledge of dancing, had been overheard at Lucas Lodge and widely remarked upon. That type of banter was perfectly fine once you were engaged, but totally at cross purposes before an offer was made. No man wanted a wife who was smarter or wittier than he was.

And was her obstinacy more in evidence than when she had refused to even consider Mr. Collins when he had come to Longbourn for the purpose of finding a wife from amongst his cousins? When Mr. Collins had learned that Jane was shortly to become engaged to Mr. Bingley, he had turned his attention to Lizzy. But any conversation that had so much as a hint of a future together was met with stone cold silence. Instead of marrying Lizzy, he had marched over to Lucas Lodge and proposed to Charlotte Lucas, and they were to be married in a month's time. That piece of good news was repeated at every opportunity by Lady Lucas.

Since there was nothing to be done about Lizzy, she would concentrate her efforts on Kitty and Lydia. Mrs. Hill, who excelled in doing the girls' hair, was now assigned to the two youngest Bennets, and when Lizzy saw Mrs. Hill walk past their bedroom with the jewelry box, she started to laugh. "Jane, Mama has determined that I am a hopeless cause, and that she will waste no more time on me. I hope I do not come to regret my decision to refuse Mr. Collins."

Jane only smiled at the absurdity of her sister's comment because she was attempting to tame Lizzy's unruly tresses, and after many minutes of effort, she finally suggested that her sister wear her hair down. They agreed upon a green ribbon that framed her face nicely, allowing her luscious dark hair to fall freely upon her shoulders. Lizzy, who had a bad habit of playing with her curls, did not know if this was a good idea.

"Yes, it is true that you play with your hair when it is down," Jane agreed, "but you are forever tucking your curls back into place when you wear it up. Since you will be playing with your hair in either case, to my mind, there is no one prettier in all of

Hertfordshire when you wear your hair down. The green gown you have chosen complements you greatly, and you will be *la belle de la danse*."

"It *is* my favorite gown."

"Yes, I know," Jane answered, aware of the reason why Lizzy had chosen that particular dress. "You will have every man at the ball asking you to dance."

But Lizzy did not care if she had every man in the ballroom asking for a dance. She cared only about one man—Mr. Darcy. This might very well be their last time together until Jane and Mr. Bingley's wedding and that was many weeks in the future.

At that moment, Lydia and Kitty came into their sisters' room to urge them to hurry. Lydia was sure that many of the officers were already at Netherfield dancing with Maria Lucas and Mary King. As Lizzy stepped out of the front door and onto the gravel path, a full moon appeared on the horizon, casting its soft glow over the landscape. The ball would last into the early hours of the morning, and Lizzy intended to dance every dance and to wear out her slippers. Because she would be so agreeably engaged, she would not think about the few hours left to her before Mr. Darcy returned to London and Miss Montford. Those thoughts were for another place where no one would see her tears.

Mr. Darcy had instructed Mercer, his manservant, to put out his very best evening clothes, and the effect of the green jacket with the black waistcoat and beige breeches was more than satisfactory. There was nothing conceited in his appraisal as he knew that he was handsome in an imperfect sort of way. A broken nose, a result of a sparring match at Jackson's Boxing Academy, had forever altered his profile, but his dark hair and gray-green eyes seemed to have appeal for the ladies, or so he had been told.

Mercer, who had been in Mr. Darcy's employ since his return from the Grand Tour five years earlier, was adept at sensing the changes in his moods. But, of late, even he was surprised by the range of his master's emotions. The day after the assembly, Mr. Darcy had ridden to Longbourn for the unpleasant task of apologizing to a young lady for a statement he had let slip as a result of his desire to be anywhere other than at an assembly in a country market town. Mercer had been anticipating that his master would return in the same mood in which he had left, but, instead, he had entered the house in a joyful mood and had climbed the stairs, taking them two at a time. The dramatic fluctuations continued, depending on whether he was discussing Letitia Montford or Elizabeth Bennet.

Pulling on his waistcoat and tightening the knot on his neckcloth, Mr. Darcy took one last look in the mirror and said, "Mercer, do you recall the saying, 'Eat, drink, and be merry, for tomorrow we die'? In my case, I would say, 'Eat, drink, and be merry for tomorrow I must go to town,'" and out the door he went in search of diversion from the events that awaited him in London.

Chapter 11

WHEN JANE HAD WRITTEN to Aunt and Uncle Gardiner to announce her engagement, she had also mentioned that there was to be a ball at Netherfield Park. Mr. Gardiner, having once kicked up his heels in the manor house before moving to London, was mildly interested in attending, but after thinking about days spent away from his business, arranging for the carriage, and having to ask his mother-in-law to come to stay with the children, he decided to stay put. However, when Mrs. Gardiner read the same letter, she started to think about what she would pack for their journey.

"My dear husband, it is not just a matter of attending a ball at Netherfield Park; you must understand that Mr. Darcy of Pemberley will be there. I grew up not five miles from his great estate, and I have very fond memories of harvest festivals held in late summer at the manor house. Although I cannot picture Miss Darcy, I do recall the young Fitzwilliam Darcy, a handsome boy, and I would very much enjoy seeing him now that he has grown to manhood."

Mrs. Gardiner continued on with detailed descriptions of

Sunday strolls along Pemberley's many streams, but it was only when she mentioned that her father had occasionally fished in the estate's waters that her husband's interest was piqued. There was nothing that gave him more pleasure than a day spent fishing, as it was the one sport that allowed him to forget about his business and all it entailed.

"Of course, it was necessary to apply to the steward for permission to fish on the property," Mrs. Gardiner cautioned her husband, "but I cannot remember it as ever having been denied."

"I wonder if the young Mr. Darcy is of a similar mind? Since we are to visit Lambton in a few weeks' time, it would be beneficial to know if that were the case. If so, I could write to the steward, and if I were in a position to mention Mr. Darcy by name, that might do the trick."

Mr. Gardiner went to the bookcase and removed Isaak Walton's *The Compleat Angler*, a book nearly as dear to him as his Bible. After scanning a number of pages, he looked up and smiled at his wife. "Mrs. Gardiner, please send word to your mother that we are in need of her assistance."

"My goodness! What has decided the matter for you?"

Turning the book so that the title faced his wife, he explained, "The Darcy estate is mentioned in *The Compleat Angler* as having some of the finest fishing in the Midlands."

While Mrs. Gardiner was thinking of which dress she would wear to the ball, Mr. Gardiner went looking for his servant. "Finch, where are my waders?"

When the Gardiners arrived at Longbourn, they were always greeted with great enthusiasm. Mr. Bennet greatly enjoyed his brother-in-law's company, while Mrs. Gardiner provided a new audience for all of his wife's stories. Despite very different temperaments, one exuberant and the other restrained, the two ladies got along quite well, and although Aunt and Uncle Gardiner loved all of their nieces, they were especially fond of the two eldest. They were greatly pleased to learn of Jane's betrothal, not just because Mr. Bingley was a man of wealth and good temperament but because Jane was in love with him. This was no marriage of convenience.

The two sisters sought some private time with their aunt, and so the trio went to an alcove in the garden. Jane, who was still giddy at her unexpected good fortunate, shared everything she knew about Mr. Bingley and his family, including his sisters' disapproval for the match. "Caroline and Louisa would have preferred someone who would have raised the family's standing in London society. Of course, I accomplish no such thing. In any event, they are to return to town after the ball."

"Where, hopefully, they will stay so that they can cause no more mischief," Lizzy added.

"And what of you, Lizzy? Now that your sister is to be married, has anyone touched your heart?"

"There are few single men in the neighborhood who can afford a wife with such a meager fortune," Lizzy quickly answered. "As for the many officers encamped nearby, I cannot see myself marrying an officer and following him from camp to camp. Therefore, as Mama often says, I am hoping Mr. Bingley will throw me into the path of other rich men. If that plan does not meet with success, then I shall rely on you, Aunt, to introduce me to eligible bachelors when I visit London."

"And what of Mr. Darcy?" Aunt Gardiner asked.

Both Jane and Lizzy exchanged glances and said, "What?" at exactly the same time, causing their aunt to study them with that peculiar look unique to mothers who think their children might be up to mischief.

"Jane mentioned in her letter that Mr. Darcy is a friend of Mr. Bingley's and that he is staying at Netherfield Park. My interest in Mr. Darcy is that I grew up in Lambton very near to the Darcy estate."

"I did not know that Lambton was so near to Pemberley, but, of course, until recently, I did not know that Pemberley even existed. Did you know the Darcys?" Lizzy asked.

"Not personally. But when Pemberley was open to view, I did go with my parents to see the house. It is a lovely Georgian stone mansion that absolutely glows in the setting sun. All the public rooms were beautifully decorated by Robert Adam, and I must admit that the pale green in their dining room has been my favorite color ever since."

"Did you ever meet Mr. and Mrs. Darcy?" Lizzy asked.

"Yes, I did. It seems that the elder Mr. Darcy and Lady Anne truly enjoyed Pemberley and spent a good deal of time there. The present master's father vastly expanded the gardens and supervised the changes himself. However, my father had moved the family to London to set up his own apothecary shop before the undertaking was finished—if a garden can ever truly be finished."

"What did they look like? Mr. Darcy and Lady Anne?" Jane asked on behalf of her sister.

"Mr. Darcy was quite tall with black hair and very hand-some. Lady Anne was petite and powdered her hair, as women did in those days, and wore those enormous hats with lots of feathers. But what I remember most about her is that she had green eyes. I had never met anyone up to that point who had green eyes."

"Her son has gray-green eyes," Lizzy told her aunt.

"Does he?"

"Yes, and he is very tall with dark hair. He too is handsome when he does not furrow his brow, which is something he often did when he first came to Hertfordshire, but not so much of late."

"If that is the case, then he must be comfortable with his company. His neighbors have made a good impression on him."

There was nothing more to be said on the subject as Mrs. Bennet and the three younger girls had found their hiding place. Mama asked numerous questions about what warehouses Jane should visit when picking out her trousseau, but before she could answer, Lydia, who was bursting at the seams with good news, told her aunt that she was to go to Brighton as the most particular friend of Mrs. Forster, the wife of the colonel commanding the regiment. As pleased as Lydia was, Kitty was equally displeased because she felt that she should have been included in the invitation. Mary was quite vocal in her disapproval of the arrangements before being quieted by her mother. From the look on Jane's and Lizzy's faces, Mrs. Gardiner understood that neither was happy with Lydia's visit to Brighton. Both considered their youngest sister to be immature and one who frequently acted without any thought about consequences. Mrs. Gardiner continued to listen attentively to what Kitty and Lydia had to say about some of the more attractive officers, including a detailed portrait of a very handsome Mr. George Wickham.

Chapter 12

THERE WAS A CLOCK in every public room at Netherfield, but the only one that kept accurate time was in the foyer. So if Darcy wanted to know just how late the Bennet family was in arriving at the ball, he would have to go out into the foyer where Bingley's sisters were greeting their guests. Because his reservoir of goodwill for Miss Bingley and Mrs. Hurst had run dry, such an action was out of the question, and so he waited.

Elizabeth had warned him that her family was always delayed, and so to pass the time, he had asked Miss Graves for a dance. But with the number of couples in attendance, every dance might last as long as thirty minutes, and he did not want to be dancing with another lady in case the Bennets did arrive. In order to avoid such a situation, he had turned to the gentlemen and ended up discussing crop yields with Mr. Patterson and the poor condition of the roads between Meryton and Watford with Mr. Everett.

After fifteen minutes of debate as to where a carriage was most likely to encounter the worst stretch of road, Darcy decided he would find a dance partner, as dancing was less demanding than his attempts to avoid dancing were. He looked about the room, hoping to find Charlotte Lucas, who had made an excellent impression on him during his evening at Lucas Lodge, but when he had finally located her, she was talking to the parson. There was something in their manner that suggested intimacy, and he wondered if Charlotte and the reverend were engaged. But if that were the case, wouldn't he have heard of it?

And then he realized what he was doing. He actually had his ear to the ground in case any of the local news involved Elizabeth Bennet. But there was more to it than even that. As was the case with Lambton, he *did* care about what happened to his tenants, the villagers, and those living on the surrounding farms, and in the case of Charlotte Lucas, because she was so pleasant, he hoped that she would marry well.

"Get thee to London, Darcy. The provinces are swallowing you up. Before you know it, you will be drinking at the public house," he mumbled to himself.

For the fourth time that evening, he refilled his punch cup and thought it very likely that when Elizabeth finally did arrive, he would be out in the bushes answering Nature's call. But then he heard the unmistakable sound of Mrs. Bennet's voice. Finally, at long last, the Bennets had arrived.

He quickly glanced in the mirror and then laughed at the ridiculousness of the situation. He had not felt like this since his years as a youth when the dancing master had finally allowed the boys to dance with the girls. While the future debutantes giggled, the boys milled about the room stealing furtive glances at the young beauties, and he smiled at the memory.

When Darcy saw Elizabeth, he took a deep breath. Before him stood one of the loveliest creatures he had ever seen, and he genuinely feared that he would give himself away. While he was enjoying the view, she had swept the hair off her shoulders, revealing a neck that he longed to kiss, that is, after he had stopped kissing her mouth. And although it was impolite to stare, he could not help himself, and even if he had been able to see only her eyes, he would still have known that she was smiling because all of her emotions were reflected in them.

"Miss Elizabeth Bennet, may I welcome you back to Netherfield Park?"

"Mr. Darcy," Elizabeth said, bowing her head and enjoying a look at his long legs. "There is such a crush of people here. We have been waiting outside for more than fifteen minutes."

"I wish I had known that."

"Would you have broken through the crowd and brought us to the beginning of the line or would you have snuck us into the hall by way of the kitchen?"

"Oh, by way of the kitchen definitely. Much more dramatic."

"Is your sister here, Mr. Darcy?"

"Georgiana was here earlier, but something happened with her dress and she had to leave. In all the time she has been gone, she could easily have made another."

"You are being too hard on your sister. Making a good appearance is so easy for a man. You put on a handsome waistcoat and coat with a fine pair of boots, and you are done. I envy you."

"You are once again correct, Miss Elizabeth, and I withdraw my criticism, especially when all of your efforts have been rewarded with such excellent results."

Darcy looked around and realized that a place had been cleared around them. Since his adoption of a good neighbor policy, he was now a source of special interest to the local population, and because of his height, he was visible to all. He decided it would be best if he visited with others in an attempt to avoid any gossip in connection with Elizabeth, but not before he had seen to his number one priority.

"Miss Elizabeth, may I be so bold as to ask for two dances this evening? I would like to dance with you before the supper break as I wish for you to meet my sister."

"I would be honored, and I would very much like for you to meet my Aunt and Uncle Gardiner who are visiting from London."

"Of course, it will be my pleasure."

"May I ask if you have already decided on the second dance?"

"If you would be so kind, may I request the last dance of the evening?" He had chosen the final dance as it would be their last and not just for the evening.

"I look forward to both dances." When she started to turn away, he called her back.

"May I ask if you know the name of the gentleman who is speaking to Miss Lucas? I feel as if I have seen him somewhere else."

"That is Mr. Collins. You may know him as he is Lady Catherine de Bourgh's vicar."

"Ah, yes. Now I remember him," he said in a flat voice.

"Did you hear Mr. Collins preach while you were in Kent?"

At this point, Mr. Darcy went silent, and after a long pause, he said, "I have been in attendance when he was preaching, but…"

"You find such discourse to be tedious."

Darcy smiled as he recalled their first conversation. "I never was one for listening to sermons. My parents insisted I sit between them in the family pew, so that I would not fidget. But how is it that he has come to be at Netherfield?"

"He is my father's cousin, and the family estate is entailed away from the female line to his benefit. In an act of generosity, he came to Longbourn in search of a wife, so that we would not find ourselves homeless in the event of our father's death."

"Surely, you are not saying that Mr. Collins was interested in making an offer to you?" he asked in genuine amazement.

"I hope I am not so unattractive as to be beneath Mr. Collins's notice."

"Are you fishing for a compliment, Miss Elizabeth? Have I not already told you that you are more than tolerable?"

"You did not always think so, Mr. Darcy. At the assembly, you easily resisted my beauty. If I recall correctly, your full statement was, 'She is tolerable, but not handsome enough to tempt me.'"

"I imagine you will probably remember that one sentence forever."

"Yes, I am sure that I will. However, it was greatly appreciated when you came to Longbourn to amend your original statement."

"It was necessary that I do so as I was in error."

Lizzy looked embarrassed. "Forgive me, Mr. Darcy. I really was not fishing for a compliment."

"I did not think you were. If you recall, at Netherfield, we had a discussion on pride versus vanity. I think we agreed that vanity *is* a failing, but I also mentioned that where there is a real superiority, pride would always be under good regulation. Although you may not comment on your own beauty, as that *would* be vanity, you may certainly take pride in your appearance as Nature has been exceptionally kind to you."

"I believe this conversation began with our discussion of Mr. Collins," Lizzy said in full blush. "He is to be married to my good friend, Charlotte Lucas."

"Ah, now I understand why people were congregating around her at Lucas Lodge. I think Mr. Collins has done very well for himself as Miss Lucas seems to be a sensible lady and that will serve him well."

"Most men are in need of sensible wives," Lizzy added, thinking of her father, "but Mr. Collins most particularly."

Knowing that the crowd had grown closer, they departed to find other dance partners, all the while thinking of the dance they would shortly have together.

Chapter 13

DARCY WAS RELIEVED WHEN his sister finally came downstairs because he had found that making himself agreeable to all and sundry was fatiguing, especially if it included a discussion with Mr. Collins about the inhabitants of Rosings Park. Darcy dearly loved his cousin, Anne de Bourgh, and although frail, she was a handsome woman. However, he had never considered her to be a candidate for being the "brightest ornament in the British court if her health had allowed her to be presented to the king and queen," and the praise Collins heaped upon his grouchy and overbearing Aunt Catherine was not only inaccurate, it was nauseating.

"Where have you been, Georgiana? I was beginning to think you had climbed down the trellis and escaped."

"Will, as you very well know, I enjoy appearing in public. If anyone could be found on the trellis, it would be you, and I apologize for the delay. While I was speaking to Mrs. Hurst, I noticed a wine stain on the lace on my bodice. I went upstairs and changed into another dress, only to have two buttons pop off, so I sat there while Mrs. Brotherton sewed on the buttons."

"Popped your buttons, did you? Are you fatter now than you were in May at the start of the season?" he whispered to his sister.

"Will, it is questions such as those that make it clear why you remain a bachelor at twenty-seven," Georgiana answered, clearly enjoying the affectionate, but teasing, relationship that had developed between them since she had come out into society. "But never mind about my weight. I would like to be introduced to Miss Bennet."

"She is dancing at present."

"If Miss Bennet is dancing, then who is speaking to Mr. Bingley?"

"Oh, my mistake. That is Jane Bennet talking with Bingley. Miss Elizabeth Bennet is dancing."

"Which of the ladies would be Miss Elizabeth?" Georgiana asked, keeping her voice even so that she would not reveal her suspicions that Will's interest in Elizabeth Bennet was more than that of her being the sister of Mr. Bingley's intended.

Georgiana immediately liked what she saw: a pretty woman with an open countenance who gave the appearance of being friendly and engaging. With the fair-haired, blue-eyed Miss Montford in mind, Georgiana realized that the ladies were as different as any two women could be. With her brother waiting for her impression of Elizabeth, Georgiana merely commented that she was very pretty. "But nothing to Miss Montford."

"If you are referring to Elizabeth's dress being made of muslin rather than silk or her wearing a rope of pearls rather than a diamond necklace, I will agree with you. However, as to physical beauty, I think Elizabeth, with her dark eyes and engaging smile, is Miss Montford's superior in looks."

"Onyx eyes."

"What?"

"I believe you referred to her eyes as being like onyx, reflecting the light."

Darcy closed his eyes and shook his head. He had been found out by his little sister and with so little effort. He told her she would have an opportunity to gauge the accuracy of his description during supper.

"I look forward to it."

With the time for their dance quickly approaching, Jane mentioned to Lizzy that with so many couples the set might last an hour.

"What on earth are we to say to each other in the course of an hour?" Lizzy asked, her voice indicating her concerns. "Since Mr. Darcy does not enjoy conversation, it will fall to me to do most of the talking."

"Mr. Darcy does not seem to mind talking to you, Lizzy. It might go quicker than you think."

Lizzy would find out soon enough, as Mr. Darcy was walking in her direction. When he extended his arm, she did feel like *la belle de la danse*. As they stood opposite to one another, Mr. Darcy commented, "Once more into the breach, Miss Elizabeth."

"Quoting Henry V's speech before the Battle of Agincourt is not the best way to start a conversation in a ballroom, Mr. Darcy. Surely, you are not equating dancing with going into battle?"

"With you, it is more like a duel. I know from past experience that you are capable of reducing conversation to its most essential elements, stripping away all layers of polite speech in favor of dealing with the heart of the matter."

"You are making me out to be a fearsome creature. That is ungenerous of you."

"On the contrary. I am paying you a compliment. You refuse to be drawn into the silly games polite society demands of us."

"We are less formal in the country, sir. When I ask a question, I want an honest answer."

"That makes you a rare bird, indeed," he commented, while passing behind her, "in either town or the country."

"As a woman, and knowing the consequences of deviating from the norms of society, I understand what you are saying. However, you are a man from a prominent family, a person of rank, and yet you still find it necessary to 'play these games,' as you put it."

"I do not endure these inconveniences for myself, but everything I say and do must be viewed as to how it will affect Georgiana. If I insult Lord High and Mighty, it may affect her prospects for making an advantageous marriage, and since I refuse to fawn and coo, I remain silent rather than risk offending with hurtful comments. Something you can attest to."

"I wonder if Miss Darcy understands the sacrifice you make on her behalf or if she would wish it if she did."

Lizzy's question went unanswered, and for the remainder of the dance, the two engaged in friendly conversation, and Mr. Darcy felt comfortable enough with his company to tweak the nose of the profligate Prince of Wales for his enormous appetite in just about everything. But he was at his most eloquent when speaking of Pemberley.

"By the end of the London season, I am so eager to be free of the noise, the dirt, the smells, and the intense scrutiny that I go directly to my estate in Derbyshire. I am very much like a man who has been breathing through a narrow funnel for months on end, but who suddenly finds his lungs filled with pure oxygen. As far as I am concerned, Pemberley is as near to heaven as you can get on this earth."

When the last notes were played and the final steps taken, Mr. Darcy escorted Lizzy to the table where they were to dine. Miss Darcy was already seated and was talking to Caroline Bingley and Mrs. Hurst, who soon departed to see to their duties as hostesses. Knowing about his intended courtship with Miss Montford in London, Lizzy was puzzled by his request that she meet his sister. She was not alone in her confusion, as Mr. Darcy was equally incapable of answering the same question.

Chapter 14

Georgiana Darcy was eager to meet the woman who seemed to have captured her brother's attention, if not his heart, and Lizzy was equally interested in meeting the young woman who brought a smile to Mr. Darcy's face whenever her name was mentioned. Georgiana had the dark Darcy hair and gray-green eyes, but little else. She was perfectly lovely and carried herself with a confidence that belied her eighteen years. But her youth was evident once she began to speak, as she talked with the enthusiasm of one who was experiencing everything for the first time.

"I am very pleased to make your acquaintance, Miss Darcy, as I have heard so much about you from Mrs. Hurst and Miss Bingley," Lizzy began.

"Oh dear!" Georgiana said with a sigh. "Now I know my virtues have been exaggerated, and my shortcomings ignored."

"Well, their enthusiasm for their subject is a compliment in itself."

"How kind of them, but let us not talk about me, but of the dance," Miss Darcy said, blushing. "I just love to dance."

"Of course, our country dances are nothing to the splendid balls of London."

"But I enjoy them so much as they provide an opportunity to meet new people. By the end of the London season, there was not one story I had not heard three or four times. I do not know why I was surprised by that, as everywhere I went I was with the same people," and Georgiana quickly glanced at Caroline and Louisa. "It is different in the country. Every year at Pemberley, we hold a harvest festival and dance. Unfortunately, because of all the rain, we were unable to host it this year. I was sorely disappointed as I find our neighbors to be refreshing in their frankness."

At that moment, Mr. and Mrs. Gardiner joined the party, and Lizzy was pleased to introduce them. She was proud of her uncle who had abandoned the safe career of a country solicitor to strike out on his own in London and had successfully established a company for the importation of coffee from plantations around the world, a topic that proved to be of interest to Mr. Darcy.

"A coffee broker! Why, coffee is my favorite brew, although I must confess I was better off before I had ever drunk a cup. Now, I cannot start the morning without it."

Mr. Gardiner smiled and confessed to the same addiction. "My wife limits me to four cups a day and nothing after 7:00 at night as there seems to be something in the drink that keeps one awake."

"Mrs. Gardiner, do you share our weakness for coffee?" Darcy asked.

"No, sir. I do not look to start new bad habits. I have enough already, especially my taste for sweets and chocolate, but I do have something in common with you as I spent my early years in Lambton. My father was the assistant to the apothecary. You would not remember him, as you would have been too young. I remember your parents with great fondness, and I am deeply attached to Derbyshire as it is the most beautiful county in England."

"Mrs. Gardiner, we are in complete agreement with you," Georgiana answered enthusiastically on her brother's behalf. "Will and I spent six weeks there after the end of the season. The views are both spectacular and inspirational. I am no poet, except when I visit the Peak, and any talent I have with a pen falls away as soon as I set foot in London."

"Mr. Gardiner and I are to visit the Peak in three weeks' time, and we are trying to convince our niece to join us," Mrs. Gardiner said.

"You really should go, Miss Elizabeth. The inn at Lambton offers comfortable accommodations, and if you mention our acquaintance, the Culvers will treat you royally."

Lizzy assured Georgiana that she would give the matter careful consideration, but at that time, the first notes of the fiddle announced that the dancing would resume. She had promised the dance to Mr. Collins, while Mr. Darcy had found a more skilled companion in the parson's betrothed. Georgiana graciously accepted an invitation from the aptly named Mr. Short, who was as tall as he was wide.

I like Miss Darcy very much, Elizabeth thought. If she were not a Darcy who lived in a mansion in faraway Derbyshire, they might easily be friends. But she *was* a Darcy and her brother *was* the lord of the manor, and nothing could change that.

When Darcy wasn't dancing, he was much in demand with the local gentry. They were impressed with his knowledge of the day-to-day running of a farm. At his father's insistence, he had served something akin to an apprenticeship to the elder Wickham as Darcy's father had emphasized that the financial well-being of the family was directly dependent upon the sound stewardship of the land and a good working relationship with their tenants. As a result, there had never been so much as a hint of discontent at Pemberley.

Before claiming his dance with Elizabeth, Darcy went out onto the terrace. If there was any doubt of an attraction between the two before this night, their time together had put an end to all pretenses. However, he had a legacy to preserve, and he could almost feel the eyes of Baron Roger D'Arcy, the first Darcy to set foot on English soil, upon him. But at that moment, his feelings for the lady were such that he wished that his ancestor had stayed in Normandy so that he might not feel this heartache.

"There you are, Darcy. Hiding from the ladies, are you?" Bingley said with a laugh in his voice. "I would imagine you have worn out your boots by now."

Darcy shook his head and smiled at the only man of his acquaintance who seemed to never have an unhappy moment, and at this particular time, Bingley was the perfect antidote for his dark thoughts.

"I must say it was damned decent of you to dance with Miss Mary Bennet. Not the best dancer. Missed a few steps here and there. But you would have hardly known it from the pleasure she had in being asked by the towering figure of Fitzwilliam Darcy. Are you done for the night?"

"No, I have one more dance with Miss Elizabeth."

"Darcy, have you given any consideration to…"

"No," Darcy said, interrupting him. "Let me stop you there

as there is nothing to discuss. By the end of the week, I shall be in London," and after patting his friend on the back, he returned to the ballroom.

While waiting for the musicians to begin the dance, Darcy admitted to his partner that he was enjoying the Netherfield ball as much as any dance in London during the season.

"Perhaps you had grown tired of too much deference," Elizabeth suggested.

Darcy laughed out loud. "You have the most remarkable observations, Miss Elizabeth. Too much deference? I had never thought of it in quite that way. But, yes, I was bored to the point of exasperation."

"But you are to return to London?"

"Yes," he said with genuine regret. "Things are not always as one would wish them to be. Sometimes, our destiny is determined long before we are born."

"Forgive me for asking a personal question, but during our time together at Netherfield, you mentioned that your mother and Lady Catherine were half sisters."

"Yes, Lady Catherine's mother was born a Denby; my mother's mother was a Devereaux."

"Did you ever wonder if there was a hullabaloo when your grandmother married a Fitzwilliam, someone who was not of Norman stock?"

"I am sure any objections were mitigated by the fact that he was to be an earl, but I have never given it any thought." The furrowed brow that revealed so much about what Mr. Darcy was thinking returned, and after many minutes of silence, he added, "Well, I imagine the Devereauxes would have thought their daughter, my grandmother, was marrying beneath her station as the first Earl Fitzwilliam was granted that title only in 1692, merely a few decades before their marriage."

A smile appeared on Darcy's face as he realized the implications of Elizabeth's question. "The Devereaux line goes go back to Baron Guillaume D'Evreux, who was in the meadow at Runnymede in 1215 when King John signed the Magna Carta. To the Devereauxes, the Fitzwilliams were parvenus."

Following that statement, the conversation reverted to those subjects that Mr. Darcy claimed to disdain. Apparently, his thoughts were elsewhere, and the best he could come up with was the number of couples who were in attendance at the ball.

While the Bennets and Gardiners waited for their carriages to be brought 'round, Mr. Darcy and Mr. Gardiner continued their discussion about coffee.

"I import coffee beans from around the world, Mr. Darcy, but to my mind, the best coffee comes from the Jamaican Highlands. It is grown in the shade, and because it is more difficult to harvest, it is rather expensive, but well worth it."

"Do you sample the brews?"

"Definitely, sir, as it is I who bears the brunt of any displeasure from the retailers. Now, when you are in London, you must come to our home in Gracechurch Street. I have a whole cupboard reserved for nothing else."

"I hope you are sincere, Mr. Gardiner, as I intend to take you up on your offer. I confess that I am fascinated by the whole process of a commodity from the far reaches of the globe ending up in my breakfast room."

At that time, Jane walked over and, after taking hold of her uncle's arm, invited the Darcys to dinner on Wednesday. "Uncle, we must allow our hosts to retire, and my father has expressed an interest in joining in your conversation. He has just now revealed that he often visited White's Coffee House as a young man whenever he was in town. Mr. Bingley has already agreed to come, although, unfortunately, his sisters will not be able to join us. Hopefully, that will not be the case with Mr. Darcy and Miss Darcy."

"I had planned to leave for London on Wednesday, Miss Bennet," and then he looked at his sister, who was imploring him with her big eyes to accept the invitation.

"Mr. Darcy, if I may speak on Mr. Bennet's behalf," Mrs. Gardiner said, "in a house full of females with no interest in angling, you will save the poor man from having to listen to all of Mr. Gardiner's fish tales—again."

After agreeing to dinner at Longbourn, Darcy looked for Elizabeth, but she had already stepped out onto the portico. Because she believed she had seen the last of Mr. Darcy, an overwhelming sadness had settled on Lizzy. When Jane informed her that the Darcys were coming to dinner, it did little to lift her spirits. It would only delay the inevitable, and it was not possible to move forward if you remained weighted to the past.

Chapter 15

THE FOLLOWING DAY, GEORGIANA and her brother took a long walk about the property, so that they might talk freely and without the constant interruption of Mr. Bingley's sisters.

"I had a delightful time at the ball. I wore through my dance slippers," Georgiana began.

"You always wear through your dance slippers. You buy them by the dozen, do you not?"

"No, I do not, but I think that is the perfect solution to my problem. I shall order them a dozen at a time in ten different colors and be done with it."

Darcy turned around and started to walk backward. When she was a child, he had done this for her amusement, and he was in an excellent mood because he was very pleased with how she had performed in public.

"Will, you are not as good as you once were at walking backward. If you do not alter your course, you will walk right into a tree."

"You are trying to make me look as you always did. But I

shall not be tricked as I have previously reconnoitered this path in case of such an eventuality." The two burst out laughing and resumed their stroll side by side.

"My dear sister, you were as charming and gracious as always, and you put a smile on more than one gentleman's face, but most especially Mr. Short's. The poor fellow was winded, but he stuck with you to the end."

"It was a capital idea for Mr. Bingley to send to London for the musicians who had played at the Clermont ball, as the music was first rate. I also thought the ladies who exhibited were quite good, especially Miss King, who performed admirably on the pianoforte. Not as well as Miss Montford, of course, but then few are her equal. However, Miss Montford cannot sing."

That was the first statement his sister had made about Miss Montford that could possibly be construed as being negative.

"But, of course, if you play three instruments, it would be unfair to expect such a person to also have an exceptional voice," Georgiana continued, "and she does speak French and Italian. On the other hand, with the exception of attending the opera, Italian is not of much use, what with Napoleon's brother-in-law and sister sitting on the throne of Naples. I mean, no one is going to the Italian peninsula any time soon."

Darcy continued to say nothing, but it was clear Miss Montford's pedestal had a crack in it.

"And there were so many fine-looking ladies at the ball. Miss Cross and Miss Maria Lucas are very attractive, and, of course, Miss Bennet is perfectly lovely as is her sister, Elizabeth. Miss Elizabeth's face is not symmetrical, but then neither is mine nor is Miss Montford's, whose nose points slightly to the right."

After hearing the comment about Miss Montford's nose,

Darcy visualized a huge chunk of stone crashing to the ground. If this conversation went on much longer, Miss Montford might find herself without any pedestal at all.

"But what is most important to me is how much a person smiles, and there were so many happy faces at the ball. It shows a *joie de vivre*."

"Ladies in the country tend to smile more and laugh more freely than ladies in town. I believe Mrs. Quilling cautioned you that a smile by an unmarried young lady is subject to misinterpretation, and one must be cautious. There are few families in the country who have the resources to hire governesses, and as a result, these young ladies do not have the benefit of their wisdom." A vision of a demure Miss Montford, with her controlled half smiles, appeared before him, as did Elizabeth Bennet, whose smiles were open and contagious.

"That is why I love being in the country. I am so very eager to go to Pemberley."

"As you know, Georgiana, I have business in town. Any plans for Pemberley will be discussed once we are in London."

After a day's rest following the ball, Lizzy's usual good humor returned. She was not one to brood or pine or cry into her pillow, and so she decided to look to that evening's supper as an opportunity to get to know Miss Darcy a little better without having to step over the flowers that the Bingley sisters laid at her feet.

Lizzy also used the dinner to get to know her future brother-in-law. She found Charles to be a delightful man, full of good humor, and perfectly suited to her sister, but he would not have done for her at all. There was no edge to him whatsoever, and although she liked a sunny day as much as the next person, life would be rather dull if it did not rain occasionally. She needed to find a man with more complexity than Charles Bingley, someone like Mr. Darcy, but available.

After supper, everyone went into the parlor to play a few rounds of whist. Miss Darcy sat at Lizzy's table and gave glowing reports of just about everything she had seen or heard or tasted since coming to the country.

"After being in town for less than a week, I was surprised when my brother told me of his plans to return to Hertfordshire. Will never did things like that before he met Mr. Bingley, but I see that Charles has found an antidote for his restlessness," and she smiled at Jane.

"Your description of Mr. Bingley's need for movement is quite accurate, Miss Darcy," Lizzy responded, "as he danced every dance at that first assembly and made an excellent impression on his company."

"And what of Will?" Georgiana asked of a brother whom she loved dearly.

"He definitely made an impression, which was remarked upon by almost everyone," Lizzy said in as cheerful a tone as she could command. "Isn't that right, Jane?" Her sister nodded, but said nothing for fear she would laugh.

"I am very glad to hear it," and after playing her hand, whispered to Lizzy, "Sometimes Will can get a bit cranky, but he is the best of brothers."

After three rounds, the ladies left the card tables in search of conversation, and the discussion eventually turned to Derbyshire. The Gardiners revealed that they had been successful in convincing Lizzy to join them for their holiday, and Jane mentioned that Charles and she would visit the Peak in the spring.

"To me, the Peak is beautiful no matter what time of year it is. The fruit trees bloom all through the spring, the heather is best seen in September, and the autumn colors are at their peak right now." Looking to Mrs. Gardiner, Georgiana asked, "Is it not possible to move up your visit as the colors will not be nearly as brilliant in three weeks' time?"

"Miss Darcy, those dates were forced upon us by the lack of accommodations at the inns. We took the first opening we could get."

"Yes, that is true. I know the inn at Lambton is very busy at this time of year. I assume you wrote to them as well?"

Mrs. Gardiner nodded.

"I would not recommend any other place in Lambton as some can be rather dirty," and then a smile crossed Georgiana's face. "You must stay at Pemberley. Although we will not be in residence, as Will has business in town, the servants will be at your service, and if you ride, the grooms will provide the perfect mount for you."

Without consulting her aunt, Lizzy answered for the Gardiners in something like a stutter. "No. Thank you, but no. It is appreciated, but it is not possible. No thank you."

Jane looked at her sister and shook her head indicating that saying "no" so many times might be seen as being ungracious, and when Lizzy looked at her aunt, she watched as her puzzled expression turned to one of understanding. Her niece was in love with Mr. Darcy.

"In years past, we have had many visitors stay at Pemberley when we were not there," Georgiana said in an effort to try to reassure Lizzy. "If Mr. Gardiner's business allows him to leave earlier, I would highly recommend that you do so and stay at Pemberley," and added, "Miss Elizabeth, it is most definitely not an inconvenience. The gardens are particularly lovely at this time of the year, and our gardener, Mr. Ferguson, dearly loves to show visitors about the estate."

"But your brother has not agreed to such a scheme, Miss Darcy," which she said with some urgency as the men were leaving the card tables. Lizzy hoped that Miss Darcy would accept the fact that her offer had been declined, but she would not.

"For a long time now, Will has told me that once I had turned eighteen, I would be the mistress of Pemberley until such time as he took a wife. Therefore, I should feel free to invite my friends to our home."

At that time, Darcy came and stood behind his sister, indicating that he was ready to leave.

"Will, the Gardiners and Miss Elizabeth are to visit the Peak in three weeks' time, and I have tried to convince them that they should move up that date as the colors are nearing their peak."

"Georgiana is correct, Mrs. Gardiner. One good storm and every leaf will be stripped off the trees. If it can be arranged, I would encourage you to do so."

"I know they would like to do that, Will," Georgiana continued, "but there are no accommodations at any of the inns. So I suggested that they stay at Pemberley."

Darcy opened his mouth to say something, but nothing came out, and after an uncomfortably long pause, Mrs. Gardiner announced they would adhere to their original plans, but thanked Georgiana for her invitation.

Because Darcy had been caught flatfooted by his sister's

offer, he was aware that his response had been less than gracious. "Please forgive me for not responding immediately, Mrs. Gardiner. I was thinking that my sister and I would be in town and unable to welcome you. However, despite our absence, there is no reason why you should not stay at Pemberley. We have an army of servants to see to your needs, and they are happier when there are guests in the house."

"Will, I believe if one of us was in residence they would accept our offer, so I shall go with them. You will be busy seeing to your business affairs, and London is rather dull at this time of year."

Instead of everyone looking at the speaker, the ladies were all looking at Mr. Darcy to see what his reaction to his sister's plan would be.

"Georgiana, there would be a lot of details to work out as I will have need of the carriage."

It was then that Mr. Gardiner joined the party, and after being informed of Miss Darcy's offer, he jumped right at it. With visions of fish practically jumping into his creel, he explained to Mr. Darcy that the carriage would not be an issue.

"I keep a carriage—not in town, of course, as the costs are prohibitive, but it only takes two days to make arrangements to have it brought in. If your concern is for your sister's safety while traveling, I have a manservant who spent some of his youth on the boxing circuit. He is a handy fellow to have about when I go down to the docks."

"It appears that all there is left to do is to work out the details," Mr. Darcy said, all the while looking at his sister.

Chapter 16

WHEN MR. BINGLEY TOOK the seat opposite to her in the carriage, Georgiana was relieved because it forced Will to sit next to her, and in that way, her brother would not be able to stare her down. But the ride was merely a brief respite. As soon as they arrived at Netherfield, Darcy said good night to Mr. Bingley, explaining that he needed to discuss some of the details for their early departure with his sister.

As soon as she went into the study, Georgiana poured a glass of port for her brother. After handing it to him, he gestured for her to sit down, but said nothing. In Will's case, silence was not a good sign.

Darcy rarely raised his voice as he considered it to be a sign of weakness. If one could not present an argument without shouting the other fellow down, then his case had no merit, and it would be a sorry day if he ever raised his voice to a woman. But he was unhappy with the latest turn of events, and he was trying to cool his anger.

"Georgiana, what do you think you are playing at?" Will

asked in an even but stern tone. "And do not look at me like that. You know exactly what I am talking about."

"Since the Gardiners already had plans to go to Derbyshire, it seemed the right thing to do. I really like them, and I am already quite fond of Miss Elizabeth."

"This is about Elizabeth, isn't it?"

Georgiana nodded. "I think you like her very much."

"Well, this explains some things," he said, standing up, and he started to pace. "Up until yesterday, Miss Montford could do no wrong, but now everything has changed. She cannot sing, speaks a language which is of little benefit to anyone, and has a nose which points to the left."

"To the right," and Will looked at her with a blank expression. "Her nose points to the right. Whenever she visits us, she always sits in the blue chair, and her nose points toward the street."

An exasperated Darcy sat back down on the sofa and started to rub his forehead. He was getting another headache. As soon as he had departed the Bennets' house, he had decided he must leave Hertfordshire immediately because he could easily have asked himself the same question: What did he think *he* was playing at? Despite having to leave for London in two days' time, he had flirted with Elizabeth. It could not be construed in any other way.

"Will, you do not love Miss Montford," Georgiana said, while moving to the sofa and putting her hand on his.

"No. I do not. But marriages between members of the upper class have very little to do with love. They are alliances made for financial considerations or dynastic or political reasons. Love may follow, but it is not the overriding reason for a man and woman to marry. You have been out in society long enough to know that."

Georgiana was ready for this argument, as she had spent the previous night in her bedchamber thinking of little else.

"You have told me that the investments you made through Mr. Bingley's financial advisor have provided you with handsome returns, so money is not the issue here. Nor is it politics, as you are a Whig and Sir John is a Tory. That leaves dynastic considerations. I understand you are the last male Darcy. If you do not produce an heir, I must leave Pemberley as David Ashton will inherit. Because of that, you have decided you must avoid doing anything that may affect my prospects in the event such a thing should happen. What we are discussing here is a matter of precedence—where my place at the table would be—below the salt as it were."

Darcy nodded, saying nothing, as he was afraid his voice would crack. He had a little sister no longer. She was an adult with full powers of reasoning and persuasion, which had lain hidden because of the playfulness of her manners.

"If I were not a consideration, would you marry Elizabeth Bennet?" Georgiana asked.

"No, I cannot," he said, shaking his head. "You must understand that there was no mistaking my particular attention to Miss Montford during the season. Our names have been linked together in the newspapers. To withdraw at this point would be dishonorable as she would be acutely embarrassed." After taking a drink, he added, "It is too late, Georgiana. It cannot be undone."

Georgiana stood up. "I am very tired, and we have an early start." After refilling Will's glass, she concluded by saying, "You do understand she will know. Oh, I am sure it will never be discussed openly, but Miss Montford will know you do not love her," and she went quietly out the door.

When Georgiana awoke, it was nearly 10:00, and she quickly called for Mrs. Brotherton. Her brother would not be happy that she was so late in getting ready.

"Miss Georgiana, Mr. Darcy departed hours ago, but he left you this note."

> *Dear Georgie,*
>
> *After thinking about our plans, I decided that it made no sense for you to go back to London, only to return to Netherfield in a few days. I will have Macy gather whatever she thinks is necessary and will send it to you by way of the Gardiners, and I will ask the Gardiners to use my carriage. Although I am sure they own a fine conveyance, I will rest easier if I know you are in our carriage. I will also send Mercer with you.*
>
> *I know that last year you were alone at Pemberley after Mr. Ferguson's wife died, and I remember your words. "Yes, I will be alone, that is, if you do not count Mr. Jackson, Mrs. Bradshaw, Mrs. Reynolds, the grooms, the maids, the footmen, etc." Besides, I am quite confident that you are capable of executing your responsibilities as mistress of Pemberley.*
>
> *Please instruct Belling that he is to see that Mr. Gardiner is properly outfitted and that he should send one of the grooms who is familiar with all of the best fishing spots. I suggest Avery or Cubbins. I doubt the Gardiners ride, and the only comment Elizabeth made about riding in my presence was that she manages not to fall off the horse. Therefore, I think it will be sufficient*

for you to have Belling take them into the District by wagon, but Mrs. Bradshaw will need to prepare a simple repast for them to take with them.

You should meet with Jackson, Mrs. Bradshaw, and Mrs. Reynolds as soon after your arrival as possible as they will need sufficient notice to provide for our guests. I will post a letter to Jackson as soon as I arrive in London, and he will inform the staff.

Regarding last night, I have one more thing to add. With rank comes privilege, but it also comes with responsibilities as well as a code of conduct.

Love, Will

P.S. Bingley is to bring the Crenshaws to Netherfield, but he has promised he will not do so until you are safely on the road to Pemberley.

Georgiana laughed at her brother's comments. He was confident in her abilities to host a party for a grand total of three people, but felt the need to provide instructions anyway. As to Will's business in London, since she could do nothing about the situation with Miss Montford, she would not think about it. Instead, she would enjoy the company of the woman he really loved.

Chapter 17

DARCY LEFT NETHERFIELD AS the first rays of the sun came over the horizon, filling in the spaces in the greenery with bursts of light. Next to the note he had addressed to his sister, he had left another for Miss Bingley and Mrs. Hurst as he had not taken proper leave of them the night before. Although he did not like Caroline and was easily annoyed by Mrs. Hurst, they knew how to keep house for their brother, and there was something to be said in praise of management skills because, with the Crenshaws' arrival, that was about to change.

Darcy did not understand why the ten-year-old twins, Gaius and Lucius, were not in boarding school. "There isn't a housemaster in the whole of England who would tolerate such behavior for one minute, no less years," he had told Bingley, who had nodded his head in agreement. Ever the pleasant fellow, Bingley had explained, "My hands are tied. I can offer Diana my advice, but I cannot force her to do anything."

"Why not?" Darcy thought. "I am being forced by convention to do something I do not want to do," and then he put his head in the corner of the carriage and went to sleep.

When Darcy arrived at the London townhouse, he found his cousin, Colonel Fitzwilliam, waiting for him. As close as he was to Bingley, it was his cousin whom he thought of as his brother. They were the same age, and as children, had spent long summers together at Pemberley or at the Fitzwilliam estate in Kent or, better yet, at the seaside in Weymouth where the Darcys maintained a villa.

"Richard, you are a sight for sore eyes," he said, patting his cousin on his back. "What brings you to London?"

"You seriously do not know?" he asked, laughing. "You sent me this extraordinary note," and he held it out so that his cousin could see that he had brought it with him, "in which you wanted to know *post haste* if there was a 'hullabaloo' when our grandparents had married. Allow me to read it:

> *Richard, My thanks for your continued service in keeping the Corsican corporal from our shores. It would be an inconvenience to be invaded by the French.*
>
> *Having lived with our grandparents for many years, do you remember if they ever mentioned a hullabaloo when they married? Old Norman stock v. upstart Anglo-Irish? Any of that? Your immediate response will be appreciated.*
>
> *Yours, Will*

"Not exactly teeming with details, is it? I must know the purpose of this letter."

"You could have written to me, Richard. Considering your military obligations, I did not expect your response to be hand delivered."

"I was looking for a break in the monotony, and I was owed considerable leave. I am so tired of sitting in a camp in Kent sticking my tongue out at the Frenchies on the opposite shore. I thought it would be exciting to be an artillery officer shooting off very big guns, but we keep our powder dry and wait. If there wasn't such a scarcity of heiresses, I would seriously consider selling my commission. But enough about me. Why do you need to know this information?"

"Answer the question, and I promise I will tell all."

"Agreed," and Richard began. "I could not remember hearing anything about a hullabaloo, so I stopped at Mama's on the way here. She had the whole story on the tip of her tongue. Our grandfather, Robert, who was not an earl at this time, married Charlotte Denby, who gave birth to Aunt Catherine, but died a few years later. Following his first wife's death, Robert went to London in search of a second wife, which is where he was introduced to eighteen-year-old Marie Devereaux. When her parents got wind that a romance was brewing, they sent Marie to live with relations in Rouen, but Robert followed her there, and they married in secret. But it did not stay a secret for long because she got pregnant with my father.

"Apparently, when the marriage was revealed, there was no hullabaloo. It was closer to an explosion. Marie was cut off from the family entirely—no money, no visits. Unlike the Darcys, the Devereauxes had remained Catholic and were appalled that their daughter had married someone who was neither Norman nor Catholic. They actually had their sights set on her marrying the Earl of Arundel, the heir to the Duke of Norfolk, the highest peer in the realm, and a Catholic to boot.

"The Fitzwilliams sent emissaries to negotiate a peace. Over the decades, remaining Catholic had done nothing for the Devereaux finances, and their Norman laurels were all that was left to them. So the earl offered them a gift of five thousand pounds; it was refused. But when he increased it to eight thousands pounds, all was forgiven. According to my mother, Marie and Robert married for love and stayed in love. Neither had any regrets."

"So Marie was prepared to risk everything to be with someone from an Anglo-Irish family that lacked the ancient ties to the monarchy that set these Norman families apart."

"It was risky for our grandfather as well," Richard answered. "Although Marie joined the Church of England after her parents had died, at the time of her marriage, she was a Roman Catholic. Two generations earlier, George I, the first of the Hanoverians, had ascended the throne in order to keep it from the Catholic Stuarts. It was a touchy time, and so I say *bravo* to both of them. But why did you need this information?"

Darcy went and poured a glass of wine for both of them and shared with his cousin the burden he had been carrying around for so many weeks.

"I have fallen in love. Head over heels. Walking on air. Can't think of anything else type of love."

"I gather we are not speaking of Miss Montford?"

"No. The lady is the sister of Miss Jane Bennet who will marry Charles Bingley in December. She is the daughter of a gentleman farmer."

"Ah, I see. The purpose of your letter was to find out if you would be betraying your Devereaux ancestors by marrying someone who is so far beneath your station in life."

"Those are not the words I would have used, but, yes, that is the question. There are damn few of us left. Only a handful of families are more than half Norman, but I am also the grandson of an earl. How would such a marriage affect Georgiana's prospects?"

"You want my advice? Well, here is what I have to say: 'bollocks.' Bollocks to the whole bloody nonsense. My commanding officer is the youngest son of a duke, and he could not find his own arse with a map. But because of who his father is, I must take orders from him even though he might possibly get my men killed. And look at my brother, Antony, Lord Fitzwilliam, who has not been in his wife's bed in a decade despite the lack of an heir. Both are pedigreed. The only problem is, they can't stand each other.

"Will, you know better than I do that the world is changing. We have rich merchants with chests full of coin, and dukes and earls with little money, and because of this, great changes are happening right under our noses. Sons and grandsons of earls are marrying the daughters of merchants, and that is the way of the future. You are uncomfortable with a possible alliance with a family not of your rank because you are in the vanguard. But be brave. Your children, no matter who the mother, will have to face even greater changes."

"Before I met Charles Bingley," Darcy said, "I had reservations about what you just described or what Sir John Montford calls 'the upward migration of the servile class which threatens England as much as the French.' However, that is not my main concern. What about Miss Montford?"

"I gather you feel committed to her because you spent so much time in her company during the season, and because of that, there are expectations?"

Richard walked over to the window and looked out into the street. He had no good news for his cousin, as he had heard

Sir John Montford speaking of Darcy at White's, the conservative Tory men's club, of which he was a member. As an officer in the King's army, it would not do to tweak the nose of his monarch, as Darcy did every time he dined at Brook's, the liberal Whig's men's club.

"What did Sir John say?" Darcy asked.

"'Darcy. Damn good sort,'" Richard said, lowering his voice in imitation of Sir John. "'Terrible politics, but a capital fellow. He will make someone a fine husband,' and then he winked at his company."

"Oh, God," Darcy groaned. "Well, there you have it. Unless something totally unforeseen takes place, you will shortly be wishing me joy," and he handed his cousin an empty glass.

After a somber dinner at Brook's, the two returned to the townhouse. For fear of being overheard, nothing had been said at the club, but over a glass of port, Richard asked his cousin the one question that had remained unanswered. Was Miss Elizabeth in love with *him*?

"I don't know," and after puzzling over it in his mind, he repeated that he did not know if she felt as he did. "You know how it is during the season. You start a flirtation, and it begins a progression. If all goes well, it will end up at the altar. I never had that with Elizabeth. Oh, there was a flirtation, but without the prospect of marriage looming in the background, it was very different. We actually had real conversations because of the lack of tension.

"Elizabeth is intelligent, charming, and perceptive. It is a pleasure to be in her company and not to be subjected to the mundane conversation that is the diet of the London salons. Richard, I cannot live on puffed-up pastries. I need meat on my plate," and looking at his cousin, he concluded, "Elizabeth challenges me. She is my equal in all things but rank."

"Will, I can see you are troubled, but from all you have said, I do not think you have injured Miss Elizabeth. She sounds as if she is a sensible woman who recognizes that her position is inferior to yours, making marriage unlikely."

"I hope you are right, Richard, because it would be a dark day for me if I believed she thought I had been trifling with her affections."

But after his cousin had retired, Darcy went over everything that had happened between Elizabeth and him. He wondered if, in his need to be near Elizabeth, he had hurt her, and if that were the case, he would hurt her no more.

Chapter 18

WHILE LIZZY WAS PACKING for her holiday to Derbyshire, Jane was sitting on the bed reading a letter from Lydia.

"Well, it seems that there is no limit to the number of dances and concerts she attends, and she goes to the shops every day and plays cards two or three times a week. She is still a flirt and boasts of it. Last week, she wrote of an Ensign Gray, and this week, she is singing the praises of Lieutenant Tenyson."

"At least she is moving up in rank. If Lydia manages to attract the attention of a captain, Mama will have Uncle Philips drawing up a marriage contract for her."

Jane knew her sister was in jest. Both sisters had strongly objected to her being allowed to go to Brighton with Mrs. Forster, who was only nineteen herself, but both had been overruled by their father.

"As long as it is not Lieutenant Wickham," Lizzy added. "While I was at Mrs. Proctor's card party, he sought me out once again for the purpose of maligning Mr. Darcy. This time his story involved the sister, Miss Darcy. He claimed to have provided endless hours of entertainment for her. I gave him no encouragement, and when I said that I thought it unfair to talk about someone who was not there to defend himself, he walked away."

"I saw that," Jane said. "He was clearly unhappy with you."

"Well, he is gone, and hopefully, we will hear no more about him. Besides, I want to think about rocks and mountains and gardens and tree-lined paths, not Mr. Wickham."

It gladdened Jane's heart to see how happy Lizzy was in preparing for her journey, especially now that she had been assured by Miss Darcy that her brother would remain in London. After first being opposed to going to Pemberley, Lizzy was now eager to visit the manor house and bask in all the delights the landed gentry took in their stride.

"Miss Darcy has mentioned there is a dappled gray in Pemberley's stables that will do very well for me, and that she will turn me into a first-rate horsewoman. She is being overly optimistic there, but I am agreeable to the idea of becoming an equestrian," Lizzy said, laughing. "She has also arranged for a picnic in the Peak District, and if we choose, she said that one of her grooms will take us to some of the caves that are actually on the Darcy property. And the gardens! If they are anywhere near as beautiful as her description, then I shall truly be in heaven. It has been two years since we visited Woburn Abbey."

Lizzy came and sat next to her sister. "It has been five days since Mr. Darcy left to go up to town, and in that time, I have recovered my senses, and I have taken stock of my prospects. Mr. Peterson was very attentive to me at Aunt Susan's in August, and when a man mentions the size of his fortune, it shows some interest on his part. I wish I had given him more encouragement, but I am confident that if he had become engaged, Aunt Susan would have written to us as she dearly loves sharing neighborhood gossip."

Looking out the window, Lizzy saw that Miss Darcy and Mr. Bingley had arrived for dinner. Both sisters hurried down the stairs, one to greet her beloved Charles and the other to make welcome a new friend.

Shortly after dinner, Mrs. Bennet gave out a cry announcing the Gardiners' arrival. Being of an amiable temperament, she loved having guests, but this time her excitement was due in large part to the mode of transportation rather than the people being transported. The Gardiners had arrived in the Darcy carriage.

Every Bennet, Miss Darcy, and Mr. Bingley went out to greet the Gardiners. Once the carriage came to a complete stop, a footman jumped off the back of the carriage and assisted a smiling Mrs. Gardiner as she exited from the luxurious conveyance. Mercer spoke with Miss Darcy, assuring her that the maid had sent the requested items and handed her a letter from her brother.

"I am sure he will begin his missive by telling me how confident he is in my abilities, and then proceed to give me a dozen more instructions as to how to entertain our guests." Mercer smiled and nodded. His master was a man who paid attention to the details, which was why he found his courtship of Miss Montford so puzzling. It was higgledy-piggledy, a word Mercer had never before thought to apply to Mr. Darcy, but he suspected that the reason for his unsettled behavior was now admiring his carriage.

Pointing at the shiny black coach with the Darcy coat of arms emblazoned on its side, a giggling Mrs. Bennet asked Mercer if she could get in, and an unembarrassed Mr. Bennet climbed in after his wife. After every Bennet enjoyed the comfort of the carriage and after every servant had taken a peek inside, all returned to the parlor for a short visit, as Georgiana needed to return to Netherfield.

But before she departed, Georgiana wanted to warn the Bennets about the Crenshaw children. After listening to tales of syrup on chairs in the servants' hall, puddles filled in with pine needles to hide the water beneath, pine cones in pillows, et cetera, Mrs. Bennet said, "Surely, Miss Darcy, you are having a little fun with us. After all, they are only children."

"They may be children, but they think and act like adults— very, very mischievous adults. If you see them near a stream or collecting acorns, be on your guard."

Jane glanced at Mr. Bingley. Surely, Charles would expect civil behavior from any guest, but most particularly from the children of his sister.

"Where is the father?" Mrs. Bennet asked.

"Safely in London at Lincoln's Inn. Apparently, Mr. Crenshaw visited Pompeii as a youth and was disturbed that so many people died. He blamed it on a lack of preparation, so he has brought up his children in a way that they might survive an epic disaster."

"But we do not have volcanoes in England. A heavy snow and a rather nasty flood are all that we have ever had in Meryton. I am afraid they will be disappointed," Mrs. Bennet said in a concerned voice.

Georgiana knowingly shook her head. "I will leave you to judge for yourselves, but as my brother often says, 'Forewarned is forearmed.' I hope you will have no need of this information, but you might want to tell your neighbors."

Chapter 19

WHEN IT BECAME KNOWN about the village that Jane Bennet was engaged to the handsome, not to mention very rich, Mr. Bingley, the news was greeted with smiles from the ladies and huzzahs from the men because Jane, along with her sister Lizzy, was among the neighborhood favorites. No one could describe Jane without mentioning the words "kind" and "sweet," but under that gentle exterior was a determination that would have surprised many.

There were many times in Jane's nearly twenty-three years when Mrs. Bennet's nerves or heart flutters had caused her to take to her bed, which usually resulted in Mr. Bennet retreating to the safety of his study, leaving the care of the younger children to Jane and Lizzy. Although the sisters shared responsibilities, it was decided that it would be best if Mary, Kitty, and Lydia looked to one person as the ultimate author-ity, and they had agreed that it should be Jane by virtue of her seniority. While Lizzy liaised with Papa, Jane would see to their mother and sometimes assume her duties. Her first meeting with the cook regarding the evening meals had been when she was thirteen.

In preparation for the arrival of Charles's sister, Diana, and her six children, Jane decided to have a talk with Mr. Bingley. She wanted to know exactly how much of what had been said about the Crenshaw children was true and how much exaggeration. When Jane asked for an accounting of any misdeeds they had actually committed, Charles had answered, "Just those done to me or to anyone?"

What followed was a litany of horrors perpetuated on family members as well as the general population by the Crenshaw brood. In a tone Charles had never heard from Jane, she asked for an explanation as to why such behavior was tolerated.

"I feel sorry for Diana because she is married to an eccentric," Bingley answered defensively. "First, Crenshaw thought he needed to prepare his family to survive a natural disaster. When none occurred, he instructed them as to what they should do in the event of a French invasion: rearguard actions, foraging, sabotage, and so on. The problem is, he considers himself to be a theorist, and as such, leaves it to Diana to execute his ideas. Unfortunately, she is always with child and has very little energy, and so the children run wild. I am the only one who will have them for a visit."

But then Bingley broke out into a smile. "I have taken the precaution of warning the staff and have given them permission to respond in kind," Charles said, "and I have doubled their monthly salary for the length of Diana's visit as compensation. Besides, I expect that my sister and her children will return to their home in about three weeks' time."

"Mr. Bingley, that is all well and good, but in three weeks, they can cause a lot of aggravation and possibly damage to an estate you are leasing. I think we should come up with our own plan and not wait upon them to act."

When the Darcy carriage arrived at Longbourn, Lizzy could hardly believe that she was going to spend her holiday at Pemberley with its extensive gardens and views of the Peak, and she had to fight the urge to giggle at her good fortune. Once seated, she found that the Gardiners and she were to share the carriage with Miss Darcy's little corkscrew-tailed pug.

"I hope you do not mind," Georgiana said. "Because I have been so busy of late, my little darling has been woefully neglected," and she kissed his nose.

Although the Bennets had four dogs, they were expected to earn their keep about the farm in return for much love and lots of meat. In town, many of the wives of the merchants kept lap dogs, mostly as an accessory, but some loved their dogs more than their husbands.

"What is his name?"

"His real name is Peeps, but Will complained that was such a silly…" and then she stopped. "It was decided that we should rename him Pepper."

For a few minutes, Lizzy's heart sank. Miss Darcy had stopped in midsentence because she knew that she cared for her brother. Although embarrassing, she decided that she would not allow it to ruin her holiday. So Lizzy asked a number of general questions about Mr. Darcy, so that Georgiana would feel she could talk freely about him.

It was a pleasant ride with Mr. Gardiner sleeping and

snoring for most of the journey, and his wife nodding on and off throughout. For Georgiana and Lizzy, it was a time to share stories of dresses, dance partners, and sore feet. Lizzy also learned some of Georgiana's personal history, including the death of her mother ten years earlier following a miscarriage.

"One of the reasons I so love to go to Pemberley is because Mama's presence is everywhere, and there is nothing sad about it. I shall show you her portraits. She was very beautiful."

She then mentioned that her father had died suddenly while Will had been on the Continent on the Grand Tour, and he had to return home immediately to assume the many duties and responsibilities of being the master of Pemberley as well as the guardianship of his thirteen-year-old sister.

"Will can be impatient, but you could not find a better brother or cousin or friend. As Mr. Bingley once said, 'When choosing up sides, everyone wants Darcy.' I think that says a lot about a person."

Following an overnight stay with the Hulston family, friends of the Darcys in Derby, the carriage continued on to Pemberley, and when the coach turned into the drive to the estate, Lizzy experienced what her mother referred to as "the flutters."

As the carriage emerged from the woods and into the light, before her, glowing in the afternoon sun, was Pemberley, the ancestral home of the Darcys. Tears came to her eyes, and if asked, she would have been unable to say if they were tears of joy or sorrow.

Chapter 20

CHARLES WAS POSITIVELY BURSTING with pride as Jane laid out her plan to retake the high ground in the war with the Crenshaw children. A day earlier, his bride-to-be had arrived at Netherfield just in time to say good-bye to Caroline and Louisa. It was their intention to be halfway to London before their sister's children arrived. Caroline's parting advice to Jane was not to sit down without looking, and Louisa leaned out the window to remind Charles to lock his door when he retired for the night. And with that, they made good their escape.

Part of the problem was apparent as soon as Jane was introduced to Mrs. Crenshaw. She was expecting, possibly six months along, and with half the day still ahead of her, she was already exhausted, and the children were prepared to take advantage of their mother's fatigue. Unfortunately, for the youngsters, the servants had planned their own welcome. Instead of being free to run amok, they were marched out the back door by the three sons of Mrs. Smart, Netherfield's cook, and into the park where Mr. Bingley's grooms were waiting for them.

But they could be contained only for so long, and during dinner in the breakfast room and away from the china, the four oldest Crenshaws came in and immediately began eating off their mother's plate and out of the fruit bowls in a foraging expedition. When they came to Jane's plate, she placed a napkin over it and informed them that what they were doing was not foraging but plundering, the latter being an act of war, and she had no intention of yielding. After an attempt by their leader, Gaius, to stare Jane down had failed, the little savages returned to the park.

By the time Jane had arrived back at Longbourn, she already had a plan in mind. The crusade for the reformation of the Crenshaws began when their Uncle Charles herded Gaius, Lucius, Athena, and Darius into his carriage, leaving only toddler Minerva and baby Julian behind, for a trip to Longbourn.

After being escorted into the Bennet dining room by the two burly sons of Mr. and Mrs. Hill, the children found that each of them had been assigned a footman who had taken up his position immediately behind the chairs of the four children.

The battle was on when Gaius refused to use utensils. His plate was immediately removed by Adam Hill, and when he attempted to leave the table without being excused, John Jr. picked him up and put him back in his seat. When he tried again, Mr. Hill, who was standing guard at the door, pulled out a tether, and the defiant one sat down quietly and asked for his plate back.

"Not today, dear," Mrs. Bennet said. "Only children who have minded their manners will have their dinner."

Lucius, who usually followed Gaius in all things, decided to cooperate because he was hungry. Breakfast had been a bowl of "take it or leave it" porridge, which he despised. "I want food," and he picked up his fork and knife to show that he would follow orders.

"*Please*. You must say *please*, Master Lucius," Mrs. Bennet told the more compliant twin.

"Soldiers don't say please," he answered in a voice revealing just how insecure he was feeling.

"Are you an officer or an enlisted man?" Mr. Bennet asked.

"An officer."

"Any officer in His Majesty's Army would be regarded as a gentleman, and as such, would know the proper manners to use when dining."

"Well, then, I am an enlisted man," he said, even less sure than when he had been an officer.

"Enlisted men follow orders," and after staring him in the eye, he continued, "or they are flogged."

A wide-eyed Lucius politely asked for a plate, and an intimidated Athena and Darius followed his lead.

There was so much to accomplish in so little time, but victory was declared when all four children asked to be excused from the table, and it had not been necessary to tether any of them to their chairs.

"You must follow through at Netherfield, Charles, or today will have been for naught," Jane said as she bid him good-bye.

"I shall see to it. I promise," and added, "By God, Jane, you are going to make an excellent mother. Our children will be models for every child in the neighborhood."

Jane guessed correctly that Gaius would organize a response in order to demonstrate his authority, and when the farmers and others traveling the road between Meryton and Watford reported especially aggressive squirrels pummeling them with acorns, the Crenshaw children were ordered out to the park to pick up the thousands of acorns that had fallen from centuries-old oaks, and when they finally waved the white flag and agreed to stop their pranks, Jane rewarded them with cake and punch.

Chapter 21

AFTER LOOKING IN THE mirror, Darcy pulled on his waistcoat and straightened his neckcloth, and upon achieving the desired effect, he asked Mercer his opinion.

"Very handsome, sir. I believe the blue coat is your second favorite."

After five years of service, Darcy had great affection and respect for his valet. His loyalty was admirable and endearing, and because of this, his master often took his servant into his confidence.

"I know that statement has a double meaning, Mercer, but I have decided that since I must do this, I shall do it properly and with dignity. Miss Montford is entitled to a proper courtship, and so I shall begin one in earnest."

"If I may speak, sir?"

"No, you may not. I have looked at this matter every which way from Sunday, but once I learned that her father was talking me up as her suitor at his club, I knew there was no escape. Besides, she is pleasant company, attractive, accomplished, and two of her sisters have five sons between them, and I must have an heir." Following a long pause, he continued, "Mercer, please hail a hackney." After taking one last look in the mirror, he added, "And so it begins."

Miss Montford looked pretty in pink. It was her best color, greatly complementing her fair complexion, blue eyes, and blond hair, and Darcy expressed his admiration for her new dress. After making sure her coiffure was new, with the curling about the face that Georgiana had described, he mentioned that as well, and after a series of such compliments, he saw it: a full smile. And she had all her teeth! Not always a given, so that was a relief.

"I see you have made some new sketches, Miss Montford." He assumed they were new, but since there were so many of them throughout the house, perhaps they had just been moved from another location. "You seem to favor St. Paul's. It is Wren's finest creation, so I certainly understand. I must say that your artwork is every bit as good as the artists who sell their prints in front of the cathedral."

"Thank you, Mr. Darcy. Papa buys the visitor's cards from the sellers for me, and I copy them in ink, charcoal, and watercolors."

"You copy them? I had not thought. Maybe you should open your own stall," Darcy said in jest, and Miss Montford responded with her half smile. So this is how it would be. Compliments merited full smiles, while jokes earned only half smiles. He would make a note of it. "You are so busy with all of your sketches, painting tables and screens, and embroidery, I wonder you have any time to read."

"I read but little, sir, as there is nothing to show for it."

At first Darcy thought she was joking, but then he took her meaning.

"It is true that there is nothing tangible produced, nothing to hang on the walls or drape over a chair, but ideas are real things. You only have to look at America, a new nation built on a foundation of ideas. Granted, they can be misused, as is the case with French revolutionaries, but they have their own power."

Miss Montford nodded. "And how is Miss Darcy?"

So much for the power of ideas. He imagined with a father as hidebound to convention as Sir John Montford was, having "ideas" might be viewed as being dangerous, and unlike the Darcy dinner table, such things were definitely not discussed.

"She is very well and at Pemberley visiting with friends."

"Miss Smythe?"

"No, actually new friends. If you recall, Charles Bingley is to marry Miss Jane Bennet of Longbourn Manor in Hertfordshire. Georgiana's guests are Miss Bennet's sister, Elizabeth, and her aunt and uncle, Mr. and Mrs. Gardiner. I found their company to be most agreeable. Mrs. Gardiner spent some of her youth in nearby Lambton, and Mr. Gardiner is an avid angler and eager to cast his line in Pemberley's streams."

"Are the Gardiners friends with the Bingleys?" she asked with that tilt of the head that made her look as if her head was weighted to the left.

"No. The Gardiners only know Charles Bingley through the Bennets. Mr. Gardiner lives on Gracechurch Street here in town."

"And who is Mr. Gardiner?"

"Who is he? Do you mean what does he do?"

The puzzled expression returned. "I do not understand that question, Mr. Darcy. What do you mean by 'what does he *do*?'"

"Are you asking how Mr. Gardiner earns his living?"

"Oh, he earns his living," she said, clearly unhappy with the answer.

Despite Colonel Fitzwilliam's claim that the integration of the wealthy merchant class with England's upper class was well under way, not everyone had heard the news. In Sir John Montford's world, merchants were "tainted by trade." If you did not inherit your wealth, you were beneath his notice—and, apparently, in his daughter's world as well.

"Mr. Gardiner is a coffee broker."

Miss Montford shrugged her shoulders, clearly not knowing what a coffee broker was or did.

"Have you ever thought about the tea you drink every day, Miss Montford? It comes from faraway lands, China, India, Ceylon, on ships with towering masts and billowing sails, hugging the coast of Africa, and following the outline of the Iberian Peninsula before veering out to sea with its destination of Bristol or London. After the ship arrives in port, the brokers go down to the docks and bid on its cargo. In turn, the brokers sell their commodities to the merchants, who sell it to your housekeeper. It is amazing to me the things we take for granted as part of our everyday lives come to us from such great distances, including our coffee and tea."

"That sounds very exciting. I have never given any thought to where my tea comes from, but I think I shall in the future."

With that slight encouragement, Darcy recalled stories told to him by his father and governess as well as the journals and accounts of the great explorers he had read while at Eton.

"Those who faced the dangers of the open seas have been a subject that has always fascinated me. As a boy, I sailed with

Captain Cook on his voyages of discovery to the South Seas and intercepted ships from the New World laden with silver and gold bound for Spain with Sir Francis Drake." After a short pause, he added, "I am speaking figuratively, of course." Surely, she knew that. Cook had died a few years before his birth, and Drake had sailed for the great Elizabeth, Regina Gloriana, in the sixteenth century.

And then the silence he so dreaded returned as Miss Montford did not know how to respond to his childhood imaginings. After a few minutes, Darcy fell back on the old reliable: the weather.

"Georgiana writes that the autumn colors at Pemberley are still quite beautiful. I think this may be the first autumn I have ever missed in Derbyshire."

"Why did you not go with your sister?"

"Because there are people I wished to see in London." *Like you, my dear. That is why I am here.* "This will be the first time my sister has acted as the mistress of Pemberley, but it is a small party and manageable for her first effort."

"I imagine you wish you were in Derbyshire since London is rather dull at this time of year."

"Yes, very dull."

"Since your sister is alone and you wish to be in the country, maybe you should go to Pemberley."

"Miss Montford, my sister is not *alone*. And I have been gone from London quite a bit of late, as you may have noticed, and I feel I may have neglected some of my... friends."

"But, Mr. Darcy, you should not neglect your sister on anyone's account. Papa would never permit me go to the country without a male relation."

Neglect? Darcy wanted to laugh. This was absurd. Georgiana was in the company of a mature young woman and her middle-aged aunt and uncle and in the midst of an army of servants. His staff could have fended off a French raid.

"I have always encouraged Georgiana's independence," Darcy explained, and then he heard a gasp from Miss Montford. With a harsher tone than he had intended, he said, "You should not be uneasy on my sister's account. There is always someone about," and then he saw an opening. "But if it would make you feel better if I went to Derbyshire, I would consider it. However, I am perfectly agreeable to staying in town if that is what you would wish."

"I can only say what my father would do, and he would go to Derbyshire to be with me."

After another fifteen minutes of weather-related discussions—Letitia was predicting cooler temperatures with some rain and snow sometime during the winter season—Darcy took his leave. When he emerged from the Montford house, a hackney pulled over, but he waved him off. He needed to walk and to think. He had finally taken the first step in beginning a courtship with Miss Montford, and after paying her what was for him an excessive amount of compliments, she had encouraged him to leave town, which he was willing to do. There was only one problem. He could not go to Pemberley.

Chapter 22

WHEN DARCY RETURNED HOME, it was to an empty house. Richard was dining at his club and would most certainly play cards, and he had given Mercer the evening off. He suspected that his valet was having a romance with a cook in one of the adjacent townhouses. Mercer, a man of forty-seven years, had never married and had once told him that he had a female acquaintance at many of the coaching inns where the post coach made its stops, but rather than limiting himself to any one lady, he had chosen to remain a bachelor. "Share the wealth, sir," he had said with a smile.

But a letter from Georgiana was waiting for him in which she related her company's first full day at Pemberley. With Mr. Gardiner fishing and Mrs. Gardiner visiting an old friend in the village, Georgiana had convinced Elizabeth to go riding.

Since it had been such a long time since Lizzy has been on a horse (she much prefers walking)...

Lizzy? Of course, Georgiana would call her Lizzy; they were friends. As far as her preference for walking was concerned, Darcy knew from their time together at Netherfield during her sister's convalescence that Elizabeth was very fond of walking. He remembered a most pleasant stroll in the park, and by the time they had returned to the house, he was in love with her.

> *...she felt the need to ride Sugar in the yard. But our dappled gray had her own ideas and went right back into the stables. Lizzy was laughing so hard that she could not get Sugar to respond, and in no time at all, they were back at Sugar's stall. You should have seen the look on Belling's face, and then, without any irony, he said, "Are you done for the day, Miss?" and we could hardly contain ourselves. It had taken Belling longer to saddle Sugar than Lizzy had been on her.*

After tucking the note into his pocket, Darcy had been on the point of retiring when Richard came home. "Tonight was not my night for cards. I am a poor man, and so I know when to leave the tables, especially when I am losing to my brother." After pouring himself a brandy and another for his cousin, Richard asked Darcy how his visit with Miss Montford had gone.

After Darcy explained the interesting turn of events, Richard said, "Darcy, you are a lucky devil. Miss Montford actually gave you her permission to go to Pemberley."

"I *can't* go to Pemberley, but if I am supposed to be in Derbyshire, then I can't stay in town either. I shall write to Anne to tell her that I wish to visit. There is no hardship there, except, of course, listening to Aunt Catherine's complaints."

"Darcy, what are you talking about? You *must* go to Pemberley."

"Out of the question," he said, shaking his head. "I will not even consider it, and if you want to know why, I shall tell you. After our discussion the other night in which we decided that Miss Elizabeth had not been injured, I came to a different conclusion. She may not have had expectations of a marriage proposal, but flirtations are hopeful things, full of promise, and I cannot believe that at some time in all those weeks that she had not looked for a different outcome."

"If that is what you truly believe, then you really *must* go to Pemberley. If her hopes have truly been elevated, then they should be brought down in increments, not in one deafening crash when you attend the wedding of her sister to Charles Bingley with your betrothed. My suggestion would be for you to go to Derbyshire and let her know that you wish to remain friends."

Darcy sat back in his chair and looked at the brandy-filled glass as the candlelight passed through it, the crystal providing clarity as to the wine's color and texture and to his thoughts as well.

"I have no one to blame for the situation I find myself in but me. I had this list in my head of what was required of a prospective bride for Fitzwilliam Darcy, and with Miss Montford, I was able to check off many of the items on the list: attractive, accomplished, good dancer, pleasant personality, an agreeable companion for Georgiana, granddaughter of an earl, and someone who moved in the highest tiers of London society. Through a process of elimination, I decided that she was the one I would marry, so that I might have a son and heir.

"Richard, if it were not so damn depressing I could almost laugh. Logical, careful, and methodical Fitzwilliam Darcy, who does everything by the numbers so that nothing is overlooked and plans are made for every contingency, messed up badly. The one thing I failed to factor in to all this courtship business was that I would fall in love with someone else."

Chapter 23

As soon as Mr. Darcy departed, Miss Montford went to the window to make sure that he was truly gone. When she saw him wave off the hackney, she was afraid he might return. But with her nose pressed to the pane, she watched as he continued walking in the direction of his house, and she let out a sigh of relief. With tears in her eyes, she went to the small sitting room adjacent to the parlor where Mrs. Redford, her companion and chaperone, sat during her visits with Mr. Darcy. This was not a secret because the rocking of Mrs. Redford's chair and the clicking of her knitting needles provided a rhythmic background to all their conversations.

Mrs. Redford, who had taken the place of Letitia's mother when Lady Margaret had died when the child was eight, came over and gave her a hug, and she clung to her companion in absolute misery. Letitia took out an embroidered handkerchief from a drawer stuffed full of them.

"It had such a promising beginning, but now..." After dabbing everything that was wet, she explained what had gone wrong. "When Papa introduced me to Mr. Darcy, I could hardly believe he was interested in me at all, but I was flattered by his attention. At first, we talked about all those things that one is supposed to talk about in a ballroom: dancing, the number of couples, the weather, plays at Haymarket, and the opera. But then things started to change. I noticed he became impatient when I talked about the weather. Then at the public ball at Merritt's, he introduced me to Charles Bingley, and Mr. Bingley asked me to dance. What could I say? He is a friend of Mr. Darcy's, and although he is most agreeable company, he is not a gentleman. And then he asked if I knew Mr. Bingley's sisters. How would I know them? We have no friends in common.

"Tonight was the worst of all. He spoke of subjects that are of no interest to me. I do not care where my tea comes from. I know little of the exploits of the explorers, and Papa absolutely forbids any discussion about America because they overthrew their lawful king. Yet Mr. Darcy admires them, and I know that Papa would find that most objectionable. And he has befriended a coffee broker person, and this man, Mr. Gardiner, and his wife are now at Pemberley with their niece, who is sister to Mr. Bingley's betrothed. He is forming a circle of friends with people not of my station. Am I to be expected to entertain them in our home? To visit them at their estates and in their homes?

"But the very worst was when he said he had always encouraged his sister to be independent and told me that she has gone to Pemberley with people new to her acquaintance and without a male relation. Will Mr. Darcy expect me to be independent? Will he put me in a carriage and send me off on my own?

"Mr. Jasper Wiggins is not like him at all," Letitia continued to complain through her sniffles. "He loves talking about the weather and is excellent at guessing the number of couples in a ballroom. Mr. Wiggins was acceptable to Papa as a suitable marriage partner for me because he comes from a prominent banking family, and his father is to be knighted. But once Mr. Darcy came to the house, Mr. Wiggins was pushed aside, and now Papa will make me marry Mr. Darcy." She then burst into tears. "And he is such a big man."

Mrs. Redford continued to listen to Letitia's complaints through bouts of sobbing, but she had already heard enough. The facts of the matter were that Mr. Darcy did not love Letitia, and Letitia was a nervous wreck around Mr. Darcy. It was obvious to Mrs. Redford that both individuals wanted to get out of the relationship. The obstacle was Sir John, who was determined to have Mr. Darcy as a son-in-law, and she knew why. If Letitia were to marry into one of the oldest families in the realm that would be a real feather in Sir John's cap. Connections—this was all about connections.

Sir John, who had spent most of the last two months in the country shooting, believed that all was well in London. He had no idea how distressed his youngest daughter was. But Mrs. Redford understood her employer and knew well his weaknesses. He was a vain, self-important man, and, hopefully, his vanity and snobbery would be Letitia's way out and, for that matter, Mr. Darcy's as well.

Chapter 24

MRS. REDFORD WAS NOT alone in her scheming. Colonel Fitzwilliam was enjoying his time away from his regiment and his commanding officer, a total incompetent, whose only rival was the Prince of Wales. The prince had come to Kent to review the troops, and with every inch of his tailored uniform decorated with unearned military honors, he had looked like a bejeweled stuffed sausage. It was at that moment that Richard had thought about selling his commission. But for the time being, his own affairs had to be put aside because his cousin was in danger of making a disastrous mistake, and because he had to move quickly, his military training would serve him well.

Richard's plan was unconventional and involved enlisting the support of his brother, Antony, Lord Fitzwilliam. Antony had married Eleanor Henley, the daughter of the 2nd Earl Henley, and with the exception of his two lovely daughters, the marriage had been a disaster. The misery of his marriage had set him on a course of reckless spending, excessive drinking, and gaming, as well as bedding half the married women in London society, resulting in more than one close call with a husband.

In order to prevent Darcy from visiting Anne in Kent, he needed a rider to go to Rosings to update their cousin on the swirl of events taking place in London, and for that, Richard was in need of the services of Gregg, Antony's manservant, an accomplished horseman. Richard brought his brother up to date on the disaster-in-the-making that was the Montford/Darcy courtship.

"This does not sound like the Darcy I know," Antony said. "But if he is not going to learn from my mistakes, then why should I help him? On the other hand, he is my cousin, and on occasion has lent me money. So I shall agree to send my man to Kent, as Darcy lacks my experience in handling unpleasant situations. However, I would like to know how Anne is going to help prevent a marriage in London when she is sequestered with Empress Catherine in Rosings Park."

"I need Anne's help to get Darcy to Pemberley. Once there, our cousin will be unable to resist the charms of Miss Elizabeth Bennet. I am telling you, Antony, he is head over heels in love with the lady. This is a Will Darcy you do not know."

Richard also took Mercer into his confidence, urging him to plant seeds of doubt about Miss Montford whenever possible, even at the risk of his master's displeasure. Mercer readily agreed, as he was a daily witness to his growing unhappiness. When Mr. Darcy had repeated a comment made by his housemaster at Eton, "You have made your bed, and now you must lie in it," Mercer had responded by saying that was an excellent lesson for a boy, but perhaps being miserable for the rest of his life might be too harsh even for his housemaster.

"And what did Mr. Darcy say?" Richard asked.

"He told me he wished to hear no more on the subject."

The next evening, after dinner, Darcy took the day's post into the parlor and was happy to see that he had a letter from Anne de Bourgh.

"Damn!" Darcy said after scanning the letter.

"What?" Richard asked innocently.

"Anne is to go to her Aunt Hargrave's and will not be at Rosings when I had planned to visit," and he read on. "However, she is eagerly looking forward to receiving a description of the autumn colors from Georgie. Very interesting since I had not mentioned that Georgie was in Derbyshire. I had intended to tell Anne when I saw her."

"I may have mentioned it to Antony, and I know he is in frequent correspondence with Anne," Richard said, quickly trying to cover up Anne's mistake. He could not blame his cousin for the slipup as she was a novice conspirator.

"Am I to believe that Antony immediately dashed off a letter to Anne to apprise her of Georgie's whereabouts? So my next question is, did you have something to do with this?" and he held out Anne's letter.

"I thank you for the compliment. If you think I am capable of informing Anne in Kent of events in London that have only just happened, you obviously think me a clever fellow." Darcy agreed that it was unlikely. "Listen, Darcy," Richard quickly added, "you cannot avoid Miss Elizabeth. Her sister is to marry your closest friend, and you will see her at the wedding, at christenings, when you visit with Bingley at Netherfield, and on many other occasions. I suggest you write to Georgiana and tell her you are coming to Pemberley for the shooting and fishing and that you will have limited contact with *her* guests."

"I don't know what else I can do. If I am supposed to be in Derbyshire, I cannot be seen anywhere in town. I am beginning to feel like an adolescent incapable of managing his own affairs." After several minutes of thought, Darcy agreed. "You have convinced me. I shall tell Mercer to make preparations for us to go to Pemberley."

Mercer stepped into the room from his listening post in the hall. "I assume that we are to leave first thing in the morning, sir. May I suggest that we travel lightly? I will arrange for a wagon to come to Pemberley the next day, carrying your trunks as well as the colonel's. In that way, we will make excellent time because we will have a lighter load."

"Mercer, tell me the truth. Had you already started packing?" There was something going on here, but he had not figured it out yet.

"Sir, part of being a good valet is anticipating the master's wishes, so I have packed some things, but not all, and there is much to be done."

"Well, it seems the Fates, being helped by others, I suspect, have conspired to have me in Derbyshire, and I will not defy them." But what would he do once he got there?

Chapter 25

WHEN COLONEL FITZWILLIAM EMERGED from the Darcy townhouse, he was expecting to get into the Darcy carriage. Instead, the Gardiner carriage awaited. Richard, who lived the life of a soldier, had no problem with the simpler conveyance. But it would be a good deal noisier than Will's well-sprung, thickly padded carriage, and he wished to speak to his cousin about Miss Montford. With Mercer present, he was unsure of how much he should say. It quickly became a moot point because, despite the noise and bumps, Mercer went to sleep almost immediately.

"Do not worry about him," Darcy told his cousin. "There are only two things that will wake him up. One is if you say his name, and the other is if the carriage makes any noise that in his many years of experience in driving a coach sounds wrong to him. He will sit straight up as if a cannon has gone off. It is amazing, but he is able to filter out all other sounds."

"Like a man who cannot hear a baby crying."

"Exactly. I will provide a demonstration of how quickly he

reacts when we get near to the inn. In any event, you may speak freely whether he is awake or not. But if you want to talk to me about Miss Montford, I must tell you I have grown weary of the subject. There is nothing more to be said."

"Will, I must speak, as I believe your happiness depends upon it, so let us look at the facts. You have paid Miss Montford only enough notice so that people suspect you are about to embark on a courtship. But even the limited amount of time you have spent in the lady's company is too much for her, which is why she has encouraged you to go to Pemberley."

"Are you saying she does not want me to court her?"

"Yes, that is exactly what I am saying. I think you quite overwhelm her. You two are so different. I wonder what you talk about when you are together."

"She likes to speak of the weather and ladies' apparel, and the opera, but after a half hour, there is nothing more to be said. The last time I called on her, I thought I should turn the conversation in a different direction. Make it a little more interesting. I had just spoken with Mr. Gardiner, Elizabeth's uncle, about how remarkable it is that our tea and coffee come from such distances."

"Did she swoon?" Richard asked, and Darcy rolled his eyes. "You spoke of tea and coffee. That is not exactly the language of love."

"I know what the language of love is, and it is nauseating. And that was not the only thing discussed. I also admired her hair and her handiwork that is prominently displayed throughout the house. You cannot look anywhere in the drawing room without having some accomplishment in view. It is like visiting a gallery. But her favorite topic is the weather. On each visit, she has commented on the chilly, foggy mornings, which are followed by afternoons with either sunny, partly cloudy, or cloudy skies with a possibility of rain—or not—followed by cooler temperatures and darkness. This is typical weather for London in late November and has been since this town was known as Londonium under the Romans."

"Those are things she has been taught to do and say. The more accomplishments a lady has, the more likely she will marry well, and being so new to society, what do you think she is going to talk about? The debates in Parliament? You are used to discussing such things with Mrs. Conway in her salon."

Darcy did not respond to Richard's comment about Mrs. Conway, his friend as well as his lover. Once he had decided to court Miss Montford, he had to stop visiting her as it would have been inappropriate, but the result was that he was starved for intelligent conversation, as well as other things.

"You speak of accomplished ladies," Darcy said. "Recently, I have changed my opinion as to what constitutes an accomplished woman. If Miss Montford played only the pianoforte, I would consider her to be accomplished because she plays brilliantly. She need not do anything else, except one thing. She *must* read books and newspapers. She *must* know what is going on in the world in which she lives. I spoke to her of the power of ideas. I gave as an example America and their remarkable experiment with a government with no monarch at its head, but she showed no interest."

"You spoke to the daughter of a Tory politician about America, a country who overthrew its king. Will, for God's sakes, that is something to debate at your club, but it is not something you discuss while courting, which makes my point.

The two of you do not belong together. I suspect she wishes to see the back of you, as much as you wish to end it with her, but she cannot because of her father."

"I *have* noticed a change," Darcy said, nodding his head in agreement. "As soon as I deviated from the pedestrian, she looked almost alarmed."

"All right then. We are making progress. Now, I am going to tell you something that you must keep to yourself," Richard said as he lowered his voice. This was something that even the trusted Mercer should not hear. "The king intends to award four baronies in order to fill the House of Lords with Tories who will maintain his policies long after he is gone. He suspects that the Whigs will continue to push for Catholic emancipation and the expansion of the franchise to vote."

"And we shall. It is a matter of fairness."

"I have no argument with that, but our king and Sir John do, which is why he will be one of the four barons."

"How do you know this?"

"Antony told me. Say what you will about my brother, but he knows what is going on in Parliament. So I took the liberty of sharing something with my brother without asking your permission."

"This better be about politics and not romance," Darcy said, and his green eyes bored into his cousin, "because anything you share with your brother has an excellent chance of ending up in *The Insider*," a scandal magazine, which he despised, especially since it had exposed his relationship with Mrs. Conway. "If this has anything to do with my courtship of Miss Montford, you have done me no favor."

"That is not it at all. Antony told me that Sir John is

boasting to everyone at White's that England will have one less Whig to make mischief once a certain event occurs."

"To hell he will. I am no Tory."

"Exactly. So I told Antony you were saying the same thing about Sir John; that is, you hoped to turn him into a Whig. Of course, I told him not to say anything to ensure that he did. My brother can be very helpful in that way."

"If we succeed in putting an end to this farce," Darcy said, "I would like it to appear as if Miss Montford and her father have called an end to it. Except for impropriety, they can say what they will about me. But this will take time to play out, and there is no guarantee of success. Because of that, I must adhere to my original plan. I shall say that my purpose in going to Pemberley is to shoot, and we shall see how much damage Antony can do in London."

"It has to succeed, Will. We are talking about the happiness of four people."

"Four? Does that include Sir John?"

"No, it includes Jasper Wiggins. Wiggins was paying a fair amount of attention to Miss Montford, but withdrew from the field once it appeared as if you were going to court her. I have made discreet inquiries, and I have learned he is still very interested in the lady, but cannot act because of you."

Darcy smiled. For the first time in weeks, he had hope, and knowing that they were drawing close to their destination, he turned to his manservant. "Mercer, we are nearing the inn."

Mercer sat up as erect as any soldier on review. "Sir? Other than the usual arrangements, is there anything you require?"

"Thank you, Mercer, but no," and Darcy laughed to himself, something he had not done in ages, or at least since the last time he had seen Elizabeth.

Chapter 26

LIZZY THOUGHT SHE HAD been as quiet as a church mouse in performing her morning toilette, but within minutes of her rising, the maid appeared to assist in dressing her. At Longbourn, although Mr. and Mrs. Hill were servants, they were so entwined with the Bennets that each thought of the other as family. During their childhood, Mrs. Bennet had instructed her girls that the servants were there "to help" not "to do," but it was the opposite at Pemberley.

Lizzy had met Ellie the night before when the maid had come to help her prepare for bed. It was all Lizzy could do to not giggle, but amusement turned to appreciation when Ellie brushed her hair and told her that she would certainly be able to tame any wayward curls.

In the morning, when Lizzy came down to the breakfast room, she found that her Uncle Gardiner had already left for his first day of fishing with Cubbins, and Mrs. Gardiner, an avid gardener herself, was getting a private tour of the gardens with Mr. Ferguson. But Georgiana, with Pepper, her pug, on her lap, was waiting for her. There were also two whippets that had the run of the house and seemed to be on some sort of mission as they went from room to room, and Georgiana explained that they were Will's dogs, David and Goliath.

"When I come to Pemberley, they think Will must be here as well, so they just keep looking for him until he does come, or I go. He would never admit it, but they are part of the reason he comes home so frequently."

Georgiana had not prepared any events for the day, but she did ask a favor. "Mrs. Reynolds is to conduct a tour of Pemberley for some visitors from the inn, and I would ask that you join them. Our housekeeper came to Pemberley from Kent with my mother when my parents married, and she delights in telling people about the family and estate. I have heard her tour so many times that I have learned it by heart. In addition to telling you about the portraits and the dimensions of the room, she will mention that my brother is the best landlord and master who ever lived, that my father was an excellent man, and that Will is as generous with the poor as my mother had been. I will not repeat what she says about me, only that she is too kind."

All was as Georgiana had said it would be, with the house-keeper pointing out some of the exceptional pieces in the Darcy collection: a Van Dyke here, a Reynolds there, and a Greek antiquity nestled in a niche. Of particular interest to Lizzy was the family portrait painted when Miss Darcy was about five and her brother fourteen. When Lizzy said that Miss Darcy resembled her mother in all things except hair and eye color, Georgiana was elated.

"Now that I have been out in society and have seen the best that London has to offer, I still think Mama was the most beautiful woman in the world. She was a little taller than you, perhaps five feet, four inches, with the tiniest waist, and she wore these enormous hats with an abundance of feathers. And I *loved* her dresses. Unlike the very straight lines of our frocks, hers were all frills and flounces, and I thought that she might take flight."

If Georgiana resembled the Fitzwilliams, her brother was all Darcy and a younger version of his father. When Miss Darcy showed her another portrait of her brother that had been painted three years earlier when he was twenty-four, she remarked on how much he had changed since becoming the master of Pemberley.

"My father died while my brother was traveling on the Continent. Will once told me that he had left Pemberley a boy but had returned as a man. You can see it in his face; he is so very serious. The management of such a large estate and being responsible for so many others, including the servants, our tenants, and me, weighs on him because he always does the right thing even when it costs him personally."

The two ladies rejoined the tour group with Lizzy only half listening to Mrs. Reynolds's recitations. However, there were two statements that did merit Lizzy's attention: "Some people call my master proud, but I am sure I never saw any such thing. To my fancy, it is only because he does not rattle away like other young men." Lizzy agreed that no one could ever accuse Mr. Darcy of "rattling away."

But it was her response to a second question that truly puzzled Lizzy. When asked if there was a Mrs. Fitzwilliam Darcy, Mrs. Reynolds had replied: "Not at present, and I do not know when that will be. I do not know who is good enough for him."

Had not Mr. Darcy gone to town for the purpose of beginning a courtship with Miss Montford? But if that were the case, then why was Mrs. Reynolds completely ignorant of the news from London? Lizzy looked at Georgiana, and seeing the confusion on her friend's face, Georgiana knew what Lizzy was thinking, but could say nothing.

A relaxing afternoon was followed by supper in the most elegant dining room Lizzy had ever seen. Robert Adam had designed all the public rooms at Pemberley, and his soft colors and classical embellishments lifted one's spirits as soon as you entered the manor house. An aura of tranquility was present in every room, and for a man with as many responsibilities as Mr. Darcy had, Lizzy understood why Pemberley would be a welcomed retreat. He had confided in her that whenever he was troubled, he returned to Pemberley because the clean air and magnificent views provided clarity, and she wondered if, instead of going to London after the Netherfield ball, he had returned to his beautiful estate in Derbyshire, if things might have turned out differently.

Chapter 27

ALTHOUGH INITIALLY A RELUCTANT rider, Lizzy was coming along nicely. When Sugar had returned to the stables that first time, the mare had stood in front of her stall patiently waiting for Belling to remove her saddle, but after Lizzy had stopped laughing over her inability to control the ten-year-old horse, she had remounted, and Georgiana and she had ridden around the lake. Now she and the old gray mare were friends, especially since Lizzy stuffed her riding coat full of carrots.

The following day, Lizzy was looking forward to another ride around the lake, but her hostess had something else in mind. With Mr. Gardiner gone off at dawn for another day of fishing, and Mrs. Gardiner once again in the gardens with Mr. Ferguson, Georgiana decided to teach Lizzy how to drive a phaeton, and she protested in vain.

"Will and Mr. Bingley race phaetons, and it is a very exciting sport. But we shall declare victory if you learn how to have the team go at a trot. It is all in the reins."

That simple statement took an hour to achieve, but when

Lizzy realized the two horses were actually doing what she wanted them to do, she was all smiles. And that day was as perfect as the one before it and the one after. No matter the weather, fog, light rain, wind, or cold mornings, Lizzy's days at Pemberley were sublime, that is, until she learned Mr. Darcy was coming.

"Lizzy, this is such good news," Georgiana said as she stood in the foyer reading her brother's letter. "Will is coming to Pemberley with our cousin, Colonel Fitzwilliam, and you will like the colonel very much. He is charming and witty and gracious as well as being an excellent dancer and card player."

Lizzy pretended to be pleased with the news, but what she really wanted to do was flee.

"Oh, this is disappointing," Georgiana said as she continued reading. "Will writes that he is coming to shoot, fish, and ride, and he has underlined all three." Turning to Lizzy, she explained, "He has not fired a gun once this season, and December is nearly upon us, so you can imagine his frustration."

"Georgiana, this may be a good time to remind you that as wonderful as our time here has been, it must come to an end. Mr. Gardiner needs to return to his business and Mrs. Gardiner to her children, and I must go back to Longbourn as my dearest friend, Charlotte Lucas, is to marry shortly."

"But I would really like for you to meet Colonel Fitzwilliam, who is a particular favorite of mine. Although Will does not say exactly when he is coming, they should be here no later than three days hence." Georgiana pleaded with Lizzy with her big eyes, which she had probably used to get whatever she wanted since she was a child, and they got her what she wanted once again.

"I shall ask my aunt and uncle if we may stay for another three days, but after that, we must go."

"Will! Richard!" Georgiana shouted from the top of the staircase when her brother came into the foyer with Colonel Fitzwilliam. "You are early," she said too loudly as she rushed down the stairs. She kissed her brother on the cheek before turning to her favorite cousin, and standing on her toes, she gave the tall, fair-haired colonel a kiss before he lifted her off her feet and hugged her.

"Let me hear it, Georgie," the colonel said, and it was not until she had said "Uncle!" that he put her down. It was a ritual they had established when Georgie, as a young girl of twelve, had developed romantic notions about her handsome cousin, and Richard, recognizing that her excessive attention was a clumsy attempt at flirting, had turned it into a game.

With Richard and Georgie happily engaged, Will let out a loud whistle that brought David and Goliath from the far reaches of the house, and when Darcy crouched down to pet his whippets, their enthusiasm knocked him over. They were crawling all over him and licking his face, and it was minutes before he could get them to settle down. This scene was repeated every time Darcy returned to Pemberley.

It was at that point that the dour Mr. Jackson arrived and, standing as erect as any sentry, waited for orders from his master. Darcy, feeling a little foolish sitting on the floor in front of his butler, finally stood up, dusted off his coat, and asked Jackson to send word to Mr. Littlejohn, the gamekeeper, that the colonel and he would be shooting later in the day.

Darcy explained to his sister that their early arrival was due to the fact that they had not come from London.

"After Mercer heard a noise he did not like, we stopped in Derby so that he could have a look at the undercarriage. We stayed with the Hulstons, and they send their regards. And where are our guests?"

"Mr. Gardiner is still in his room. He has been out fishing every day, and I think he finally exhausted himself. He certainly exhausted Cubbins. Mrs. Gardiner and Mr. Ferguson have become the best of friends, and it is so very touching to see the two of them talking about plants and flowers. Since Mrs. Ferguson died, he has barely put two sentences together, but now the words are flowing."

"And Miss Elizabeth?"

"I believe she is walking near the gazebo. I did not go out with her today because I was preparing for your arrival, but you have caught me unprepared."

"No worries, Georgie. We are here for the shooting. Continue to see to your guests as you have done all week, and Richard and I will take care of ourselves. Please excuse me, as I want to spend a few minutes with Mr. Aiken before I meet with Mr. Littlejohn."

Will was barely out the door when Georgiana turned to the colonel. "What news from London?" and Richard brought his cousin up to date on the unhappy Miss Montford, Georgiana's equally miserable brother, and the plan he had put into action with Lord Fitzwilliam.

"Oh dear! Are we seriously relying on Antony to solve our problems? He is usually the source."

"Georgie, you know he is an incurable gossip, and we are relying on him to do just that."

"And Will is agreeable to this plan?" When the colonel nodded, she said, "He must be desperate to be free of Miss Montford if he is deliberately involving Antony. Your brother gets under his skin like no other. When we were at the Clermont ball, Antony had a wager with Sir Edgar about the color of Lady Eleanor's eyes and asked Will to settle the bet. Antony lost!"

"Well, it has been awhile since they have been together—years in fact. But never mind that. If Antony performs as expected, your brother will be in his debt."

"He will not like that."

"But he is willing to do what he must to be rid of Letitia Montford in a manner that will not embarrass her."

"Which will free him to be with Elizabeth," Georgiana said with a smile.

"Exactly."

Chapter 28

AFTER DARCY HAD FINISHED meeting with his steward, he went to the stables with David and Goliath in lockstep behind him. While he waited for the gamekeeper, he asked Belling to bring out Macbeth, his favorite horse, but one who was starting to show his age. When he had left for town, the black stallion had been favoring his back leg.

"He's been treated royally, sir, and he's got used to it. If he give you any trouble about being ridden, it's because he don't think he has to earn his keep no more."

Darcy smiled and then ran his fingers along the white blaze marking on his forehead, and after looking into his eyes, he saw that there was still a fire in them. He knew Macbeth had a lot more to give before being put out to pasture. Darcy had always been attracted to animals with spirit, and he had a good eye for it. David and Goliath had been the runts of the litter, but you would never know it from the way they ran at the bigger dogs, including his father's Great Dane. The horses he loved the most were those who wanted to show him what they could do.

As Belling took Macbeth's tether from him, a splash of color at the top of the hill caught his eye, and he immediately recognized Elizabeth Bennet's blue coat. It was the same one she had worn when she had walked to Netherfield to visit her ailing sister.

"Sir, that lady is Miss Darcy's friend, Miss Bennet," Belling said, following his master's gaze. "She walks up there every morning and usually runs down the hill going at a right good gait. She probably ain't doing it today because of last night's rain making the grass as slippery as ice. She'll be coming this way because she gives Sugar a few carrots before going up to the house." Before taking Macbeth back to his stall, Belling asked Mr. Darcy if he should send Cubbins to see what was keeping Mr. Littlejohn.

"No, that is not necessary. I am in no hurry."

As much as Lizzy liked riding Sugar, walking remained her greatest pleasure, and she enjoyed walking to the top of the hill where a gazebo provided a vista of the surrounding countryside. From this vantage point, Lizzy had a clear view of the manor house and gardens, and she would wait for the reds and yellows of the gardens below to rise out of the mist in tiny bursts of color. It was her favorite thing to do at Pemberley.

But as she waited for the first signs of the endless rows of chrysanthemums to emerge, she realized that today everything would change. It was the last morning in which she could roam the grounds freely as Mr. Darcy was expected in the late afternoon. Upon his arrival, all formalities would have to be observed, or she might shock the lord of the manor with her casual dress and bonnet left behind on her dressing table and long braid hanging down her back.

Since Mr. Darcy would be arriving later in the day, Lizzy thought she might ride Sugar around the lake. She had not gone out yesterday because of storm clouds. Now that the morning mist was rising, it looked as if this would be a good day to go riding, and it would be her last opportunity to be with the aging mare.

As she approached the stable, she looked down at her muddy boots and the dirty hem of her coat, and she remembered the time she had arrived at Netherfield in her soiled frock. "Six inches deep in mud," she had heard Caroline Bingley say, followed by Mr. Darcy's remark that he would not approve of his sister going about in such a way. "Well, you may have something to say to Miss Darcy about where she walks," Lizzy said to herself, "but I am not going to let a little rain and some puddles keep me from walking on such a beautiful morning, especially with winter just around the corner. So there, Mr. Fitzwilliam Darcy of Pemberley."

As Lizzy walked the path leading to the stables, she was met by a growling David and Goliath, and when she took another step, they started to bark at her, which was unusual. In fact, she had never heard so much as a yelp from either dog. She then remembered something Ellie had said: "If you want to know where Mr. Darcy is, all you need do is find David and Goliath." After hearing Mr. Darcy's voice ordering his dogs to stop barking, she came to a complete stop and tiptoed her way back down the path.

"Miss Elizabeth," Mr. Darcy said, poking his head around a bush.

"Mr. Darcy," Lizzy said, bowing and wishing for all the world that she had worn her bonnet so that he might not see her wild hair or how embarrassed she was to be found in such a state.

"I thought we agreed at Netherfield that if you wished to go unnoticed, it would be best for you to stay off the gravel," and looking at her hem, he said, "and I see you are still having difficulty avoiding puddles."

"We had a brief storm last night, and the path leading to the gazebo is quite muddy as a result," Lizzy said, pointing up the hill to the cause of her less-than-ideal appearance.

What was he doing here? And why was he so handsome with his amazing eyes, which were gray today, having taken on the color of the sky, and even with his long riding coat, she could see how well his breeches fit him. *Oh God, do not look there*, she thought. *You are already blushing, and you are at risk of embarrassing yourself even more than you already have*, and she looked everywhere but at him.

"You were not expected until this afternoon, Mr. Darcy," she said, talking to the bushes in a voice that was almost an accusation.

"I am sorry to disappoint you by coming so early, Miss Elizabeth, but I have only come from Derby, not London. We actually should have arrived last evening."

"Well, if you had, sir, I would have been properly dressed today," and she flipped her braid over her shoulder. Looking at her hem, she added, "I would most certainly have kept to the gravel paths if I had known I was to encounter the lord of the manor."

"You look fine, Miss Elizabeth," he responded, and then he could stand it no longer, and he went to her and took her in his arms. He kissed her, and just as he had imagined a hundred times, she clung to him, savoring every kiss and pressing in against him.

"Mr. Darcy, Mr. Littlejohn is here," Belling said, interrupting a beautiful daydream.

"Tell him I will be with him in a few minutes, Belling," Darcy answered, annoyed by the interruption, but grateful that he was wearing a long coat. Turning his attention once again to Lizzy, he asked her what she had been doing during her time at Pemberley. "Other than stuffing Sugar full of carrots."

Lizzy smiled. He was trying to put her at her ease, and she felt some of the tension leaving her neck and shoulders.

"Belling took us by wagon to visit White Peak, and we had a lovely picnic. Your sister spent a whole day teaching me how to drive a phaeton. Please do not laugh," she said when she saw his smirk. "I can now handle a pair of horses quite well as long as they are old and will only be asked to go around the lake."

"It is for the purpose of teaching novices how to drive a phaeton that we keep the older horses in the stable," he said, still laughing at the thought of an inexperienced Elizabeth driving a pair of horses, "and I commend you for trying. Anything else?"

"Not really. My uncle is determined to fish in as many streams on the property as possible, and my aunt cannot be kept from the gardens. So we have been quite content to remain at Pemberley."

"So you have enjoyed your time here?"

"Who would not? When we leave on Thursday, I will know exactly how Adam and Eve felt when they were expelled from the Garden of Eden," and for a second, a wave of regret passed over her as she thought about what she would leave behind.

"I understand from Miss Darcy it is your intention to engage in only manly pursuits," Elizabeth teased. "No lawn bowls or strolls around the lake for you and the colonel. You have come for the shooting and to ride and fish. But, perhaps, we may pass each other in the gallery, or I may see your coattails as you go out one door and I come in another."

"Miss Elizabeth, I have come for the sport as I have not shot a gun this season, and I rarely ride in town as parading about in parks is not for me. So please do not think I am trying to avoid you."

Lizzy laughed. "You would not have to avoid me, Mr. Darcy. This is your home. It is I who must give way."

This statement caused his whole demeanor to change. "Surely, you do not think I would want you to leave Pemberley because I have come."

"No, I do not think that, but then we do not know each other very well. Can either of us be certain of what the other would do in any given situation?" and Lizzy took a step back, uncomfortable with the direction the conversation had taken.

But Mr. Darcy closed the gap between them, and after taking Lizzy by the forearm, he looked at her with an intensity she had not witnessed before and said, "You know me well enough."

But Lizzy did not think she did. If she had, then she would know why he was in Derbyshire. "I do know some things about you that I did not know before coming to Pemberley."

"Such as?" he asked, unsure of what she might say. Her statement that she did not know him had stung.

"That you know how to play the pianoforte and can perform duets with your sister."

Darcy let out a sigh of relief, and after letting go of Lizzy's arm, he said, "Georgiana is a wicked girl for telling you such a thing. I play badly and for an audience of one—my sister."

"But now that we know your secret, you will be hard-pressed to avoid our requests for a tune."

"Miss Elizabeth, I see that you have been able to indulge in two of your most favorite things while at Pemberley: teasing and walking."

"But it was your sister's hope that I would be so comfortable at Pemberley that I would act in exactly the same manner as I would if I were at Longbourn."

"I agree with Georgiana. I would not want you to change because you have come here," including wearing your hair down, he thought. He would love to be the one to take her hair out of its braid and to brush it himself, but those things were reserved for a husband. "You may be very sorry you have discovered my closely held secret, Miss Elizabeth, because you will now be forced to listen to my flawed efforts on the pianoforte. Last time I played a tune, David and Goliath ran out of the room."

With an impatient Mr. Littlejohn within her view, Lizzy said, "I will leave you to arrange for your shoot, Mr. Darcy, and look forward to tonight's entertainment."

"Consider yourself warned," he called after her, and he turned his attention to manly pursuits, so he might not spend the whole day thinking about Elizabeth Bennet.

Chapter 29

As Lizzy approached the manor house, she saw a handsome gentleman walking toward her. Assuming that he was Colonel Fitzwilliam, she stopped and waited while he approached and decided that she would never again leave the house without a bonnet.

"Colonel Fitzwilliam at your service," the man said and made a deep bow. "Please forgive me for not seeking a proper introduction, but I have heard so much about you, Miss Bennet, that I have circumvented convention."

"I am pleased to make your acquaintance, Colonel Fitzwilliam, as Miss Darcy speaks of you with the deepest affection."

"I am fortunate in having two wonderful female relations, Miss Anne de Bourgh of Rosings Park in Kent being the other one, and I see too little of both." Holding out his arm, he asked if he might walk with her back to the house.

"But weren't you on your way to the stables to join Mr. Darcy? He is arranging for the shoot with Mr. Littlejohn, and I have no wish to detain you."

"I will be with Darcy all afternoon, and why should I stand by while my cousin discusses the specifics of the shoot if I can enjoy the pleasure of your company?"

"I am afraid Miss Darcy may have exaggerated my attributes."

"I do not think so, and Miss Darcy was not my only source."

So Mr. Darcy had spoken about her to his cousin, which meant what? Lizzy could feel something like resentment building up inside her. She wished that Mr. Darcy had stayed in town, so that she might enjoy the rest of her holiday and not have to think about what had happened in London.

"So you are here for the shooting, Colonel."

"Yes. Finally. In years past, we would come with a party of five or six gentlemen, but Darcy has been off his game throughout the season. His friends finally tired of waiting for him to make the arrangements and went elsewhere, and I am sure there were those in the village and on the farms who were getting quite nervous that he had not been here because the birds are distributed to the families of the servants, his tenants, and the poor of the parish. Even with that, you will not hear a bad word spoken about him. When something important happens in the village or the neighboring farms, he wants to know of it, and if he can help, he will. His sister is of a similar mind. She just smiles more than her brother."

Lizzy was glad that Mr. Darcy didn't smile more often because, when he did, it made her go weak at the knees.

"Mr. Darcy would be very flattered if he heard you praising him so highly."

"On the contrary," he said. "Darcy is modest about his achievements and the good works he does. The only time he brags is when he talks about cricket. He was a superior batsman at Cambridge, and he likes to speak of the time that Cambridge beat Oxford in three successive matches. Other than that, he is not one to run on about his accomplishments, but then, still waters run deep."

Upon reaching the house, Lizzy excused herself as she needed to see to her toilette. From the window of her apartment, she could see Colonel Fitzwilliam walking back to the stables. Lizzy had once heard Mr. Bingley describe Mr. Darcy as a big, tall fellow, but the colonel was taller and broader than his cousin and had blond hair and sky blue eyes. It seemed as if the Fitzwilliam family at large was made up entirely of good-looking people, and it would be no hardship to spend an evening in the company of that gentleman.

"What were you saying to Elizabeth?" Darcy asked Colonel Fitzwilliam.

"I introduced myself. I have heard so much about her that I did not wait for a formal introduction."

"You introduced yourself? Where are your manners?"

"Oh for God's sake, Darcy! She was not offended. You are in the country, where things may be less formal. Your rigidity is what got you into this predicament in the first place."

Darcy had to acknowledge the truth of this. If he had not been such a stickler for protocol, he would never have gone back to Miss Montford after having met Elizabeth.

"Well, what do you think?"

"I think it is a fine day for shooting—not a dark cloud in sight. At what time will Mr. Littlejohn have everything ready?"

"Damn you, Fitzwilliam. You know what I am talking about."

The colonel pointed to the path leading from the stables. "Let us walk," and after they had put some distance between themselves and all the grooms hurrying about the yard, he continued. "I think she is lovely and engaging, and I formed that opinion only by walking with her as far as the house. Now that I have met her, I think we must revise our plan and not wait upon Antony. As soon as we return to London, you must visit Miss Montford and tell her that there will be no courtship. I am sure she will be relieved, and you must be strong enough for both of you and stand up to her father."

"I have already decided to do just that. I must have been temporarily insane to think Antony could be of any use to me, and besides, this is something I must do myself."

"When did you have this epiphany? You said nothing while we were in route to Pemberley."

"When I saw Elizabeth. All the things that had been running through my mind helter-skelter came into alignment. This whole marriage business is not about Letitia. It is about Sir John and me. It is not for my personal qualities or rank that he wants me to marry his daughter, although I am sure my name and fortune were part of the equation. He is determined to have me renounce the heresy of my politics. He wants to be able to crow that Sir John Montford was able to show an ardent Whig supporter the error of his ways. Poor Letitia. She has been a pawn in a rather unpleasant game of chess. Torn between father and husband, she would have been perfectly miserable.

"Richard, what is today? Monday? Well, the Gardiners and Elizabeth are leaving on Wednesday, and I shall be right behind them on the road to London. I am going to call on Miss Montford, and I will reassure her that all the blame will fall on me. And I will apologize profusely for misjudging… everything. In trying to do the right thing, I came very close to ruining her life. She would never have been happy with me, nor I with her."

"*Bravo!* All I can say is go to it, and the quicker the better."

"But what do I do in the meantime?"

Fitzwilliam started to kick the gravel, trying to think of how best to proceed. "Egad, what a mess! I suspect Miss Elizabeth knows that you have been courting someone in London, so if you flirt with her, you will appear to be a total cad. On the other hand, you cannot ignore her as she is a guest in your home. Even if we should spend the whole of the day in shooting or riding, we must eat supper together, and then there are the evening's entertainments.

"I would suggest that you act as you usually do when you are in an uncomfortable situation: be reticent, unavailable, and closemouthed. Keep any conversation civil, but distant, and spend as much time as you can with the uncle," which was all well and good, but they had neglected to tell Georgiana of their plans.

Shortly after Lizzy returned to her room, Ellie came in followed by two footmen carrying a copper tub, and after setting out everything necessary for the bath, she ordered the young men to carry a screen over to the window. Lizzy was still getting used to the idea of someone other than her sister or mother washing her hair and scrubbing her back, but Ellie executed the task without making her feel uncomfortable. If all of this pampering kept up, she would soon need the servants to spoon feed her her meals.

"What dress should I wear this evening, Ellie?"

"Well, I like the yellow one very much, and Miss Darcy has a rope of pearls that will go with it quite nicely. And with your pretty curls, you might think about wearing it down."

Lizzy was pretty sure that was Mr. Darcy's preference as well, and for that reason, she thought it unwise. Why should she do anything to attract his attention? In two days' time, she would leave Pemberley, and he would return to London—again. And in the near future he might possibly come to visit Mr. Bingley at Netherfield, and then go back to London—again. And the highs and lows she was experiencing as a result of his coming and going were beginning to wear on her.

"I know Colonel Fitzwilliam is partial to ladies who have their hair down," Ellie said, interrupting her thoughts, "and I wouldn't mind if someone as handsome as the colonel paid me a bit of attention over supper or cards."

And then Lizzy thought, why not? If the colonel liked women with their hair down, she would leave it down. What would be the harm in having that gentleman pay her a "bit of attention," as Ellie put it? Anything beyond a friendship was not possible as he was destined to marry a woman of wealth and rank. But so was Mr. Darcy, and it did not stop him from flirting.

"All right then. I shall wear the yellow dress with Miss Darcy's pearls."

"And your hair, Miss?"

"I shall wear it down."

Chapter 30

"I WISH YOU HAD said something earlier about playing cards," Georgiana said to her brother. "I have already planned out the whole evening. Isn't it the responsibility of the mistress of Pemberley to make all the social arrangements, that is, *until you marry?*"

That last bit made Darcy smile. His sister had a subtle way of moving him in the direction she wanted him to go.

"Yes, it is, but I absolutely refuse to play charades."

"I would not ask you to as I know how you detest it. I can assure you it is an entirely musical evening."

"Which reminds me. I have a bone to pick with you. Why did you tell Miss Elizabeth I play the pianoforte?"

"Because you do."

"As you well know, I play at the most basic level and only because Mama insisted I should learn and would stay in the room to make sure I practiced."

"You are not being asked to play Mozart, so please unfurrow your brow. It will be fun. I promise."

While Darcy was dressing, he was hoping Elizabeth would not wear her hair down because her long dark tresses would make him want to look into her eyes, and his efforts to be anything other than a good host would collapse. Because he did not want to send the wrong signal, he needed to be in complete control tonight. It was only a few more days before he would be able to go to London and sort things out, but his hopes were dashed as soon as she walked into the dining room. He had thought green her best color, but now he decided it was yellow.

While Ellie had been curling her hair, Lizzy was planning how best to act during supper. Of course, she would be civil to Mr. Darcy, but she would look at him only when necessary. Instead, she would concentrate on getting to know the colonel better. However, those plans failed immediately because tonight Mr. Darcy looked as handsome as she had ever seen him. She did not think it possible for him to be more attractive than when he wore his green coat, black waistcoat, and tan breeches, but tonight he had chosen a black coat with trousers, and there was an elegance in his appearance that caused her heart to skip a beat.

"I know your older sister is to marry Mr. Bingley," the colonel said to Lizzy who was seated next to him at supper, "but do you have any other sisters?"

"Yes, I have three younger sisters, all at home, except my youngest sister, Lydia, who has gone to Brighton as a guest of the wife of the colonel of a militia regiment. However, that is about to change as I have just received a letter from my sister, Jane, saying that our father has sent for her."

Aunt Gardiner nodded her head in approval at her

brother-in-law's action. In her opinion, Mr. Bennet should never have approved of the scheme in the first place because there was always the possibility of someone of such a tender age getting into trouble in a town filled to overflowing with young men.

"Longbourn must be a positive bevy of beauties if your sisters favor you," the colonel said.

Lizzy blushed at the compliment, but considering that Colonel Fitzwilliam must have dined with some of the most beautiful women in society, she was quite flattered by his attention. This exchange did not go unnoticed by Darcy, who was trying to catch his cousin's eye. Since he was prevented from showing any special attention to Elizabeth, he thought Richard should do the same. Instead, Colonel Fitzwilliam was openly flirting with the woman Darcy was in love with.

"Colonel, I know you have an older brother who is the Earl Fitzwilliam, but are there others?" Lizzy asked.

"Yes, I have two sisters, but just the one brother, and with a brother such as him, one is enough. I assume you read *The Insider*, Miss Bennet?"

"I must confess, with some embarrassment, that I do, but for those of us who live in the country and who go up to town only once or twice a year, we must have some entertainment."

"I am pleased to hear my brother's antics have some value, if only to entertain."

"Not just your brother, as there are others for whom the printers must buy their ink by the barrel," Lizzy said, thinking of the Prince of Wales and his brothers.

"Do you pity me then, Miss Bennet? As a younger son, I am destined to a life of self-denial and dependence while my brother has his every wish granted. As milord frequently says, 'Richard got the looks and hair while I got everything else.'"

Lizzy laughed at his comment. She had read enough about Lord Fitzwilliam to know he had no interest in his own wife but could not stay away from anyone else's, and that he played at high-stakes card games where he would lose a fortune one night and win it back the next.

"Truthfully, Colonel, when has a want of money ever prevented you from going wherever you chose or procuring anything you wanted?"

Darcy laughed to himself. He had warned his cousin that having a conversation with Elizabeth was quite different than anything he was used to because she always spoke honestly.

"There is truth in your question," the colonel answered, "but our habits of expense make us too dependent. Unlike my cousin here, younger sons cannot marry where they wish."

Georgiana, seeing that her brother did not like Richard's last comment, interrupted by relating news from Longbourn that Lizzy had shared with her. "Elizabeth, please tell my brother about the Crenshaw children."

"The Crenshaws? Those hellions?" Richard said in a surprisingly animated manner.

"Yes, one and the same," Georgiana answered, "but I have good news. The beasts have been tamed."

"I do not believe it," Fitzwilliam and Darcy said in unison.

"They are beyond reformation," Richard said. "If I were of a litigious bent, I would have sued their father for destruction of private property. They put some putrid plant in my new boots, making them perfectly useless. When Darcy and I got our hands on those twins, we took them up to the house by the scruffs of their necks to their mother, and do you know what she said? 'They are infiltrators executing acts of sabotage behind enemy lines.' And Darcy said to the two boys, 'Do you know what happens to saboteurs when they are caught?' but then the mother saved them by telling them to go to their rooms. She then assured me that her husband would pay for a new set of boots, but he must not have known where to send the cheque because I never got it. Bingley made good on it."

"Richard, I am sorry. I did not intend to upset you," Georgiana said in a soothing voice, "but it is true. The beasts roar no more."

"And who accomplished this miracle?"

"Miss Jane Bennet."

Darcy broke out into laughter. "Richard, now I am sure Georgie is joking. I know the lady, and an unkind word has never passed her lips."

"I thank you, Mr. Darcy, for being so complimentary of my sister," Lizzy interjected, "but I can assure you that Jane did succeed where the colonel and you could not, and she did so by the use of her reason."

Darcy sat back in his chair and gave Lizzy a look that clearly showed he did not believe a word of it.

"We anticipated your skepticism, Mr. Darcy, and so I have brought Jane's letter for you to read. How such a feat was accomplished begins halfway down the page."

After reading all of the details of the singular afternoon at Longbourn, Darcy nodded his head in approval. It was true. Miss Bennet had succeeded where everyone else had failed. After putting down the letter, Darcy briefed his cousin on its contents and said, "Well, Fitzwilliam, we must give Miss Jane Bennet her due. She was very clever. I would have thought it would have been easier to raise Lazarus than to get those twins to behave."

"Call me a doubting Thomas," Richard grumbled, "but I would have to see them in action to believe it. Never mind. I never want to be in their company again." Everyone laughed at the absurdity of such young children having so many adults tied up in knots.

"So, Mr. Darcy, will you concede that, in this case, brains succeeded where brawn had failed?"

"I readily concede that female ingenuity won the day, Miss Elizabeth, and I would not debate the point in any event as I have been on the losing end of every argument since I first met you."

"If you truly believe that, Mr. Darcy, then your losing streak has come to an end because, in this case, I agree with you."

"I will make a note of it in my journal."

"Will, I think you are deliberately putting your fingers on the wrong keys," Georgiana said in frustration. "We have played this duet numerous times."

"But not for more than a year, and despite what you say, I am not doing it on purpose."

"Georgie, do you have the music for 'I Saw Three Ships Come Sailing In'?" Richard asked in an attempt to stop the sparring. "Will knows how to play that tune, and I will accompany him." Georgiana quickly went through her music chest and found the sheet music for the carol.

"Richard, that is an excellent suggestion," Georgiana said, "as tomorrow is the first of December and St. Nicholas's Day is but six days off. It is the perfect tune for the season," and Georgie left her brother so that he might perform.

"I am warning you, Mr. and Mrs. Gardiner and Miss Elizabeth, that I play badly," Darcy said, and looking at his sister for a reprieve, which she refused to grant, he told her, "Put Pepper out of the room or he will start barking."

"Don't worry, Darcy. I intend to sing very loudly to cover your poor performance," his cousin teased him.

After Darcy had finished, he asked Mrs. Gardiner what she thought.

"The colonel has a fine baritone."

"You cannot avoid the question, Mrs. Gardiner. What did you think of my playing?"

"Sir, I will tell you what I tell my children: Practice, practice, and more practice will get you the desired results."

"Gently put, Mrs. Gardiner," Darcy said with a smile.

Aunt Gardiner turned to her niece. "Elizabeth, dear, will you sing, 'I Liked But Never Loved Before'?"

"Oh, no, not that maudlin ballad," Mr. Gardiner groaned. "Please forgive my wife. She has an insatiable appetite for songs about lost love and other tragedies that will have everyone in tears."

"I am only asking for the one ballad, Mr. Gardiner."

"Very well, Aunt, if you will accompany me," Lizzy said, agreeing to her request. Lizzy had a pleasing alto voice and, like her aunt, had a weakness for romantic ballads, and no sheet music was needed as they knew the song by heart.

"I liked but never loved before
I saw thy charming face;

Now every feature I adore,
And dote on every grace.
He never shall know the kind desire,
Which his cold look denies,
Unless my heart that's all on fire,
Should sparkle through my eyes.
Then if no gentle glance return
A silent leave to speak,
My heart which would forever burn,
Alas! Must sigh and break."

Lizzy bowed her head in appreciation of the applause, and although she knew it was unwise, she looked at Mr. Darcy and felt tears welling up in her eyes.

"As you can tell, my uncle was correct, at least as far as I am concerned," Lizzy said. "These love songs always make me cry."

Mr. Darcy sprung out of his chair and handed her one of his handkerchiefs, and looking at her, he shook his head ever so slightly, as if to tell her that she need not cry and that all would be well.

Georgiana, who had organized the night's entertainment, signaled for Avery and Potter, two of the footmen, who were accomplished fiddlers, to come in. The chairs and tables were quickly moved to the side, and the footmen began with a lively Scottish air. For the remainder of the evening, Lizzy was able to forget that the following day was to be her last at Pemberley.

Chapter 31

THE PREVIOUS EVENING, GEORGIANA had suggested that the last day of their guests' visit should be spent exploring one of the many caves in the Peak and mentioned Thor's Cave, which was considered to be one of the most spectacular caves in all of England.

"Georgie, that is not possible," her brother said. "With the short days and the vagaries of the weather, it cannot be done," which his sister already knew.

"Maybe we should go Shepherd's Cave? That is within easy distance of the house."

Earlier in the day, while her brother had been otherwise engaged, Georgiana had conspired with Richard, and behind closed doors, the pair had plotted how best to get the two together and had settled on Shepherd's Cave.

Since meeting Lizzy, Georgiana regretted her role in promoting Miss Montford to her brother. When she first had visited with Letitia, she found that she was not a particularly good conversationalist but believed that would change once a friendship was established. On her second visit, Letitia had played a sonata by Beethoven so exquisitely that she had been moved to tears. At that time, she decided that this sweet, accomplished lady would be kind to her brother, which was of utmost importance to her because she did not want someone like Augusta Selridge or Caroline Bingley for Will. It was only after experiencing Lizzy's wit, intelligence, vivacity, and wonderful curiosity did Georgiana realize she had been championing the wrong lady.

"As you know, Richard, it is very tight in the cave, and as they make their way to the rear, they will be close enough to embrace." With her vivid imagination, she could picture her brother taking Lizzy in his arms, and while so entwined, the colonel and she would slip away, leaving the two to speak of their love for one another. Richard agreed that it was their best opportunity to have them in such close proximity, but warned his young cousin that her brother was capable of many things, but making an open display of affection in front of others was not one of them.

Before Darcy would agree to such an excursion, he felt it necessary to explain to his guests that the only way to reach the cave was on horseback followed by a quarter-mile walk.

"Shepherd's Cave is nothing to compare to Thor's Cave, but we on the eastern side of the Peak have a few interesting caves of our own. Archaeologists from Cambridge have studied it and concluded that the cave has been in use for thousands of years, as there are a number of primitive drawings on the walls from pre-historic times. As interesting as they are, it is the stalagmites and stalactites caused by deposits of calcium-rich water dripping from the ceiling on to the floor of the cave that are truly fascinating."

"Mr. Darcy, you need not convince us of the worthiness of your choice, as Mr. Gardiner and I will not be going," Mrs. Gardiner responded. "Because it was mentioned in *The Compleat Angler*, my husband has already made plans for a fishing excursion near the Milldale bridge with Cubbins, and I promised Mr. Ferguson that I would spend my last day with him in the Chinese garden."

After learning that the Gardiners would not be going, everyone looked to Lizzy.

"I have never been to a cave of any kind. So this is of interest to me, and I would enjoy seeing it. My only request is that I be allowed to ride Sugar. We are old friends now."

Darcy silently thanked his sister for suggesting the excursion, and once again he had to admire her maneuvering, as he knew full well that the desired end had been Shepherd's Cave all along. But that was something he would keep to himself, as he was pleased with her results.

Aunt Gardiner was not blind to what was going on around her but had said nothing because she could not imagine that Mr. Darcy of Pemberley would show such an interest in Elizabeth. Having grown up within a few miles of Pemberley, she was well aware of the prominence of the family, their extensive holdings, and wealth. Mr. Darcy also moved in a world so different from Lizzy's that it would be an extraordinary event if he were to honor her with an offer of marriage. But after last night, when Lizzy could not hold back her tears because of her feelings for the gentleman, and when Mr. Darcy utterly failed to hide his love for her, she felt that she must speak.

"Did the dancing go on for much longer after Uncle Gardiner and I retired?" Aunt Gardiner asked, and while Lizzy finished her toilette, her aunt noticed the puffiness around her eyes and had no doubt that her niece had been crying.

"For about another hour. I do not know where I got the energy to continue, but Colonel Fitzwilliam is so entertaining that I did not want the night to end."

"And Mr. Darcy?"

"Aunt, I know why you have come," Lizzy said, "and I want to tell you that I am fine. In the past, I have shed some tears over Mr. Darcy, but last night I cried myself to sleep, and when I awoke very early this morning I said 'enough.' Nothing was ever going to come of this flirtation anyway, so I am ready to move on and put all thoughts of him from my mind. Jane writes that I have received a letter from Mr. Peterson, who is a very respectable man and one who owns a large farm near Watford. I was reluctant to encourage him because he had lost his wife a little more than a year ago, and his children are so young. But if he thinks he is ready to begin anew, I will receive him."

"Please forgive me for being so forward, my dear, but what you and Mr. Darcy have between you is hardly a flirtation. The man is besotted, and I saw this despite his efforts to disguise it."

"I am sorry to hear it because Mr. Darcy is to become engaged to a lady from London named Miss Montford."

"Then why is he here and not in town?"

"I cannot explain his behavior, and it puzzles me exceedingly. If the matter of their courtship is still not settled, he should have remained in town and seen to it, and if the matter is settled, then he should not have come at all, knowing that I was here as the guest of his sister. But there are different rules for the Mr. Darcys of the world. In his sphere, he may come and go as he pleases, while I must sit and wait and say nothing."

"Lizzy, I understand there are different rules for people of rank and always have been, but I cannot reconcile the Mr. Darcy I have come to know with the callous man you are describing. I think Miss Montford and he may have come to an agreement not to proceed with a courtship, which would explain why he is here and not in London. I know nothing of the Montfords, but I suspect the problem might lie with her parents. They may want to press forward because an alliance between their families would be quite a feather in the Montfords' cap."

"I am sorry, Aunt, if you think I have been too harsh because Mr. Darcy is guilty of nothing. He never made any promises to me of any kind. Our relationship, if you can call it that, has consisted entirely of a handful of conversations and even fewer dances, and he most certainly may come to his own home whenever he chooses. I just wish he had waited a few more days, so that I would not have been here."

"But, Elizabeth, I think the reason he came now is because he cannot stay away from you. When he arrived, he declared that he had come for the shooting alone, but he will not shoot today as he is going with you to Shepherd's Cave."

"But it does not matter if he chooses to come or not," Lizzy said, shaking her head as if to dislodge any thought of Mr. Darcy. "Today is my last day in Derbyshire, so I intend to enjoy the company of Miss Darcy, who is very agreeable, and Colonel Fitzwilliam, who is charming, and Mr. Darcy as well." Lizzy walked to the window, and while gazing at the vast gardens and the woods beyond, she said, "Being at Pemberley is like going to sleep in my own bed and awaking in a beautiful and exotic foreign land. It makes for a pleasant dream, but reality comes with the first light."

Chapter 32

IT SEEMED THAT THE Darcys had clothes for every occasion, including a chest full of dresses, boots, bonnets, and breeches for when they went "caving." But Lizzy had never worn uglier clothes in her life. When they arrived at the stables, the outfit actually got worse because, once they were in the cave, Lizzy would need to put on a wide-brimmed farmer's hat that was coated with coal tar to make it waterproof. Mercer had come up with the idea for the coating during his years as a coach driver, and now he was inflicting it on his master's guests.

"The ceiling of the cave drips, miss, and you don't want that mineral water plopping down on your head and ruining a pretty bonnet," Mercer explained.

"Do not worry about your appearance, Lizzy. The men do not look any better," Georgiana said while glancing at her ugly brown riding coat. When the two gentlemen came out of the stables carrying their farmer's hats, Georgiana started laughing. "Well, we may now proceed, as Farmer Will and Farmer Dick have arrived," which made Darcy laugh. He found his sister to be delightful, and his most unguarded moments were when he was with her.

Because the trailhead was two miles away, Mr. Darcy had decided to travel there by carriage in case it should start raining and had sent the horses ahead with the grooms. As soon as Lizzy got in the carriage, Miss Darcy and the colonel's plans became evident. The colonel chose to sit with his cousin, requiring Mr. Darcy to sit next to Lizzy. But as much as she liked the pair of intriguers, she could not support their efforts to bring Mr. Darcy and her together. It was time to put the gentleman behind her.

Once the wagon reached the trailhead, Darcy, who left nothing to chance, wanted to go over every detail with the grooms before sending them back to the stables, and while they waited for him, Lizzy went over to Sugar.

"Sugar is also the favorite of my nieces, the daughters of Lord Fitzwilliam," the colonel said after watching Lizzy stroke the dappled gray's face.

"Do they come here often?"

"Not often enough, as their father tries Darcy's patience like no other. Usually, it is I who brings them, but, occasionally, Darcy will gather them up when Georgie and he are coming for a few weeks. The girls have drawings of Sugar on the walls of their nursery."

"Sugar is perfect for me. With her wide girth, I feel quite secure."

"Ah, a wide girth! That puts me in mind of my Aunt Catherine," and Lizzy stifled a laugh. "That may seem unkind, but every time I look at Sugar, I cannot help but think of the august personage of Lady Catherine de Bourgh, as they are both broad abeam."

"I have never met Lady Catherine," Lizzy said, ignoring the

colonel's comment about his aunt's girth, "but I might possibly in the near future, as my good friend, Charlotte Lucas, is to marry her vicar in a week's time. I understand he is invited to Rosings Park every Thursday for the purpose of editing his sermons, and he is asked to stay for supper."

"Good God! You are a relation to Mr. Coggins?"

"His name is Mr. Collins, and he is my father's cousin. I do not know him very well as he has visited Longbourn only a few times."

"This is astounding!"

"That your family and mine have a connection through Mr. Collins?"

"No, that his sermons are edited—certainly not for length."

"Colonel Fitzwilliam, you are making me laugh when I should not."

"You must understand, Miss Elizabeth, that one needs a sense of humor in order to have an aunt such as Lady Catherine. I have never met anyone who knows so little about so many things and is more than willing to speak about them at length, and her influence is felt far beyond Rosings Park."

"Is she in the commission of the peace?"

"No, but she is an active magistrate in her own parish, and whenever her tenants are quarrelsome, discontented, or too poor, she goes forth into the village to settle their differences, silence their complaints, and scold them into harmony and plenty."

"Mr. Collins shared a great deal about your aunt and Miss de Bourgh during his visit to Longbourn."

"If Mr. Collins was truthful, then you know that mother and daughter are like night and day, Anne representing the day. Unlike her mother, Anne knows a lot about a lot of things and has a wonderful wit. Unfortunately, she is very frail and travels little. I hope you will have an opportunity to meet her because you would get on very well."

By that time, Darcy signaled that they might proceed, and he helped Lizzy to get on Sugar. "Squeeze the saddle with your legs if you feel as if you might fall off," and after handing her the reins, he added, "and tighten up on the reins. You hold them too loosely."

Well, this was a great start as it appeared Mr. Darcy was already annoyed with her, and they had not even arrived at the cave. Just as well, she thought. "I don't want to talk to you either." But Darcy was not annoyed with Lizzy, but with his cousin.

"Richard, when we have an opportunity, you will have to explain to me how your flirting with Miss Elizabeth advances my cause."

"Because if she is talking to me, then she is not looking at your scowling face," Richard quickly rebutted, "and I readily admit I am attracted to her, but not in the way you think. We are kindred spirits as we both must wait for events to come to us. As a woman, she may not speak freely, and because I am a younger son, I am dependent on the kindness of my relations to keep me out of poverty. And please do not think me ungrateful because your allowance permits me to live in some degree of comfort, but sometimes this dependence on others sticks in my craw. But enough of this complaining. Today is a day for exploration, so onward to the cave!"

The first half mile of the trail allowed for two horses to ride in tandem, and so Richard took the opportunity to ride next to Lizzy. Scanning the expanse before her, she asked if all this land was a part of the Darcy estate.

"Most of it. What is not Darcy land belongs to the Ashtons, and Lady Ashton is Darcy's aunt. However, if you go back in time, you will find the Darcy family's holdings were in Hampshire, not Derbyshire, along with a barony. But the Darcys are a stubborn family, which cost them greatly, and that is why I am grateful that I am a Fitzwilliam."

"May I ask what happened to cause the loss of the title and properties?"

"When it was wise to be a Protestant, the Darcys remained Catholic, an act of conscience and admirable, but they paid a price for it. Because of that, their properties in the south were confiscated during the Commonwealth and never returned to them after the Restoration of Charles II as other people, more important than the Darcys, wanted it. Instead, thousands of acres here in Derbyshire were substituted. But at that time, it was a wilderness, and the family had to start from scratch. As for the title, it went to another.

"Will is no different than his stubborn ancestors and continues the contrarian tradition. When it would serve him well to be a Tory, he remains a Whig. And speaking of wilderness, that is where the Whigs will be for years to come, and when the Prince of Wales ascends to the throne, Darcy will not profit, as he has made it known that he disapproves of the size of the prince's allowance. He speaks his mind but, as I said, at a cost."

"Yes, he does speak his mind. I was on the receiving end of it when we first met at an assembly. He mentioned within my hearing that as far as my beauty was concerned he found me merely tolerable and not handsome enough to tempt him to dance."

"Good grief! Even for Darcy, that is a bit much."

"Yes, but the next day, he came to my home to apologize, and it has become something of a joke for us."

"I can assure you, Miss Bennet, that Mr. Darcy now finds you to be much more than tolerable."

"So he has said on occasion. How much farther is it to the path to the cave?"

"The trail will narrow shortly, and then we will need to walk from there," and he thought that Darcy had better move quickly. Time was running out, and he was in danger of losing the girl.

Chapter 33

It was an easy ride to the trailhead, allowing Lizzy to take in the vista spread wide before her. She had visited many beautiful places in England, but there was something about the rugged beauty of the Peak District that enthralled her. Man's hand was less evident here, and it was Nature stripped to its essentials that she found so compelling.

Accompanying the foursome was a lad of little more than ten. "This young man is Ben Avery, Ellie's brother," Darcy said by way of introduction. "He has been given the important job of carrying the torch when we go into the cave." After tousling the boy's hair and sending him on his way, Darcy shared with Elizabeth that Pemberley was awash in Averys. "In addition to Ellie, there is a sister who is a maid, their cousin John was one of the footmen who played the fiddle last night, and you practically trip over Averys when you are in the stables or carriage house. However, I imagine having an unlimited supply of Averys will soon change as a flannel manufactory has opened nearby, and one groom has already resigned his position to go to work there.

But I believe in progress, and the factory will provide much needed jobs for those in the Derwent Valley." He then pointed in the direction of the path. "But please allow me to go ahead of you."

"Do you feel safe with me walking behind you, Mr. Darcy, on such a narrow path and on an incline?" After seeing how he had acted with Ben, her heart had warmed, and she felt the beginning of a thaw.

"Perfectly safe, Miss Elizabeth, as there are too many witnesses about," and he returned her smile.

It was good to see Elizabeth smile because the whole idea of his coming to Pemberley had been a total disaster. Darcy could not even remember the reasoning behind it. It would have been better if he had remained in London, dealt with Miss Montford, and rode posthaste to Pemberley to be with Elizabeth. Instead, he found himself starring in a bad play with no third act.

And why had he thought it was a good idea to go to a cave? Instead of slip-sliding his way through a wet cavern, his preference would have been to stroll a woodland path. Better yet, he would take Elizabeth's hand, walk into the woods, make a bed of leaves, and make love to her. Of course, such a thing only occurred at night—every night—as he lay awake in his bed. In his imaginings, Elizabeth and he had made love in every room at Pemberley, and their lovemaking had now moved to the gardens.

When they arrived at the mouth of the cave, Darcy handed each of the ladies their farmer's hat, and Georgiana and Lizzy broke into giggles at the sight of the horrid things.

"Georgiana, all I can say is that I hope the hat looks better on me than it does on you."

"Sorry, Lizzy, but you are no example of *haute couture* either."

While the ladies were laughing, Darcy and the colonel decided how best to proceed.

"Fitzwilliam, you go first, followed by Miss Elizabeth, and then…"

"I am not going first, Darcy. I am the tallest. The last time I went into that cave, I got a nasty scratch from one of those calcium icicles. I suggest you go first, and if you bump your head, I will know where to duck. Miss Bennet should follow you, then Georgie, and I will protect the rear."

"Protect the rear? From what? Wayward sheep? Never mind. Let us proceed."

Little Ben, with his torch, was the first into the cave, and when all were inside, Darcy explained that the front part of the cave was used by shepherds as a place to sleep at night and to shelter during a storm.

"You can see some tally marks scratched into the wall, which I am sure were used to count sheep as recently as this summer. The interesting part is through here."

Lizzy crouched as she passed through a narrow opening before emerging into a much larger room smelling of minerals and accompanied by the sound of the drip, drip, drip of water. Ben's torch revealed large cones of calcified water rising up from the floor and bursting forth from the ceiling. Lizzy looked around and was filled with the wonder a child experiences when presented with an unexpected gift.

"Remarkable."

"Yes, it is, but there is something even more remarkable beyond," and he directed Ben to proceed. Taking her by the hand, Darcy led her to an inner cavern where there were pictures of animals drawn with charcoal on the walls of the cave. Although the pictures were more representational than realistic, Lizzy got chills thinking she might be looking at something that was 5,000 years old.

"The archaeologists from Cambridge believe this room served a sacred purpose because the animals depicted here are either predators, such as wolves and bears, or animals that would have required great courage to hunt, like elk or wild pig, and the cavemen, with their spears, are definitely on the hunt. There are finer caves with better drawings in England and certainly on the Continent, but I take some pride in this little depository of the history of an ancient people being so close to where I live."

While Lizzy took her time in studying the sketches, Darcy was thinking about how he could kick himself for wasting such an opportunity. Here he was in a dark cave standing next to the woman he loved, and he was regaling her with stories about wild pigs and a primitive people who lived in caves and wore animal skins. He had done the same thing with Miss Montford. Was it any wonder she had looked frightened when he had discussed the American and French revolutions and the great explorers? And now he was doing it again.

"Mr. Darcy, did you read in the London paper that a young girl in Dorset, I believe her name is Mary Anning, discovered the fossilized skeleton of what appears to be an ancient crocodile? It fell from a cliff following a storm. Can you imagine?"

"You read about such things?"

"Why does that surprise you? Because I am a woman?"

"You are right. I should not be surprised, but there is so much about you that does surprise me."

Seeing that the couple was getting along famously, Georgiana signaled to her cousin that they should leave. "Will, Richard and I will wait for you outside. There is a steady dripping on my head, and I have seen all of these drawings, but please take your time."

And Lizzy and Mr. Darcy did. He stood as close to her as he could without scandalizing the young Avery. Even with that ridiculous hat on, she looked beautiful. He watched as the flames from the torch cast her profile in flashes of shadow and light, and he had to fight the urge to take her in his arms. Instead, he shared all that he knew about the cave and the valley below. After they had returned to the first room, Darcy stopped Lizzy before she could go out.

"Elizabeth, I am truly sorry…" but then he said no more, and after a long pause, Lizzy spoke.

"Mr. Darcy, I can see that you are troubled, so perhaps I can put your mind at ease." Believing that he was apologizing because nothing could ever come of their relationship, she told him about Mr. Peterson. "There is a certain gentleman who owns a large farm near Watford, and he has expressed an interest in calling on me. He is a fine man and a worthy suitor."

Darcy was dumbfounded. How could such intelligence possibly ease his mind?

"Please explain to me how revealing the presence of a suitor waiting for you in Hertfordshire is supposed to put my mind at ease? It does no such thing."

If Darcy was dumbfounded, Lizzy was shocked by the vehemence of his response and felt the need to defend herself. "I only mentioned Mr. Peterson because I thought you were unhappy with your performance regarding… I thought you might have felt that you had given me the wrong impression about… Oh, never mind."

Once again he stopped her from leaving. "There are complications."

"Complications? Forgive me if I appear confused, sir, but it is my understanding that you are about to become betrothed to a lady in London. There is nothing complicated about that."

"No."

"No? No what? No, you are not about to become betrothed? I see that you hesitate. I would think that such a question could be easily answered with a simple yes or no."

"There is nothing simple about this whole matter."

"I beg to differ. If I had been asked the same question, I would have had a ready answer."

If Georgiana had imagined listening to the sound of cooing lovebirds coming from inside the cave, she was quickly brought down to earth by loud voices speaking in anger.

"Richard, they are quarreling."

"I would not call it quarreling. It sounds more like fighting to me. Apparently, Miss Elizabeth has tired of our games."

"Ben, go into the cave and ask Mr. Darcy if he needs a light to find his way out," but the boy stood frozen as he had heard the same angry words coming from the cave. "Tell Mr. Darcy that I sent you. Now please go."

As soon as Ben went into the cave, Lizzy and Darcy went silent, and Darcy told him that he would be out shortly.

"Elizabeth, I am trying. I can assure you that I am trying."

"I do not understand what you mean."

"If I may speak to you in private this evening, I would appreciate it."

"Fine," and out she went.

As soon as Lizzy emerged into the light, she immediately

began praising the cave to Miss Darcy and Colonel Fitzwilliam because if she did not talk about all that she had seen, she would start crying out of pure frustration. After lauding all of the cave's treasures, she quickly began to walk down the path to where Sugar was tethered. For fear that she might kick Darcy, the colonel assisted Lizzy onto the mare. Nothing was said during the ride down to the carriage and little on the ride back to Pemberley, that is, until they came into view of the stables.

"Oh, no!" Georgiana said and looked at Richard.

"Oh, God!" Richard answered when he saw what she was looking at.

At that point, Darcy turned around and uttered a very audible "Damnation!"

"What is wrong? Has something bad happened?" Lizzy asked, thinking that something terrible had occurred at Pemberley during their absence.

"Yes, Miss Bennet. Something *is* wrong. My brother, Lord Fitzwilliam, has decided to pay us a visit."

Lizzy turned around to see the stable grooms unhitching a matched pair of white horses that had been pulling an ebony carriage with the coat of arms of the Fitzwilliam family on its side, and just from the little bit she had heard of Antony, Lord Fitzwilliam, she agreed that this could not possibly be a good thing.

Chapter 34

As soon as the carriage came to a stop, David and Goliath were doing circles and flips to show their master how pleased they were to see him, but Darcy hardly noticed his dogs' acrobatics. Even before he saw Antony's carriage, his unhappiness with how the excursion to Shepherd's Cave had gone was visible on his face. Now with the prospect of spending the evening with his rake of a cousin, his visage was all storm and thunder.

After Mr. Darcy helped Lizzy out of the carriage, he told her that he was looking forward to seeing her at supper, although his countenance appeared to be saying something else entirely. She quickly made her way into the house only to encounter Lord Fitzwilliam. But her mind was too unsettled to attempt to tackle a conversation with the earl, and she made a quick bow, mumbled "milord," and went right upstairs.

Georgiana would have made good her own escape if she had not also run headlong into her cousin, who was standing in the foyer looking confused as his eyes followed Lizzy running up the stairs.

"Georgiana, my dear, how lovely to see you. One of your servants just ran past me. I must say that even for a Darcy that is a damn liberal policy allowing a servant to use the front hall stairs."

After kissing his extended cheek, Georgiana explained that the lady was Miss Elizabeth Bennet and a guest, and after looking at her outfit, he asked if the usual tradition of handing down her used clothing to the maids had been reversed to accepting them from her servants.

"We are dressed this way because we went to Shepherd's Cave."

"Oh, sorry I missed that," he said, rolling his eyes, "but I had a pleasant conversation with Mrs. Gardiner." After seeing her expression, he reassured her. "Do not worry. I have not been here long enough to outrage anyone. Jackson has not even had time to follow your brother's standing order to dilute the port."

Georgiana was so rattled by Antony's sudden appearance that the remark went right over her head. "Antony, what are you doing here?"

"I was just about to ask that question myself," Darcy said, entering the foyer with David and Goliath right behind him. It always amazed Georgiana how easily his dogs sensed their master's changes in mood, and they now stood behind him like sculptures guarding a pharaoh's tomb.

"I came to find out what is going on," Antony said while deliberately ignoring his brother, who was vigorously shaking his head in an attempt to quiet him.

"What makes you think something is going on?" Darcy asked.

"Why else would Richard have sent my man to Kent for the purpose of delivering a letter to Anne with instructions to wait for an answer and to return to London immediately?"

After seeing Darcy's expression, Richard asked, "Can't I write a letter to my cousin?"

"Of course you can," Antony answered for his brother. "But why was it so important that Darcy be kept from going to Rosings Park? I suspect it has something to do with that badly dressed lady who just ran up the stairs."

"Will, may I please get out of these dirty clothes?" Georgiana pleaded, and she tried to slip away, but Darcy caught her by the arm and suggested that they all adjourn to the study for a family discussion.

Once there, Richard tried to extract his young cousin from the mess they now found themselves in. "Listen, Will, Georgie did not have anything to do with the part about Gregg riding to Rosings Park with a letter for Anne."

"Which part *was* she involved in, if not that?"

"I swear, Will," Georgiana said. "I have done nothing behind your back. My only involvement in any scheme was to invite Elizabeth and the Gardiners here to Pemberley and to suggest the excursion to the cave, both of which you knew about."

"Do I know the lady who is the cause of so much intrigue?" Antony asked, and all three answered with a loud "no."

"Antony, I know you did not come all the way from London just to catch up on family gossip," Will continued. "So, tell me. What the hell are you doing here?"

"That is not very nice, Will, especially since I have news to share."

"So share it." Darcy's patience was wearing thin, and his eyes, which could change with his mood, were now gunmetal gray.

"With pleasure. A few nights ago, Richard came to White's, and after we got Gregg off on his midnight ride to Kent, he worked the conversation around to politics. As you know, my interest in politics is only exceeded by my interest in women. There were rumors that you might be courting Letitia Montford. I say 'might' because your attentions to the young lady have been irregular at best, and you have everyone playing a guessing game.

"After beating around the bush, Richard finally got to it. He said that even though Sir John and you were polar opposites on the most important issues of the day, you were hoping to change that. You had gone so far as to say you were determined to secure Sir John's support for some legislation the Whigs were supporting regarding the expansion of the franchise to vote.

"Knowing that I cannot keep a secret, I understood my brother wanted me to spread this about, and so when Sir John came in the next evening, I told him what Richard had said. He sucked in his breath and forgot to breathe, and turned blue, not his best color, I might add. But then he asked where you were. When I told him, Sir John asked for me to give you a message."

"Which is?"

"He wants you to pay a call on him as soon as you return to town. He called you a young whippersnapper. I have not heard that word since I asked my father for an increase in my allowance when I was nineteen. Now, I believe I have performed admirably, so may I have a glass of port—from your reserve, Will—not the special port you keep just for me?"

Even considering the source, Darcy decided that this was good news. If his friendship with Letitia could be ended as a result of her father's disapproval of his politics, then it would turn out all right *if* his behavior since the ball at Netherfield had not caused irreparable harm in Elizabeth's eyes. As far as Darcy was concerned, he could not get to London to see Letitia fast enough and get this whole sorry affair behind him.

As soon as Lizzy reached her room, she rang for Ellie and asked that arrangements be made for a bath.

"Right away, miss, and a letter's come for you. It is on the table in the foyer. Should I get it?"

"I am sure it is from my sister Jane, so it can wait. I am much more interested in getting all of this dirt off me."

Lizzy felt an overwhelming sense of fatigue and was looking forward to soaking in a warm bath. Hopefully, she could wash away all the anger she was feeling for Mr. Darcy. But when Lizzy entered her apartment, she found her Aunt Gardiner waiting for her.

"I fear that I am intruding, as I am sure you are tired," her aunt stammered, "but I am actually hiding out in here."

"From Uncle Gardiner?"

"No, your uncle has not returned. I am speaking of Lord Fitzwilliam," and she clutched the lace on her bodice. "Elizabeth, he is a total rake. He had me blushing like a new bride. As your guardian, I do not want you anywhere near that man."

"I don't think you need worry," Lizzy said, taking off her coat. "From what I have heard, he would be more interested in you than me. Apparently, he draws the line at seducing maidens."

"Oh dear! You do not really think that he would try to…" but Aunt Gardiner could not finish the sentence.

"I have never met him, but I think he is probably more talk than action. I imagine one cold look from Mr. Darcy will settle him down nicely. But what did he say to you?"

"I am embarrassed to repeat the conversation," but with the slightest smile on her lips, she related the hour she had spent in Lord Fitzwilliam's company. "I have never been in the presence of an earl before, and I did not know what to say. In fact, he told me I was saying 'milord' too frequently. He appreciates his rank being acknowledged, but to his mind, a few 'milords' are sufficient," and Ruth Gardiner started to giggle like a young girl. "Actually, he is wickedly charming. I can imagine him getting his way more often than not."

"But tell me what he said."

"All right. After all, you are more than twenty years old and not a child. As I said, I did not know what to say to him because of his rank, and so I asked him about his family. He told me that he had two delightful daughters, ten and twelve, who were the apples of his eye. After we had exhausted the subject of his children, I told him that I had met the colonel and asked if there were any other sisters or brothers. 'Yes,' he said, 'I have two sisters. The younger one thinks I can do no wrong, while the older one thinks I can do no right. The older one actually got it right.'

"That is exactly what he said, but then he went on. 'My parents had four children, one right after the other, and then no more. I wonder what happened there?' Well, I blushed from head to toe at the implication that they no longer… Anyway, after he saw me blushing, he said, 'Tsk, tsk, tsk, Mrs. Gardiner, I wasn't thinking of that at all.'"

Lizzy started laughing. "I think he was trying to fluster you as he has a reputation to protect—that of being a rascal."

"Well, my dear, if he wanted to see me flustered, he suc-ceeded. I will tell you that I shall have Mr. Gardiner beside me throughout the evening, and if he must leave me for even a moment, I shall seek you out."

"You would do better to find Mr. Darcy. That gentleman was in ill humor when I left him, and I doubt he is in the mood for any of his cousin's antics."

Chapter 35

SHORTLY AFTER MRS. GARDINER returned to her room, her husband came bounding in after an excellent day of fishing on the River Dove. Although he had been gone since dawn on this his final excursion, he was overflowing with energy and was looking forward to sharing his day at Viator's Bridge with his wife. Instead, Mrs. Gardiner demanded his immediate attention.

"May I clean up while you tell me about your exciting day in the gardens, Mrs. Gardiner? Certainly, any words that fell from the lips of that laconic Scotsman would be more interesting than anything I had to say about fishing in a spot mentioned in *The Compleat Angler*." Mrs. Gardiner was so eager to share her experience with her husband that she entirely missed the sarcasm contained in his remark.

"This is not about Mr. Ferguson but Lord Fitzwilliam, who, by the way, is very handsome and has the same amazing blue eyes as his brother." When she had finished detailing her interesting conversation with His Lordship, Mr. Gardiner burst out laughing.

"Why are you laughing? This man is an avowed philanderer, and everything he says is a *double entendre*."

"My dear, this shows that our randy earl has excellent taste in women. I would take his flirting as a compliment as he is known for having affairs with some of the loveliest married women in England."

"He is an adulterer! Are you not shocked?"

"Yes, he is an adulterer and, from what I understand, quite beyond redemption when it comes to women, wine, and gambling. However, I am not shocked at his behavior as this is quite common among the aristocracy. But did you really blush like a new bride, and you the mother of four?"

"Absolutely! What would you expect me to do when his conversation was replete with sexual innuendo? I shall admit he has a very ingratiating way about him, and I can just imagine a woman looking into those blue orbs and forgetting herself. Of course, I am not referring to myself, and may I state in the strongest language possible that such a conversation rightly belongs exclusively within the confines of the bedroom of a husband and his lawfully wedded wife."

"Ruth, we are in a bedroom, and I am your husband and you are my lawfully wedded wife," and with a wicked smile, he asked, "so may I speak of such matters?"

After seeing the look in her husband's eyes, Mrs. Gardiner started to laugh. "Edward, remember yourself. It is the middle of the day."

"I shall close the drapes."

"We must dress and go down for dinner."

"I shall be quick," and Ruth Gardiner fell back on the bed laughing, and her husband soon joined her. After they had finished making love, Mr. Gardiner wondered if it would be possible to arrange for his wife to sit next to Lord Fitzwilliam at supper.

"Did you take your bonnet off while you were in the cave, miss?" Ellie asked Elizabeth. "Because it looks as if someone emptied a salt cellar in your hair."

Lizzy confessed that she had removed the farmer's hat before leaving the cave. Not only was it ugly, but it prevented her from seeing Mr. Darcy's face. She knew he had been watching her, and when he had moved closer to her to explain the drawings on the cave's wall, she felt a growing heat spreading throughout her body. But she could not decide if it was a good thing or a bad thing.

However, there was no question that telling Mr. Darcy about Mr. Peterson had been the wrong thing. His response was totally unexpected. Instead of his seeing that she was providing him with a graceful exit and relieving him of any self-recrimination, he had become angry when he thought she might have a possible suitor. Good grief! What was she supposed to do? "Get thee to a nunnery"? And what did he mean when he had said he "was trying"? Why was it that a man of sense and education, who had lived in the world, found it so difficult to speak in declarative sentences that did not require an interpreter?

Ellie had already laid out the dress Lizzy was to wear that evening, and she could hardly look at it without thinking she was a character in a fairy tale, the one in which a village maiden marries the prince and lives happily ever after. Shortly after their arrival at Pemberley, Georgiana had shown Lizzy some of the dresses she had worn during the season, all of which had been made by a famous designer who had fled Paris and the Terror in France. One of the dresses was an exquisite russet gown with gold thread woven into the bodice and with gold tassels hanging from the short sleeves.

"This was the dress I wore to the Smythe's ball a year ago. I had not yet come out into society, and it was something of a practice ball for those girls who were shortly to make their debut."

"Georgiana, I think it is the loveliest gown I have ever seen."

"I agree with you, but the color was all wrong for me, but it was my fault as Madame Delaine had warned me I was too fair for such a color. Obviously, I did not take her advice, and as a result, I have a gown I shall never wear again. It would be unfortunate if someone did not wear it, so I would like for you to have it."

Lizzy smiled at the generous offer. She could not even guess at the cost of the gown, but she could easily imagine that it cost more than she would spend on all her frocks in the course of a year.

"That is most kind of you, Georgiana, but I am afraid I cannot accept it."

"I thought you might say that, so I shall tell you that if you do not take it, I shall give it to Mrs. Brotherton, who will sell it. This is something I do for her because she does so much for me, but the thought of some stranger wearing this particular gown when I have a friend who would look absolutely stunning in it distresses me." And there were those big eyes again. Lizzy felt sorry for whomever she married as the man would never win an argument when she could put on such a look.

"Let us compromise. I shall wear the dress tonight, but tomorrow I shall return it to you. May we agree on that?"

"Yes, that is the perfect compromise," and Georgiana was sure her brother would be glad that she had struck such a deal.

After a decade of handling the reins of a post coach, Mercer had accepted the position of serving as valet to Mr. Darcy. This was not the first time he had served in such a position, but his previous employer had been such an arrogant bastard that he had gladly returned to driving a coach and six. In the five years since accepting the position with Mr. Darcy, Mercer had developed a deep affection for this young man, and whenever he recognized that his master was troubled, he did his best to help him work his way through it. Tonight was such a night.

While soaking in a tub, Darcy had unburdened himself to his manservant concerning the fiasco in the cave. "I know I acted badly, but when Elizabeth said she had been encouraging the attentions of another man, I responded quite harshly."

"Sir, from what you've told me, I don't think she was telling you that she had encouraged another man. She was saying that you shouldn't feel bad about not being able to court her because she had a suitor in the wings."

"Is that supposed to make me feel better, Mercer?" He turned around and looked up at him. "Seriously?"

"Yes, sir, 'cause if she had already received the gentleman, then what was she doing in Derbyshire? No, to my mind, she was telling you that, come what may, she was going to be all right."

Darcy chewed on that for a while and decided Mercer was probably correct because he did not think Elizabeth capable of being unkind, and it would have been a great unkindness if she had used the farmer from Watford as retaliation for his cock-up in London.

"I know, sir, that you do not think it right to say anything to Miss Elizabeth until you have settled the problem with Miss Montford, but I think that if you put on your best face tonight, she might figure out that you are going to do your very best to take care of the matter once you get back to London. And, besides, I know the lady cares for you."

"How do you know that?"

"I seen it at the Netherfield ball. After I took care of all my duties, I went downstairs to listen to the music and to watch the dancing like I always do, and I seen how she looked at you. I've had enough women look at me like that to know what I'm talking about. That was the look of love, sir."

"You and Lord Fitzwilliam with all your women," Darcy said, laughing. "At the moment, I have two women in my life, and it is one too many."

"Speaking of Lord Fitzwilliam, I know how he gets under your skin, and forgive me for saying so, but it shows on your face. Whenever you are in his company, you furrow your brow, and it stays that way."

"You sound like my mother. She often said the same thing. Apparently, I was born frowning."

"What you've got to do, sir, is keep Miss Elizabeth in the front of your head all night and ignore His Lordship."

"Ignore His Lordship? That is like saying ignore that cliff up ahead."

"But you can do it, sir. I think you have to because this might be the last time you see the lady for a while. Even if everything goes well in London, it'll be several days coming and going from town before you will see her again, so it is very important that you leave Miss Elizabeth with a good memory of you. And smiling would help."

"All right, Mercer. I shall keep in the forefront of my mind the memory of our time together at the ball at Netherfield. You say that she looked at me as if she were in love. Well, I can assure you that one of us definitely was."

Chapter 36

It had occurred to Darcy to ask Antony to comport himself in a manner befitting a peer of the realm. But that would be the same thing as asking a leopard to change its spots, and so he had said nothing. In any event, he had witnessed how expertly Elizabeth had handled Caroline Bingley at Netherfield Park, and he hoped she was up to the unique challenge of conversing with Lord Fitzwilliam. Hopefully, Georgiana had warned her about him because she had them sitting together at supper. His sister was probably correct in thinking he was more likely to be on his best behavior with an unmarried woman than with Mrs. Gardiner. Despite Georgiana's youth, rumors of her cousin's reputation had reached her ears.

Darcy was waiting at the bottom of the staircase for his guests, and from the look on the faces of Mr. and Mrs. Gardiner, it appeared that each had had a good day—he at Viator's Bridge and she in the gardens with Mr. Ferguson—because they were both obviously in a stellar mood.

After greeting the Gardiners, he stood waiting for Elizabeth.

After pulling on his waistcoat, tugging at his neckcloth, and checking his cuffs for the tenth time, he looked up to see Elizabeth descending the stairs, and the sight took his breath away.

"Miss Elizabeth, you look exceptionally beautiful tonight." Although she was wearing her hair up, some of her curls fell softly on the back of her neck, and the effect was perfect. And he too felt something stir, and he hoped it would go away quickly.

"Thank you, sir. Your sister was kind enough to allow me to borrow her dress." Surely, it was all right to acknowledge she was wearing Georgiana's dress. After all, he had paid for it.

"An excellent decision. My sister was perceptive enough to realize how lovely it would look on you."

"We have come a long way, Mr. Darcy, since the Meryton assembly when you were of a different mind."

"Yes, but you know me well enough to know that I praise only that which I truly admire."

At that point, Colonel Fitzwilliam came into the foyer, and he looked glorious in his brilliant red regimentals. The colonel truly was—what was the best word to describe him—oh, yes, gorgeous, and a smile came to her lips. She could easily imagine women stopping and staring at him whenever he came into a room.

"Miss Elizabeth, you are absolutely luminous tonight," the colonel said, bowing. "'She doth teach the torches to burn bright.' You see, I am not as guarded in paying compliments as my cousin here. When I have such beauty before me, I do not pick and choose my words. I announce it to the world."

"Colonel Fitzwilliam, I can see the influence spending an afternoon with Lord Fitzwilliam has had on you, but your praise is appreciated."

"I admit that it is a Fitzwilliam trait to speak freely, and it is one of the few things Antony and I have in common."

"However, with regard to Mr. Darcy," Lizzy said, "since he is so judicious in his use of compliments, I would find myself quite flattered to have earned even one."

"Did I hear my name mentioned?" Antony said as he joined the party. Lizzy quickly judged His Lordship to be quite handsome, but was surprised to find him out of fashion as he was still wearing the colorful jacket and waistcoat of the fops who had preceded the fashion followers of Mr. Beau Brummel. She wondered if the reason for his out-of-date attire was that he had not paid his tailor.

Taking Mrs. Gardiner's hand, His Lordship kissed it, and he kept his lips pressed to her ungloved hand for so long that she had to gently pull it away.

"Did you have a pleasant afternoon, Mrs. Gardiner? Did your husband regale you with his fish stories, including the big one that got away, or was he able to catch it?"

"Milord, I was *very* pleased with my catch," Mr. Gardiner answered, and when Lord Fitzwilliam left their company to seek an introduction to Elizabeth, Mrs. Gardiner whispered to her husband, "Do you see what I mean? He is scandalous."

"Well, my dear, I am not going to say anything to him."

"Because he is an earl?"

"No, because I am in his debt," and he said this with a gleam in his eye, and Lord Fitzwilliam, having seen it, winked at him.

After they were seated at the dining table, Antony complimented Darcy on his company. "With so much beauty in Derbyshire," he said, bowing his head in the direction of each of the three ladies, "I have no reason to go back to London."

"Please feel free to make yourself at home, Antony. Unfortunately, we are all departing tomorrow," Darcy said.

"Surely, not on my account."

"Believe it or not, decisions are made every day that do not require taking you or your whereabouts into consideration."

"Really? Well, I shall then take every opportunity to enjoy the time we have together."

Antony behaved himself all through supper because he knew that Darcy could hear everything he said. There were few people whose presence gave him pause for thought, but his dour cousin was among them.

"Miss Bennet, are you positive we are not acquainted?" the earl asked as soon as they had removed to the drawing room.

"Quite sure, milord. I only know you from the newspapers and magazines."

"Ah, *The Insider*. My reputation has preceded me."

"I was referring to the more serious London newspapers. They have written extensively on your call for an accounting of the money spent on the war."

"How boring. I would rather you have read *The Insider*."

"I do read *The Insider*, milord, but it is not reliable. For example, you could not possibly have been at White's and Boodles and Mrs. Arbuthnot's salon all at the same time."

"I have a reputation as a rapscallion to protect, and I fear you are damaging it."

"If that is the case, you are already too late. My aunt shared some of your conversation from this afternoon in which you spoke so affectionately of your daughters. I cannot believe a man who told such tender stories about his children can be a complete rascal."

"Miss Bennet, you have found my one weakness, my darlings, Sophie and Emmy."

"I consider myself to be an optimist, milord, and if there is one good thing about a person, surely there are others."

Standing up, Lord Fitzwilliam said, "I must quit your company immediately, my dear, or you will have me down on my knees at the altar of the Abbey repenting like Henry II, which I do not want to do. I can assure you it is much more fun to be a sinner than a saint. But let us have some music. My cousin has opened the ballroom for our pleasure. Perhaps we may convince the talented Miss Darcy to play something so that we might dance."

Upon entering the ballroom, Lizzy gazed in wonder at the crystal chandeliers and polished wood floors, and when she looked at the marble fireplaces, the flames made the cherubs carved into the mantle look as if they were dancing.

Mrs. Gardiner offered to play so that the others might dance, and Darcy was about to ask Elizabeth for a dance but found the colonel was quicker on his feet. Darcy shot his cousin a withering look, but the colonel paid no notice. He liked beautiful women, and he liked to dance. Darcy would have to bide his time.

After waiting his turn, Darcy first apologized to Elizabeth in case Lord Fitzwilliam had said anything offensive during supper or in the drawing room and offered a preemptive apology in the event he should embarrass her at any time during the remainder of the evening.

"I suspect his reputation is exaggerated," Elizabeth answered.

"I am not sure I can agree with you, as he has worked hard to deserve it."

"Can a man who is so fond of his children be all bad?"

"No, of course not. But he could be so much better. It is a point of irritation for me to read in *The Times* an excellent speech that he had made in the Lords, with everyone praising him, and then to learn that following his oration, he headed straight for the gaming tables. But you are right in one thing. He is devoted to his daughters and quite a different person in their company. Like Sophia and Amelia, there are those who have such power over the hearts of others."

Lizzy looked into his eyes, and they were the beautiful green she had discovered on that long-ago morning when he had come to Longbourn to apologize. In his elegant suit, he was so handsome, and he had her heart beating faster than was comfortable. She looked away so that he might not see what she was feeling.

Lord Fitzwilliam was an excellent dancer, and after stepping lively to a number of the more familiar tunes, he suggested they all try something new.

"There is a lovely dance called the waltz, which is very popular on the Continent."

"Antony, if it is on the Continent, with battles being fought everywhere, how could you possibly know that?" Georgiana asked.

"Because I have a friend in London who is an émigré from Vienna. She got tired of war, war, and more war, and snuck out of the country."

"I am familiar with the music as there are waltzes in Mozart's *Don Giovanni*," Georgiana said. "But even if I have something in my music chest, no one here will know the steps."

"Except me, my dear. You see, my friend has been giving me private lessons," and for the first time that evening, Darcy adopted that stare which could bore a hole right through a man. Ignoring his cousin, Lord Fitzwilliam continued, "The dance calls for the gentleman to take the lady's right hand and hold it thusly," and he raised his arm to slightly below shoulder height, "and he then places his hand on the lady's waist, while she puts her hand upon his shoulder. The dance begins with sliding steps followed by a bit of a hop. It is actually quite easy."

Mr. Gardiner stared aghast at His Lordship. "Milord, I am not sure if you are to be taken seriously. Surely, no father or husband would approve of his daughter or wife performing such a dance in a public venue?"

"Oh, I would. Lady Eleanor may dance with whomever she chooses in any venue she chooses. But, Mrs. Gardiner, if you would permit me, I will provide you with a demonstration. It is not nearly as scandalous as you think."

Georgiana jumped out of her seat and said to her cousin, "Antony, I am quite interested in new dances. Would you please show me the steps?" When she took Antony's hand, she whispered, "I am begging you. Please behave. Do you not have lady friends in London with whom you could practice the waltz?"

"Of course, my dear. But you have identified the problem. They are in London, and I am here."

Rather than risk being asked to dance again, Mrs. Gardiner quickly offered to play the tune to the best of her ability. All watched as Lord Fitzwilliam made elegant turns with his young cousin. Elizabeth viewed the performance with admiration as the couple executed the simple steps quite nicely.

"It is actually quite lovely," Lizzy remarked. "I do not know if I would approve of it in a setting less intimate than this one, but it is elegant."

Upon hearing that Elizabeth liked the display, Darcy stood up and offered his hand to her. "Miss Elizabeth, would you do me the honor of dancing with me?" In short order, they were moving about the room as if they had been dancing together forever, and she wished it would go on forever. But when the music stopped, Richard bolted out of his seat and asked Mrs. Gardiner for a reprise of the waltz, so he might dance with her. As much as Lizzy liked the colonel, she wished he would go away.

Everyone was having such a good time "waltzing" that Lord Antony finally convinced Mrs. Gardiner to dance, and her husband was pleased to see his bride of more than a dozen years looking so beautiful on the dance floor. The evening ended with Lizzy and Darcy dancing the last waltz, and instead of holding her hand out as he had previously done, he wrapped his hand around hers and brought it to his chest and laid it against his heart.

While Darcy had been dancing the waltz with Elizabeth, his need for her to become a part of his life had moved into every fiber of his being. As a result, he was experiencing the acute frustration of someone who was being denied the one thing he wanted more than anything else. With Elizabeth returning to Longbourn in the morning, it was critical that he speak with her tonight because he needed her reassurances that she would not give Mr. Peterson any encouragement.

After the Gardiners announced that they were retiring, Darcy was hopeful the others would do likewise, but the brothers

Fitzwilliam were enjoying their port while talking military strategy and the war on the Peninsula, in which the British were suffering large casualties as a result of dysentery, the bane of any army. However, as soon as Georgiana heard the word "dysentery," she popped up and said she was ready to go to her bed, and Lizzy felt that she must leave as well.

Darcy followed the ladies into the foyer, and after kissing Georgiana good night, he asked Elizabeth if he could have a word with her. Because there was no time left for any misunderstandings, Lizzy took one step up on the stairs, so she could see his eyes. But, apparently, the particular word he had been searching for eluded him, and he remained silent and just stared at her. And so she would begin.

"I cannot praise Pemberley enough or your sister, who was a most gracious hostess, and I am indebted to you for taking me to Shepherd's Cave and for your hospitality last night and this evening. I can say without hesitation that I will remember my time here at Pemberley for all of my life."

"But I hope you will soon return to Pemberley," Darcy said, surprised that she thought she might not be coming back.

Lizzy looked at him with a puzzled expression. "I do not think that likely, Mr. Darcy."

"Elizabeth, I know there has been a lot of confusion, but I want you to know that I am taking steps..." and he took her hand in his.

Lizzy waited for him to finish the sentence, but he said nothing. Why could he just not tell her what he was doing? Say what he was feeling? Why was it necessary to have all of this suspense?

"Mr. Darcy, you have me at a disadvantage as it appears you

know things that I do not. So let me say this. Picture, if you will, a castle on a hill with a village below. Dividing them is a deep chasm. If the two are ever to come together, it must be bridged, but you cannot span a chasm in a series of small steps. You must do it in one great leap of faith. There is no guarantee of its success, but it is the only way."

"I understand. I truly do. But I must ask for your continued patience. I leave for London in the morning, and the matter that awaits me there will be settled. I am looking forward to a time when I may speak freely—when nothing binds me to silence."

Lizzy saw the struggle in his eyes and leaned forward and put her cheek against his and rested it there for a moment before wishing him Godspeed and a successful journey.

Chapter 37

AFTER THE MAID HAD helped her out of her dress, Lizzy went to the dressing table so that Ellie could take down her hair. This was the part of having a maid that Lizzy had come to enjoy the most—someone brushing her hair. At home, Jane and she took turns, but here, she had the pleasure of someone running a brush through her hair night after night and doing so until asked to stop. But after tomorrow, she was back to taking turns with Jane.

"I hope you don't mind, miss, but me and Lucy, Mrs. Gardiner's maid, snuck downstairs and had a peek at the dancing. I never seen anything like it before."

"Were you shocked, Ellie? Because, at first, I know I was. But the movements are so elegant. It is as if you are floating on a cloud, and everything is spinning all around you. It is exhilarating."

"I was there when Mrs. Gardiner was dancing with His Lordship, and because her dress is wider than yours or Miss Darcy's, it made it look like she was a spinning top—but a beautiful one. And I saw you dance with the master, and you were a right handsome pair."

Lizzy steered the conversation away from Mr. Darcy. She felt it inappropriate to discuss the master of Pemberley with one of his servants, but she could not help but be pleased with Ellie's comment.

Just before leaving, her maid reminded her that the letter that had come for her that morning was on the writing desk.

"Thank you. I had forgotten. I am sure it is from my sister," and she was equally sure that Jane was writing to tell her that Lydia was doing her best not to return home from Brighton.

But after retrieving the post, Lizzy decided that she wasn't quite ready to read her sister's letter. Instead, as she lay on the bed staring at the pleated rose canopy, she remembered her last dance with Mr. Darcy and the feel of his hand around her waist and how he had brought her closer to him with each turn until they were only inches apart. The only way Mr. Darcy could have been closer to her was if he had actually pulled her into an embrace. She then remembered the previous night's dream when Mr. Darcy had come to her bed, and she went over the scene again and again. Turning on her side, she pulled the pillow to her and dozed off in Mr. Darcy's arms, and Jane's letter lay unread on the bed.

"Richard, Antony, let us have a brandy in the study," Darcy offered. Hearing the word "brandy" was enough to get His Lordship on his feet. After taking a drink, he remarked, "It is excellent, Darcy. Do you have it smuggled in from France?"

"My man arranges it. Apparently, Mercer has contacts on

the coast from his coaching days, and because of Napoleon's wars, the importers of wines and spirits from France are the ones who are suffering. It is my way of showing my support for the merchant class."

"As a Tory and one who rarely supports any Whig policies, I must say I agree with this one," and Antony raised his glass to allow the light to pass through the liquor. "If I had any ready cash, I would go and talk to Mercer myself." Because Darcy made no cutting remarks about his profligate ways and seeing that he was in an agreeable mood, Antony decided to tease him. "Darcy, I feel I must point out that you are now twice in my debt."

"Twice? How so?"

"The first, Sir John Montford, you already know. As for the second, if I had not suggested dancing the waltz, you would not have had that lovely creature in your arms."

Darcy looked at Richard. How much had he told his brother about his feelings for Elizabeth?

"Oh, do not look at Richard. You never could hide your emotions. That is why you do not win at cards."

"I see you are enjoying yourself at my expense."

"I have to admit that I am. I do not think I have ever seen you more vulnerable. It almost makes you human and, therefore, much more like me."

"I wouldn't go that far."

"Your being human or much more like me?" and the three men laughed. It was a rare event, but Darcy had to admit he owed the earl a debt of gratitude.

"May I take you up on your offer to stay at Pemberley for a few days? I am rarely in the country these days because Briarwood is falling apart, and it is damn depressing to hear my steward drone on and on about all that needs to be done on the outside and then to have to listen to the same thing from my butler and housekeeper. I have stopped reading their letters."

"Yes, Georgiana will be here for another two weeks or so. Now that she has the responsibilities of the mistress of the manor, she wants to learn the ropes and will spend her time with Mrs. Reynolds and Mrs. Bradshaw."

"But, hopefully, she will not have those responsibilities for much longer as you will be bringing your bride to Pemberley."

"Before you announce my engagement to the world, Antony, may I remind you that there are things to be done in London first?"

"I agree there are loose ends that need to be tied up, but surely the matter is settled in favor of Elizabeth?"

"Yes, the matter is settled in my mind, and I am eager to be in London to settle it in fact. But until I have spoken to Miss Montford or her father, I do not want anything regarding the matter spread abroad."

"I look forward to wishing you joy, and I might add that I envy you. My parents determined who my bride would be, and look how well that turned out! And poor Richard over there must marry a woman of wealth. You, however, will marry for love."

"Before we break out the champagne, Antony, tell Will what is going on in London," Richard said. "It may affect his plans, and you know he will say nothing."

"Yes, I can see how that might happen," and Antony revealed the continuing tragedy of George III. "Apparently, the death of Princess Amelia has pushed our king over the edge. He is no longer capable of ruling, and there will be no coming back this time. The wheels have begun to turn to make the Prince of Wales his regent, and it will happen early in the new year."

"I am very sorry to hear it, but how does this news affect me personally?"

"The king's list will remain unchanged, and Sir John Montford will be given his barony. However, his ties are to the king, and he has said some imprudent things about the Prince of Wales. Once the prince is made regent, he will cut everyone who ever criticized him."

"That is no hardship on my part. I do not run with that crowd."

"Will, don't you see what could happen?" Richard asked. "Once Sir John learns that his friendship with the king will not work in his favor, he might be willing to overlook your politics in order to access your connections, and he may insist on your marrying his daughter."

"But you just said no announcement is to be made regarding His Majesty until after the new year, so Miss Montford and I will have parted company long before then."

"Darcy, Darcy, Darcy! Sometimes your naïveté amazes me," Antony said. "London leaks like a sieve. The news is already starting to come out, and Sir John is likely to hear of it. So be sure that ending your courtship with Miss Montford is your first order of business, or it may end up being your last."

Chapter 38

Lizzy was still clinging to her pillow when she heard
Colonel Fitzwilliam and his brother come up the stairs. She
did not mind the disruption because her waking thoughts
were even more pleasant than her dreams, and flashes of
the evening passed through her mind: the dance, the touch,
looking into his eyes and seeing hope there, and resting her
cheek against his. If only he had kissed her, the evening would
have been perfect.

When Lizzy turned on her back, she felt the crush of Jane's
letter beneath her, and since the candle by her bed still burned,
she began to read it.

> My Dear Sister,
> I hope you are enjoying your stay in Derbyshire
> and that it continues to be the ideal holiday for you.
> Although I regret writing anything that might take
> away from the pleasure of your visit, I must write of
> my concerns about Lydia. In her last two letters, she

mentioned that a particular lieutenant was paying her a good deal of attention, someone she already knew from Meryton. She then wrote to Kitty to say that the officer's first name began with a "G," and when she next wrote, she indicated that his last initial was "W." When I asked if the initials, G.W., belonged to Mr. Wickham, Kitty said that they did.

Lizzy, what possible reason can George Wickham have for paying so much attention to Lydia? We know her to be a silly girl, ill educated, and more importantly for Mr. Wickham, lacking a fortune.

I know Mr. Darcy gave you no specifics when he told you to be wary of anything Wickham had to say, but the implication was that he was not to be trusted. I spoke of my concerns to Papa, but he insists Lydia's lack of fortune will protect her, especially since she is under the protection of the colonel. And I asked if such protection would protect her from a determined seducer, and, Lizzy, he actually laughed. He still sees Lydia as a child, and intellectually I agree with him. But physically, she is a woman. Papa did agree to write to the colonel to tell him he is sending Adam Hill to Brighton to escort Lydia home. But what if it is too late? If our father will not act, what can be done? Please write as soon as possible as I am greatly troubled by this news.

Love, Jane

As soon as she had read the last word, Lizzy was on her feet searching for her dressing gown. She needed to know from Mr. Darcy what injury Wickham had caused his family because she was convinced that it had something to do with Georgiana. When she went into the hallway, she ran straight into Mercer.

"Mr. Mercer, has Mr. Darcy retired for the night?" she asked in a quaking voice.

"Not yet, miss, but he was about to. Is something wrong?"

"Possibly. Would you please ask Mr. Darcy if I may speak with him?"

When Mercer went into the study, he found his master had removed his jacket and taken off his neckcloth and was staring into a snifter of brandy, watching as the amber liquid lapped the sides of the glass. This was something he often did when he needed to think.

"Are we ready, Mercer?"

"Sir, Miss Elizabeth is in the foyer asking to speak to you. She is quite disturbed."

Darcy jumped to his feet, and with no regard to his appearance, he went into the foyer and found Elizabeth in a considerable state of anxiety.

"Good grief, Elizabeth, what is wrong?" and he directed her to a sofa in the study. "Mercer, stay close."

"Mr. Darcy, I have had a letter from Jane concerning my youngest sister, Lydia, who has been visiting with Colonel Forster and his family in Brighton. Apparently, she has met Mr. Wickham there, and it appears that for the last couple of weeks he has been paying her quite a bit of attention. I remembered your warning to me about him, and after being in his company on a number of occasions, I had the impression that he is not to be believed or trusted. But I am hoping he is not a bad man, merely an exaggerator and a flirt. May I ask you to read Jane's letter, so that you might reassure me that he has no designs on my sister?"

Darcy took the letter, and it was as expected. To him, Wickham's intent was clear: the seduction of Elizabeth's youngest sister.

"But why?" Lizzy asked, unable to hide the anguish in her voice.

Darcy placed his hand on her cheek and, looking into her tear-filled eyes, explained the ugly truth. "It is because you believed me and not his lies, and this is his way of punishing you." When Lizzy began to cry, he pulled her into his arms and rested his head upon hers. She fit perfectly, as he knew she would. He ran his fingers through her long dark curls and kissed the top of her head, trying to give her some comfort, but there was little else he could do at that moment.

Taking her by the hand, he led her to the chair closest to the fireplace, and he thought how beautiful she was, and despite her sadness, the pleasure he felt when holding her in his arms. But there was business to be done, and after handing her a glass of wine to calm her, he went into the foyer where Mercer waited.

"Bring His Lordship's man to the study immediately. After you have done that, prepare for our departure to Brighton, and we shall be moving with all possible speed."

Returning to Elizabeth, he found her standing in front of the fireplace staring into the fire, and although she was no longer crying, the pain she was feeling was clearly visible on her face.

"Please come and sit down. I want to tell you of my plans," and with her hands between his, he began, "First, I am reasonably confident we have some time. Because Wickham intends a seduction and not an elopement, he will be unable to return to his regiment. Thus, he must plan his every move to avoid risk of discovery. I have sent for His Lordship's man, who is an expert horseman, and he will ride to Brighton with a letter from me alerting the colonel as to Wickham's intentions."

"But it is the middle of the night."

"Please remember he is Lord Fitzwilliam's man, and he is used to being summoned at such times and moving expeditiously."

Lizzy nodded that she understood.

"Mercer and I will leave at first light and go straight through to Brighton, and I will act as a representative for your family until such time as your father can determine the course of action he wishes to pursue. I would ask that you write a letter to your father tonight, stating in the clearest possible terms that Lydia is in danger and that I can testify to that fact. You and the Gardiners will return to Longbourn as planned, but your letter will go by express rider." He then took her hand and kissed it. "We must move quickly, Elizabeth, so please go write your letter, and I will do the same. Bring it to me as soon as you have finished."

When Darcy opened the door to the study, Gregg was waiting for instructions, and he was already dressed ready to ride. After being informed of the particulars, he left to go to the stables, and Darcy thought that no matter what Antony was paying him, it was not enough.

Darcy sat down at the desk in the study to pen his letter to the colonel. He gave no particular examples of Wickham's unscrupulous behavior, but instead asked the colonel to rely on his reputation as surety until he could talk to him in person. As soon as the ink had dried and he had sealed it, he handed it to Mercer to deliver to Gregg.

Darcy waited at the bottom of the stairs for Lizzy, and as she descended, she practically took them two at a time and was waving the letter in the air, trying to get the ink to dry faster.

"One of the grooms will take this into Lambton early tomorrow morning and hire an express rider. It will be placed in your father's hands long before you arrive at Longbourn. By the time you get home, Mr. Bennet will have made his plans. I think that is all we can do tonight to assist Lydia, but I need to speak to you before I leave. Will you join me in the study?" And he gestured for her to go in ahead of him.

As soon as they were seated on the sofa, he began, "Before I leave for Brighton, I would like to share some things with you that may explain some of my actions. Allow me to begin by saying that only a male can inherit Pemberley. This stipulation means that I must have a son. However, because I was comfortable with the designated heir to Pemberley, I was in no hurry to marry. David Ashton is a good man, forty-five years of age, fond of Georgiana, and one who gave every indication of being a lifelong bachelor. However, shortly before the start of the season, he informed me that he was to marry a niece and ward of the Duke of Rutland, who owns property that abuts Pemberley. Consolidating our two estates has been a wish of the duke for as long as I can remember.

"As soon as I learned of the engagement, I knew I had to find a wife. If I have learned anything from Antony's marriage, it was that the woman I married must, at the very least, be kind. It ranked higher in importance to me than beauty or accomplishments. So after reviewing all of my options, I settled on Miss Letitia Montford.

"I will admit that I was not the best suitor. After returning to London following the Netherfield ball, I realized that I was comparing everyone to you—and not just Miss Montford. No lady was as witty, intelligent, or pretty as you were. No one could make me smile or laugh the way you did," and taking Lizzy's hand, he said, "You have ruined me for every other woman."

"If you are looking for an apology, you will have to look elsewhere," Lizzy said, as she ran her fingers along the back of his hand.

"Even though I did not love Miss Montford, I continued with the courtship for fear she might be humiliated if I withdrew my attentions, and she had done nothing to deserve that. Fortunately, I have meddling relations who would not let me jump off that cliff. Richard, Georgiana, and Anne did things behind my back, including making arrangements for you to come to Pemberley, with me to follow. Another person who helped considerably was Miss Montford herself. I know you were surprised to find me at Pemberley, but I had been encouraged to come here by Miss Montford."

"I do not understand. She *wanted* you to leave her?"

"Yes. She wished me to be anywhere but in London. I think I actually frightened her."

"I can understand that."

Darcy laughed out loud. "Even in the present circumstances, your wit does not desert you. But do not expect me to believe for one minute that you are afraid of me. You have had me on my heels since I sat across from you in the parlor at Longbourn."

"If you have adopted a more humble posture because of me, Mr. Darcy, I am glad to have been of service."

"Elizabeth, when the dust settles, I will have to ask myself why I am deliberately seeking the companionship of someone who will always get the better of me. But as to Letitia Montford, I do believe she would release me immediately, but I am unsure if her father would be willing to do the same. But I no longer care what Sir John thinks. I have decided that this courtship must end as Miss Montford would be perfectly miserable with me, and she could never make me happy. There is only one person who can do that, and I am looking at her."

Taking his cue from the look in her eyes, he did what he had wanted to do ever since that afternoon at Longbourn, and he took her in his arms and he kissed her and kissed her again, and after parting her lips with his tongue, he felt the response of her warm lips tasting his. She moved her hands to his face and traced his lips with her fingers, and then she put her arms around his neck and kissed him again before resting her head on his chest. For many more minutes, they sat there quietly in each other's embrace, but Darcy knew that there were so many things that needed to be done before he could leave in the morning. And so he stood and brought her to her feet and kissed her in one long kiss because he did not know when he would feel her lips again.

"I am to Brighton in the morning and then to London for that business of which we just spoke. But at the earliest possible moment, I will come to you, and I promise you, no more small steps. I plan to bridge the chasm that separates us in one giant leap of love."

Chapter 39

DARCY, DRESSED IN HIS traveling clothes, was on his way to Antony's room when Lord Fitzwilliam stepped out into the hallway.

"Sneaking out of your own house, Darcy? That is very odd."

"Actually, I was coming to see you, but what are you doing up at this hour?"

"It should not surprise you that I am a light sleeper. Always listening for the door, you know."

After Darcy explained what was going on in Brighton, and with Lord Fitzwilliam's own daughters in the forefront of his mind, a look of disgust appeared on the earl's face. "I despise that sort of behavior. A sixteen-year-old girl is a child. Say what you will about my *affaires de coeur*, the ladies are all over the age of twenty-five."

Darcy disagreed with Antony's view of what was honorable behavior, but it was no time for a discussion on morality.

"I have come to tell you that I was in need of Gregg's service, and he is on his way to Brighton these past two hours. But I do not know if even so able a horseman as Gregg can get there in time to disrupt Wickham's plan. After all, Brighton is two hundred miles away, and the man must rest."

"Do you know how Gregg came to be in my service?" Antony asked.

"From his size and his equestrian talents, I suspect he was a jockey at some point."

"*Exactement!* He jockeyed for my father, and I was at the races at Canterbury the day he took a nasty spill. My dear *pere* put him to work in the stables until he recovered and was able to race again, but when he finally hung up his whip, I took him into my service as I was now Lord Fitzwilliam. Before Gregg, I never could keep a manservant. Not everyone likes surprises. Anyway, I needed someone who was a fast thinker as well as being fast on his feet and on a horse and while running down alleys. But as to the matter at hand, Gregg has raced from Cornwall to Perth and knows every highway and byway in the realm and every coaching inn where he can change horses quickly. Once he gets near to London, he will hire a hackney and that will allow him to sleep all the way to Brighton. Rest assured. He will get your message to Colonel Forster."

"God only knows if all this rushing about will do any good. But that is out of my hands, and I must do what I can. Mercer and I are on our way to Brighton. I have left instructions with regards to Georgiana with Jackson, and any help Richard or you can provide would be appreciated. If my sister no longer wishes to stay at Pemberley, please see her back to London."

"Of course. No worries on that or any other matter."

"Antony, when this nasty business is concluded, I would like to talk to you about a whole host of things."

"I know one of the things that has caught your attention is my attire. I am well aware that I am out of fashion, and you assume that it is because of money owed to my tailor. That is part of it. However, since the rise of Mr. Beau Brummel, every man in London looks exactly like every other man in London, and I do not like the idea of not standing out in a crowd. And as for having a 'talk,' we must first establish the definition of the word 'talk,' as your interpretation leans heavily towards 'sermonizing' while mine does not. But that is not what is important right now, so off you go and good luck!"

When Darcy arrived at the stables, Mercer had everything ready for their departure. They would travel with no luggage, so they might go farther and faster before having to change horses. The senior Belling and his son, Tom, were both capable drivers, and there wasn't a conveyance that Mercer could not drive if necessary. But there were so many variables: the horses, the weather, the conditions of the roads, and on and on, but fortunately, his arrival was second in importance to Gregg's.

As they drove out of the Pemberley estate, through Lambton, and on to the London road, he thought that the speech he had given Elizabeth about there being enough time to intervene before Wickham could put his plan into action was just that—a speech—for the purpose of bucking her up. Who could possibly say what a man would do who would exact his revenge through an innocent girl? But he was sure of one thing: If Wickham succeeded in seducing Lydia, he would track him down to the ends of the earth.

When Colonel Forster's servant roused him from his bed at 1:00 in the morning, he told him that he better have a damn good reason for doing so. After reassuring Mrs. Forster that it was regimental business, she went back to sleep, and wearing his robe and night cap, he went downstairs to find out what fire was burning and where.

The man standing before him, encased in a thick layer of dirt, astounded him when he informed him that he had been traveling for a full day and had come from Derbyshire on behalf of Mr. Darcy of Pemberley, cousin of His Lordship, Earl Fitzwilliam.

Fumbling for his spectacles, he read the letter Gregg had presented to him, and with each sentence, his pallor grew paler until all color had drained from his face. He immediately went and knocked on the cook's door and asked Mrs. Grant if she would go upstairs to make sure that Miss Lydia was in bed.

"I want you to look at her face—not at a bundle in the bed—to see if she is breathing."

Mrs. Grant, whose knees creaked as loudly as the stairs, returned to report that Miss Lydia was sound asleep, and she had stood there for a full minute watching the rise and fall of her chest. After apologizing for disturbing her, the colonel bade her good night.

"Mr. Gregg, you have served Mr. Darcy well, and he has asked that I make sure you are fed and properly boarded," and he instructed his servant, Walters, to see to the man's needs. After doing so, Walters was to come to the colonel's study as he was to deliver a message to Captain Wilcox, the officer in charge of the guard, for the purpose of finding Mr. Wickham.

The colonel had no doubt that Captain Wilcox would find the bastard, and once he had him, he would be confined to quarters with a guard posted at his door. In his note, Darcy had instructed the captain that no one was to say anything to Wickham. "I shall be doing all the talking in the morning," the colonel mumbled.

There was nothing more to be done at such an hour, so the old campaigner took a blanket from the bedroom chest, placed a chair in front of Lydia's door, and went to sleep dreaming of his life before he had married his nineteen-year-old bride.

Chapter 40

DESPITE IT BEING A very cold morning, as soon as the carriage turned down the drive to Longbourn, Jane came out onto the porch to meet the travelers. After an exchange of greetings, she got right to the heart of the matter. "The express rider came early this morning, and Papa is prepared to leave immediately and is relying on Uncle Gardiner for the use of his carriage as far as London."

"Of course," Uncle Gardiner said immediately, "but I shall go with him as he will be in need of a sympathetic ear. This matter must be weighing heavily upon him."

Jane thanked her uncle for his not unexpected kindness.

"We are eager to hear whatever news you have from Pemberley," Jane said to Lizzy.

"And I will be glad to share it, but why are we standing outside in the cold?"

"Because Mr. Collins is here," Jane said in a voice that indicated this visit was just as welcome as the last. "He arrived in Hertfordshire four days ago in preparation for the wedding and had been staying with the Lucases. Although he claims that he is not a superstitious man, he thought it best not to see the bride the day before the wedding, so he has come this morning to Longbourn."

"I thought you were not supposed to see the bride the day *of* the wedding?"

"Mama told him that, but he insisted he was right and she wrong. But never mind Mr. Collins, Papa is in the library waiting for you."

When Lizzy went into the room where her father sought refuge from his family, she saw a man who had aged in her absence. She had no doubt he was blaming himself for their current circumstances, and she could provide no comfort on that subject because it was true.

"My dear, I am pleased to see you, but as you know, I must leave immediately. Do you have anything to share that might assist me in this unpleasant task?"

Lizzy explained that Gregg had left during the night and was to go straight through to Brighton, while Mr. Darcy was to follow in the carriage. "Mr. Darcy feels it important for him to be there to impress upon the colonel the seriousness of the situation as only he can provide information about Wickham's past offenses."

"So Mr. Darcy is certain that a seduction was planned?"

"He did not say it outright, but I suspect this feigned elopement would not be Wickham's first."

"Well, that settles it, and I am off. I leave you to care for your mother and, unfortunately, to amuse Mr. Collins."

After seeing Uncle Gardiner and her father off on their journey, Lizzy went to look for her mother, fully expecting to find her in her room suffering from a case of nerves. Instead, she was in the front parlor speaking with Mr. Collins, and when Lizzy joined them, she immediately jumped up, kissed her daughter on the cheek, and whispered in her ear, "Mum's the word."

Despite the drama swirling all around her, Mrs. Bennet's composure in dealing with a difficult guest confirmed what Jane and Lizzy already knew. Her attacks of "nerves" and the onset of the "flutters" were merely theatrics for the purpose of gaining attention from her family. This scene proved that she was quite capable of remaining calm, especially when the marriage prospects of her daughters might be in jeopardy.

During dinner, little was said by anyone other than Mr. Collins. Because Lizzy had spurned his attentions, most of the conversation was directed at her, and when he talked about Lady Catherine de Bourgh and her generosity in making the parsonage comfortable for his "beloved Charlotte," Kitty let out a groan.

"Mr. Collins, why don't you tell Lizzy and Aunt Gardiner all about your esteemed patroness," Kitty said. "You would not wish to deny them your detailed descriptions of the fireplace at Rosings or the extensive gardens or its paths, and don't leave out your own view of Rosings from your study or how you have mastered the proper amount of compliments to be paid and deference to be shown to Her Ladyship or how her daughter, Miss Anne de Bourgh, frequently passes the parsonage on her way to the village and how she drives her own phaeton and…"

If Lizzy had not kicked Kitty under the table, she would have continued. Mr. Collins could be exasperating, but he was their cousin, and one who held their future in his hands.

Kitty's suggestion thwarted Lizzy's plan to withdraw immediately after dinner, and she was forced to listen to Lady

Catherine's vicar praise everything his patroness said or did. It wasn't until Mrs. Bennet pointed out that the groom-to-be had a very busy day in front of him that he retired.

As soon as Mr. Collins was out of the room, Mrs. Bennet collapsed into her chair. Fortunately, Aunt Gardiner offered to see her sister-in-law to bed. Lizzy gave her a look of such gratitude, and her aunt responded with a knowing smile.

"Lizzy, do you think Mr. Darcy's efforts will succeed?" Jane asked as the sisters burrowed into their bed and snuggled together for warmth.

"I do not know, but I am hopeful because Mr. Wickham has no idea that anyone is aware of his plans. But enough about Lydia. Charlotte is to be married in the morning and you in two weeks' time, but everyone is talking about Lydia."

"Charlotte's wedding is to be a simple affair with only family and close friends invited to the wedding breakfast. Mr. Collins said that Lady Catherine is insisting that a habit of economy be established from the very start, and I think it is what Charlotte prefers. You know she does not like being the center of attention."

"True enough. So, tell me, how do things go with Mr. Bingley?"

Even in the dimly lit room, Lizzy could see her sister's smile. "I think about Charles all day long, and I want to be with him all the time. I will be very happy when our wedding day has come. He is only gone to London for a few days, but I miss him terribly."

"Jane, has Charles ever kissed you?"

"Yes, but ever so briefly, because Mary and Kitty or Mama are always about, and it is the same at Netherfield. Although the Crenshaw twins have been sent to boarding school in Scotland, their mother and the other children are always about. Charles does write very nice love letters intimating that he wishes we had more time together alone, but that is it. Why are you asking? Have you been kissed?"

"Yes, I have. Truthfully, I do not know what I was expecting a kiss to feel like, but it was better than anything I could have ever imagined. When Mr. Darcy swept me up in his arms, I felt a sensation that went throughout my body, and I have to admit that it was most pleasant."

"Oh, Lizzy, I am so happy to hear that you found it to be pleasant. I have to admit I am a little nervous about my wedding night. It is so strange to me that something that is absolutely forbidden to me on Friday will be required of me on Saturday. And it is not as if I do not know what is going to happen. After all, we do live on a farm. I just do not know how it all comes about and what is required of me."

"I do not think all that much will be required of you, Jane. When Mr. Darcy kissed me, he held me so closely that I felt something hard against me that had not been there a minute before."

"What was it?"

"A bedpost." And the two sisters exploded into laughter. "Other than kissing him, I did nothing. It seems to be a miracle of Nature, and one that comes in a goodly size."

"Lizzy, I cannot believe you are saying these things, but I am glad you are. All I know is that when Charles kisses me, it is not enough. I want more."

"Well, no need to worry, Jane, because I am quite sure Mr. Bingley will be happy to oblige."

Chapter 41

ALTHOUGH MERCER HAD DONE everything he could to expedite the journey, there was no avoiding the stops necessary to change the horses. The carriage had to be checked to make sure a wheel wasn't loose or an axle bent, calls of Nature answered, and simple meals eaten as well. But when they arrived in Brighton shortly after 10:00 in the morning, nine hours behind Gregg, his efforts were rewarded. As soon as Darcy entered the colonel's residence, he was immediately reassured by Colonel Forster that Wickham's plans had been thwarted, and after receiving such information, Darcy asked Mercer to see to the drivers and to get some rest.

"My aide will assist you in that," and the colonel ordered Lieutenant Dickinson to take the men to the kitchen for a large bowl of Mrs. Grant's soup and the meat pies she had prepared for them. "I have ordered supper for you as well, but I am sure you are eager to have a report on Miss Lydia and Wickham."

As soon as the colonel had finished reading the letter from Darcy, a search for Wickham had been undertaken, and he was found within the hour at a sporting house. The next morning, Wickham had been interrogated by the colonel, but denied any plans to leave Brighton with Lydia, insisting that all he had done was to renew an acquaintance that he had formed while encamped near Meryton. When confronted with details of assignations provided by Lydia and documented in her diary, Wickham admitted he had had some harmless fun with the girl. However, he continued to insist his purpose had never been the seduction of one so young and concluded by saying that he had never intended to marry Lydia Bennet.

At that point, the colonel had stood up and said, "That is the first statement you have made that I actually believe." After informing him that he was confined to quarters indefinitely, Colonel Forster left.

"The long and the short of it, Mr. Darcy, is that your letter prevented Wickham from carrying out his plans. When Miss Lydia came down to breakfast this morning, her room was searched, and an overnight bag was found. When asked for an explanation, she revealed all. She was actually quite proud that she had been able to secure the affections of such an admirable fellow. Even after we told her unequivocally that he had said it was never his intention to marry her, she just laughed, explaining that was what he had to say in order to protect his position in the regiment. To my utter astonishment, she actually thinks our discovery of her plans merely delays the marriage, and the nuptials will take place quickly 'now that everything is out in the open.'"

From the room above, a loud cry could be heard, and Darcy looked to the colonel for an explanation. "That is our young lady grieving for her lover. That caterwauling has been going on all morning. 'My dear Wickham,' she cries, 'when will you come for me?' She sobs and moans for about fifteen minutes and then takes a rest before starting up again. My wife attempted to console her, but because she is with child, her nerves were fraying. So she has departed and our housemaid, the poor girl, is sitting in the room with Miss Lydia."

"Thank you, Colonel, for your quick response. You have saved that girl from certain ruin," Darcy said, standing up. "I believe her father is on the road to Brighton as we speak, but since I have no way of knowing when he will arrive, I intend to talk to Miss Lydia after I have eaten and have had the use of a wash basin. The young lady needs to know Wickham's history, and although I doubt it will do much good, she will hear it."

Lydia looked startled when the maid opened the door to reveal Mr. Darcy. She had heard the colonel talking to someone, but when she did not recognize the voice, she assumed it was one of the soldiers who had been running back and forth to headquarters. The colonel had told her he was not budging from the house until he had safely delivered her to her father. He had then droned on about "a betrayal of trust and violating the rules of hospitality," and other such drivel. Didn't the old goat remember what it was like to be in love, especially since he had married a woman half his age?

Grabbing a wooden chair from the hallway, Darcy brought it into the room and sat opposite to Lydia, and he thought what a little shit she was. There wasn't an ounce of remorse in her demeanor. Instead, she was trying to defiantly stare him down, and he wanted to laugh—he of the furrowed brow, steel gray eyes, and look of thunder yielded to no one—except Elizabeth.

"Let us get right to business, Miss Lydia. First, if you intend to reproduce the hysterical crying I heard when I first entered this house, your confinement will continue, and I am sure that at this point it is getting rather close in here."

"You can't talk to me like that," Lydia said, outraged. "You are not my father, and you are not my guardian. I know about these things because my uncle is a solicitor."

"Secondly, I see you have not eaten your breakfast," he said, looking at the untouched tray on the side table. "There are three hungry men in the kitchen who have been traveling for more than a day because of your thoughtless actions, and they will be glad to have the extra rations. Of course, that means you will go without any nourishment until breakfast."

"Mr. Wickham told me how arrogant you were and how you denied him his proper inheritance," Lydia said, practically spitting out the words, "and he warned me that everything that comes out of your mouth when talking about him are lies."

"Lies. That is a good place to start because, Miss Lydia, you have been used most grievously. You have your sisters to thank for your rescue. When Jane read of Wickham's excessive attention to you, she wrote to Elizabeth at Pemberley. Unfortunately for Wickham, but fortunately for you, I knew the truth about his meanness of character."

Lydia turned her back to him and went to the window.

"And I have the documents to prove it, and since you have a solicitor in the family, he may wish to examine the receipt for three thousand pounds paid to Wickham by me in lieu of a living or another receipt for one thousand pounds as settlement of my father's will. That is a lot of money, Miss Lydia. Where is it?"

Lydia turned to face him, and he could see by the look on

her face that he had succeeded in planting seeds of doubt. But a defiant Lydia insisted that she would have married him anyway.

"You see, Miss Lydia, the problem is, he would never have married *you*. You do not solve his problems. He is knee deep in debt, and if the colonel cannot bring charges against him, he will turn him over to the debtors' courts. Since he has no way of coming up with the many hundreds of pounds he owes, probably just here in Brighton alone, he will be sent to debtors' prison. Wives are allowed to join their husbands if they can pay for their board, but I would not recommend it. Marshalsea Prison is right on the Thames, and it gets very cold there, and the dampness creeps right into your bones."

Chapter 42

THE ONLY OTHER TIME Darcy remembered being this fatigued was when he had received word that his father had died. Richard and he had been on the Grand Tour, and they were making their way south through France with a destination of Nice when the news had reached him. With his sister's well-being in mind, Darcy had made record time in reaching the port of Calais, but then there was still the Channel crossing and the long journey to Derbyshire. When he had finally arrived, he was unshaven, bedraggled, and in need of a bath, much as he was now. Thank goodness he was back in his own home, and he would shortly be asleep in his own bed.

"Will, let me have Mercer draw you a bath," Georgiana said to her brother, who was slumped in a leather chair in the study, saying he was too dirty to sit anywhere else.

"No. Please don't. He is more tired than I am."

"Then I shall ask Rogers."

"No, first I want to have something to eat, then a bath, and then I am to bed, hopefully, until late tomorrow morning. I am weary to the bone. I do not even know how long it has been since I left Pemberley."

"This is the sixth day since you departed, but tell me what happened in Brighton. Hopefully, you were in time."

"We were in time. When I left Miss Lydia, she was sobbing in her father's arms. Mr. Bennet was very grateful for my intervention, but all he wanted to do was to get his daughter home. I assume your return to London was uneventful?"

"Perfectly so," Georgiana answered. "The three of us left the day after you did. Richard has returned to his regiment, and as for Antony, well, he is staying here—not permanently, of course, but please allow me to explain."

"Please do." Darcy was so tired he did not have the energy to protest.

"Before leaving London, Antony hired an agent to find someone to take up the lease on the townhouse, and in the short time we were gone, the agent found someone—a Mr. Whitby. Antony says he's as rich as Croesus and made his money in hemp, whatever that means."

"Whitby supplies the Royal Navy with much of its rope. Through Bingley's financial advisor, you and I are venturers in his concern, and he has done very well by us."

"Antony said he asked a ridiculous amount for the lease, and Mr. Whitby did not bat an eye when the agent mentioned the amount of the rent. They are to go to Briarwood, and our dear cousin is hoping the gentleman will buy the manor house. I received Mr. Whitby here for dinner, and I watched as Antony shamelessly told that unsuspecting man that he could not part with the Fitzwilliam estate unless he knew it was in good hands. With tears in his eyes, he explained what a great loss it would be for him and his family, when you and I know he would walk away from it if a buyer could be found who would provide for the servants and settle his accounts."

Darcy did not care if Antony sold Briarwood. The house was an architectural hybrid combining Jacobean and Georgian elements and doing justice to neither. Antony had once compared it to one of the Prince of Wales's rejected mistresses: no longer young, beautiful, or wanted.

"But Antony is looking for other accommodations? Yes?"

"Yes. He said he could not live with you as you remind him too much of his mother."

"Good. Anything else I should know?"

"Have you heard about the king?"

"What about the king?" Darcy asked, but he already knew the answer. If Georgiana had heard of the madness of King George, then so had everyone else.

Georgiana had first heard the whispers and rumors during a stop at an inn north of town, which meant that the news had already spread into the suburbs and surrounding countryside. By the time the travelers had reached London, pamphlets depicting the king as nearly blind and completely mad were being sold on the streets.

Many were predicting that as soon as the prince was named regent there would be a major shift in the political landscape. Although it was true that the prince was more liberal than his father, once the Prince of Wales became regent, Darcy believed that he would see things differently. Power was intoxicating, and history had proved that monarchs never seemed to have enough of it.

"There have already been a few changes," Georgiana said,

and she shifted uncomfortably in her chair. "I might as well tell you now, Will. Sir John was here yesterday. Fortunately for me, so was Antony."

Darcy sat up in his chair. "Is he still angry with me?"

"To the contrary, he said he was looking forward to having vigorous debates with you, and that he was not so set in his ways that he could not learn a thing or two from a younger man."

Darcy burst into laughter. The thought of Sir John, a dyed-in-the-wool Tory, listening to anything he had to say was a bright spot in an otherwise gray landscape.

"Sir John is willing to be educated by me! I would sooner believe the prince had taken a vow of chastity," and he continued to laugh to himself. "Just think of the irony, Georgie. Lydia Bennet goes to Brighton, delaying my return to London just long enough so that, in Sir John's eyes, I go from being an arrogant whippersnapper who is courting revolution to someone he wants to exchange ideas with."

"What are you going to do?"

"I am going to go to bed, and tomorrow I will visit with Miss Montford or her father and advise them of my intention to withdraw from whatever they thought I had been doing."

"I do not think you should go to see either Montford tomorrow. You will still be very tired, and Antony says Sir John can be very abrasive and is known to shout when he does not get his way."

"That is excellent advice, and I shall take it. But I shall delay no longer than that as every day I do keeps me from Elizabeth. At this point, I do not even care what Sir John or anyone else thinks or says about me. Besides, I deserve it. The only thing I have done right since I met Elizabeth was to go to Longbourn to apologize for being an arrogant... Well, an unpleasant fellow. Since that time, it has been a comedy of errors, and it must come to an end."

Georgiana could hardly bear to think of someone speaking ill of her brother. But then an idea came to her that would avoid putting Will's good name at risk. While her brother rested, she would go to see Miss Montford, and during her visit, what could be more natural than to have the names of one's friends come up in conversation? Georgiana smiled at the thought of how Miss Caroline Bingley might actually end up facilitating the union of her brother and Miss Elizabeth Bennet.

Chapter 43

WHILE PREPARING FOR HER visit with Miss Montford, Georgiana thought about the differences between the two families. While the Montfords refused to associate with people like the Bingleys, the Darcys befriended them. She understood from Will that this was a recent change, which had begun when their father had invited members from the Lunar Society to Pemberley. The elder Mr. Darcy had so admired these men of science that their modest beginnings were of no importance to him, but such changes took time, as was demonstrated by her brother's attentions to Miss Montford. He had only singled her out because he wanted Georgiana to make an advantageous match from among England's elite families, and that required that he make a good match himself. But his sacrifice would have been too great. Why should he forego his own happiness for the sake of hers?

When the hackney came to a stop in front of the Montford house, Rogers took Miss Darcy's card and presented it to the butler. It was a long while before Rogers returned with permission for Georgiana to come in, and when she went into the parlor, she was greeted by Mrs. Redford, Letitia's companion.

"Miss Darcy, how good of you to call. Unfortunately, Miss Montford is unwell today, and she could not receive you personally. However, she suggested that I visit with you."

What Mrs. Redford could not say was that when Letitia had learned that Miss Darcy was waiting in her carriage, she had refused to receive her because she was afraid that action might prompt her brother to call as well.

Georgiana suspected there was nothing wrong with Letitia that her departure would not cure. This was very disappointing because her plan could not go forward without Letitia. After pleasantries were exchanged, Mrs. Redford asked the purpose of Georgiana's call.

"I am having a few friends to tea this week, and I thought Miss Montford would like to meet them."

"That is very thoughtful of you, Miss Darcy. Was it your intention to tell Miss Montford who you would be inviting?"

Was that a leading question, Georgiana wondered? It certainly sounded like one.

"Perhaps you were thinking of inviting Mr. Bingley's sisters," Mrs. Redford said, trying to help Georgiana along.

"Yes, as a matter of fact I was. Miss Caroline Bingley and Mrs. Louisa Hurst would be two of my guests."

This was very good news, Mrs. Redford thought. Letitia had been greatly upset by Mr. Darcy's alarming revelation that he considered Mr. Bingley to be a gentleman and his sisters genteel.

"May I share any of the names of your other guests with Miss Montford?" Mrs. Redford asked, continuing to prod and encourage.

Georgiana did not know what to say. If she had been able to speak to Miss Montford, inviting Miss Bingley and Mrs. Hurst probably would have been sufficient for her purposes. However, Mrs. Redford was asking for additional names, but everyone else of her acquaintance was of the genteel class.

"Miss Darcy, I understand you have just returned from Pemberley where you were entertaining some new friends."

"Yes, Miss Elizabeth Bennet and Mr. and Mrs. Gardiner." But the Gardiners did not advance her cause, which she was sure was also Mrs. Redford's, because Mr. Gardiner was a gentleman, and her puzzled expression prompted Mrs. Redford's response.

"I believe Mr. Gardiner is a coffee broker and often visits the docks."

Georgiana nearly jumped out of her seat. "Yes, that is true, and although a gentleman, Mr. Gardiner *earns* his living," and Georgiana experienced the same happiness a student feels who has given the correct answer and has pleased her tutor. Buoyed by her success at guessing what Mrs. Redford needed to know, she added, "I could also invite Mrs. Crenshaw, Mr. Bingley's older sister, who has very odd ideas with regard to the rearing of children. You might have heard about her sons, as they were reprimanded for throwing rocks at the squirrels in Hyde Park, but she may have gone to Scotland."

Mrs. Redford smiled at this charming young lady whose purpose was to get her brother out of his unhappy courtship with Miss Montford.

"I think we have enough with Mrs. Hurst, Miss Bingley, and Mrs. Gardiner."

Georgiana gave a sigh of relief as it was obvious Mrs. Redford was trying to extricate Letitia from a relationship that could in no way make her mistress happy. "I hope you understand that my brother would never deliberately hurt Miss Montford."

"I know that, dear. I was always in the next room, and although it had a good start, it became clearer with each visit that their differences were too great. I think it is important for you to know that Letitia's mother died when she was only eight, and her father's world view is all she has ever known."

Georgiana squeezed Mrs. Redford's hand. "Miss Montford is most fortunate in having you as her companion. I have only recently found the perfect companion, and I rely on her heavily as her advice is always sound and in my best interest."

When Georgiana reached the front door, she asked Mrs. Redford if she thought the guest list would be sufficient to solve their problem.

"I do not know, Miss Darcy. All I can tell you is that Sir John will hear of it, and then the rest is up to him."

Chapter 44

TODAY WAS A DAY to rejoice and be glad for Charlotte Lucas was to wed Mr. Collins. While each member of the Bennet family made ready for the nuptials, they were all talking about which of the groom's many annoying habits, his poor table manners, incessant talking about Rosings Park and all things de Bourgh, nightly readings of *Fordyce's Sermons*, or his constant humming and whistling, that they would now be spared.

Jane and Lizzy were discussing that very topic when they heard a loud cry from Mr. Collins, and Jane, who had finished dressing, hurried down to see if the parson had been injured. Instead, she found her cousin staring at a letter that had just been delivered by John Lucas.

"What is the matter, Mr. Collins?" When he did not answer, Jane turned to Charlotte's brother. "John, what is this about?"

"My sister took ill this morning with a fever, and the wedding has to be postponed for a few days. My parents aren't feeling all that well either, but no one is dying," John said, while looking at a crying Mr. Collins.

Jane took the letter from her cousin's shaking hands, and it was just as John had said. Charlotte had to keep to her bed but anticipated a full recovery in a few days. In fact, she had written, "I wish to emphasize in the clearest possible terms that the wedding is only delayed, not canceled." By that time, Lizzy had come downstairs, and after reading the letter, she understood that that particular sentence had been included because Charlotte was aware that Lizzy considered Mr. Collins to be one of the stupidest men in England.

"Of course, this means Mr. Collins will be with us until Charlotte recovers," Lizzy said when Jane and she were alone again.

"I hope it does not snow as that will keep Charles in town," Jane said, looking out the window at a gray December day, her statement indicating just how little interest she had in their annoying cousin. "Lizzy, come to the window. I do believe that an express rider has turned into the drive."

"Even better. That is Mr. Gregg, Lord Fitzwilliam's man. Let us hope he is the bearer of good news."

Lizzy and Jane were not the only ones who had noticed the rider coming up the drive, and Mrs. Bennet, followed closely by Aunt Gardiner, practically grabbed the letter out of Gregg's hand, and when Mrs. Bennet clutched it to her bosom and let out a sigh of relief, all knew that Wickham's plan had failed.

"Say nothing. We do not want Mr. Collins to know," she cautioned her daughters. "Thank heaven, my dear Lydia is safe. That wicked man's plans have come to nothing."

Leaving her mother to Jane and Aunt Gardiner, Lizzy

directed Lord Fitzwilliam's manservant to the kitchen. "I imagine you are in need of nourishment, Mr. Gregg."

"What I lack in height, I make up for in appetite, miss," he said, laughing.

When Gregg went into the kitchen, Mrs. Hill could see that this was a very hungry man, and in no time, he was diving into a plate full of eggs and bacon.

"Mr. Gregg, I cannot thank you enough for the arduous journey you undertook on behalf of my family."

"Glad to do it," he said, after swallowing a mouthful. "I used to ride for the senior Lord Fitzwilliam, but I got too rickety to do it every day and had to hang up my silks. But I like a bit of excitement now and then."

"So you must enjoy being in Lord Fitzwilliam's service."

"That I do, miss. That I do. But if truth be known, because of his little girls, he's been on his best behavior of late, so this was a nice change." Gregg then recounted the long journey from Pemberley to Brighton and the look on Colonel Forster's face when he read Mr. Darcy's letter. "He went from having no color at all to being as red as those uniforms you see everywhere in Brighton. He was fit to be tied." But then Gregg stood up, and reaching into his jacket, he said, "I almost forget, miss. I've got a letter for you from Mr. Darcy."

When taking the letter from Gregg, Lizzy tried not to look overly eager, but after excusing herself, she went up to her room and anxiously opened the first letter she had ever received from Mr. Darcy.

"There you are," Jane said, coming into their bedroom and sitting next to her sister. "I wanted to tell you that despite her complaints, Mama is fine, but intends to keep to her room to avoid Mr. Collins."

"I look forward to the day when I can stay in my room and have everyone wait on me hand and foot because of *my* nerves," Lizzy said, and Jane picked up on the note of unhappiness in her sister's tone.

"What do you have there? Is it a letter from Mr. Darcy?"

"You may read it. It will not take long."

> *Dear Miss Elizabeth,*
>
> *I am happy to advise you that when Lord Fitzwilliam's man arrived in Brighton, your sister was asleep in her room. However, it was subsequently learned that an "elopement" had been planned. It is your father's intention to depart for home in the morning. I will remain in Brighton for another day before returning to London. Once I am in town, I will write again.*
>
> *Yours, F. Darcy*

Jane, who was the recipient of many romantic notes and letters from Mr. Bingley, could understand her sister's disappointment, but it was no secret that Mr. Darcy kept his emotions under regulation.

"Lizzy, do not read too much into this."

"That would be difficult to do."

"But you must think of the circumstances under which the note was written. Mr. Darcy wrote quickly so that Gregg could be on his way to deliver the good news to us, and I am sure that there were a lot of people in the house, affording him no privacy in which to write a more personal letter."

Lizzy nodded. She had no wish to worry her sister. She had enough on her hands with their mother in bed with a case of nerves and Mr. Collins loose in the house audibly lamenting the separation from his beloved Charlotte.

"Mr. Collins!" Lizzy said, jumping out of her chair. "We forgot about Mr. Collins. Lydia and Papa will be coming home tomorrow. You know our sister well enough to anticipate the drama that will unfold. Mr. Collins cannot stay here or everyone from here to London will know of our troubles. Jane, what are we to do?"

Lizzy was right. Lydia would make no effort to rein in her emotions, no matter who was in the house, and she could just picture her loudly pining over the loss of her dear Wickham. Mr. Collins had to go. But where? And then Jane smiled. "I know exactly where Mr. Collins can go."

"Mrs. Crenshaw, allow me to introduce my cousin, Mr. Collins. He was to be married today, but his bride is unwell, and the wedding has been postponed."

Mr. Collins gave a wan smile. He was uncomfortable being introduced to a woman who was clearly nearing her time of confinement, but Mrs. Crenshaw's genuine warmth and sincerity soon put him at his ease.

"When I received Jane's note asking if I could accommodate you for a few days, I was very happy to do so. With Charles gone, it will be good to have the company as I enjoy conversation very much."

Since Jane had hosted the four eldest Crenshaw children at Longbourn, much had changed. Charles's sister had tearfully confided in Jane that she was tired of being the leader of a "pack of wolves," as her husband characterized their family, but that everyone else described as a bunch of barbarians. She knew the children could be brought to heel because she had once employed a Scotsman, Mr. Campbell, who had performed miracles, even with Gaius and Lucius. But when her husband continuously interfered, Mr. Campbell had tendered his resignation, and the wolf cubs were released to run wild once again.

Jane had provided the encouragement necessary for her future sister-in-law to exercise greater control over her family. Without bothering to consult her husband, Mrs. Crenshaw had rehired Mr. Campbell, giving him full authority over the children, and had enrolled Lucius and Gaius in the same boarding school the tutor had attended in Scotland. As Mr. Campbell had explained, "Mr. Crenshaw wishes for his sons to be Spartans, and I can assure you the environment at Glenkill meets the very definition of Spartan." She had bid a tearful good-bye to an anxious Lucius and a defiant Gaius, but she was convinced they would survive the ordeal and would be all the better for it.

The two chatterboxes struck up an immediate friendship, and as Jane departed, she could hear Mr. Collins describing the fireplace at Rosings and Mrs. Crenshaw offering to lend the parson her copy of Rousseau's *Social Contract*.

Before climbing into bed, Jane watched as Lizzy reread Mr. Darcy's note. It wasn't the brevity of the note that was so distressing; it was the signature, "Yours, F. Darcy," that was the source of her unhappiness.

"Jane, I do not know what I was expecting, but it wasn't this. That is how someone would sign a business letter."

"Are you concerned about the depth of his regard for you?" Jane asked.

"I don't know. What I do know is that his moods change as quickly as the weather in the Peak. And this matter with Lydia. Is there anything that better illustrates the shortcomings of our family than his having to travel all that distance to save our sister from ruin? He must be asking himself, where was her mother? Where was her father? More importantly, does the possibility exist of another scandal in the family?"

"Lizzy, I understand your concerns, but despite the failings of our family, which Mr. Darcy was well aware of, he surrendered all when he fell in love with you."

"Did he?"

"Yes, I am sure he did. It is just that he is methodical—no false starts. He wants everything just so before he will proceed."

"Yes, I agree. Mr. Darcy is a cautious man—one who takes only small steps." As Lizzy lay there in the dark, she thought, so much for spanning a chasm in one giant leap of love.

Chapter 45

DARCY STARED AT THE writing paper hoping for a bolt of inspiration to hit him as he was bereft of ideas. He was not a man of words—either verbal or written. He said what needed to be said, and no more, and there were times when his taciturn nature had worked to his advantage. On the afternoon when he had gone to Longbourn to apologize to Elizabeth for his rudeness at the assembly, the conversation had turned to his intolerance for idle discourse. If it had not been for that, he would have quickly left her parlor, and possibly, just as quickly returned to London. So a case could be made for the employment of an economy of words, although he doubted Elizabeth would see it that way.

Out of the corner of his eye, Darcy caught sight of his cousin, Lord Fitzwilliam, dressed in all his sartorial splendor in a peacock blue coat with an embossed design, matching blue breeches, and a gold waistcoat. There were few in London society who could successfully get away with dressing as their fathers had, but Antony was one of them.

"Greetings, my dear cousin!" he said as he dangled a calling card in front of Darcy. "I dined at my club this afternoon, and guess who was there? Never mind. You do not have to guess. Sir John Montford. If you look at the back of the card, you will see it is his intention to call tomorrow afternoon at 4:00. Why so late, you ask? It is because the rotund gentleman does not miss a meal, and any time sooner would have interfered with his two-hour midday dinner."

4:00? So much for setting out for Hertfordshire tomorrow, Darcy thought.

"What are you doing there—writing a love letter?" Antony asked, while peering over Darcy's shoulder. "All you have is the salutation."

"Yes, I know it needs work," Darcy said, only partly in jest.

Antony pulled a chair over so that he was sitting right next to his cousin and offered his help. "I have lots of experience in this area, and I can assist you." Since Darcy was suffering from a severe case of writer's block, he accepted Antony's offer. "It should be easy to compliment someone as beautiful as Elizabeth Bennet. For example, you might say that her dark eyes hold the secrets of the universe."

"What the devil does that mean?"

"That she is mysterious."

"But she is not mysterious. She is open and honest—something I greatly admire."

"Is that what you want to write?"

Dear Elizabeth,
  Allow me to compliment you on your openness and honesty.
                                    Sincerely, Fitzwilliam Darcy, Esq.

"Don't be ridiculous. But I have never understood why someone would write a letter telling another person what they look like. Elizabeth does own a mirror."

"Oh, this is going to be harder than I thought," Antony said, groaning. "It is not what she looks like in the mirror; it is what she looks like in your eyes."

Darcy thought about her dark eyes, and if they did not hold the secrets of the universe, they certainly held the secrets of his heart.

After watching Darcy jot down a few of his thoughts, Antony asked, "Have you kissed her?"

"Why?"

"Because if you have, you may write of how you felt when your lips met hers—the heat, the passion, all thoughts deserting you, except those of her, and how at that moment, the two of you became one—inseparable and complete."

"That is very nice, Antony. I can see how that would be a pleasing sentiment."

"Sarah Compton loved it."

"Good God. I am not going to write to Elizabeth using words you have written to your mistress."

"Former mistress. And what is the difference between using my words or copying out one of Will Shakespeare's sonnets?

Shall I compare thee to a Summer's day?
Thou art more lovely and more temperate:
Rough winds do shake the darling buds of May."

"That *is* a beautiful sonnet," Darcy said defensively. He had been thinking about copying out that very poem.

"It is beautiful, and if you want, I can go down to the park and some talented person will have already copied out Sonnet Eighteen for you in a beautiful hand, and for a few pence more, you can get a sketch to go with it of some artist's concept of Summer personified." Despite his excellent advice, Antony could see that the man was still struggling. "For goodness' sake, Darcy, all you have to do is think about that lovely creature during your most romantic moment together. Then pick up the pen and write."

"Well, you have given me some ideas, so I thank you."

"Before I go, I want you to know I will be leaving shortly. I have taken rooms in Kensington to be nearer to a dear friend."

There was no doubt Madame Antonia Konig, lately of Vienna, was the dear friend he wanted to be nearer to, and Darcy's expression said it all.

"Darcy, I know what you are thinking. Kensington! Ugh!"

Darcy just shook his head in disbelief. Only Antony would consider his move from Mayfair to Kensington to be the greater evil than the reason for the move—his mistress.

"I can see you do not approve. I had hoped that since your heart has so recently been touched, you might understand. But since you do not, please allow me to explain. I am deeply in love with Antonia, but because I am bound to the Evil Eleanor, I cannot marry her—which I would do if I did not have this mill-stone of a marriage around my neck. And there are other reasons. Because Antonia lives near Kensington Park, I was able to introduce Emmy and Sophie to her, and they got along famously. It is nice for my children to see a man and woman together in the same room without furniture being thrown about."

"I am happy for you, Antony," Darcy said, surprised at

his own change of heart. "I know you never wanted to marry Eleanor, and it has been a disaster for you from the beginning. And you are right. Love does change you."

Antony came over and put his arms around his cousin and hugged him.

"For God's sake, Antony, you are not French."

"I know. If I was, I would have kissed you."

After Antony left, Darcy returned to the task at hand: writing a love letter to Elizabeth. But with his cousin's advice fresh in his mind, he had no difficulty in choosing the moment to inspire him. It was in the study at Pemberley when Elizabeth had come to him seeking his help. When she came into the room, her hair was flowing over her shoulders, and her robe, obviously thrown on in haste, had fallen open, revealing the nightgown beneath. For a mere second, with the glow of the fire behind her, he had seen the outline of her body, and he had to fight his desire to pick her up, take her to the sofa, and make love to her. With such a glorious image in the forefront of his mind, Darcy picked up the pen and began to write.

Dearest Elizabeth,

Although we are apart, you are always in my thoughts. You are the first thing I think about in the morning and the last before I close my eyes. Even in my sleep, you are with me, as you inhabit all my dreams. The remembrance of you in my arms is what sustains me. Is it wrong of me to tell you how much I want to kiss you, to hold you, to feel you against me?

That is not something a gentleman should write, but your power over me is such that I want to be with you every minute of every hour so that we become one— "inseparable and complete." Those words come from another, but they fit so well with what I am feeling that I believe they were composed for me, if not by me. The hours go slowly, but soon I shall be in Hertfordshire. Once we are together, it will require an act of God to separate us.

Love, Will

Darcy called for his manservant. "Ask Rogers to send that by express rider and make sure that it goes out today." Well satisfied with the results, Darcy sat back in his chair and, after thinking about the contents of the letter, decided that he was rather good at this business of writing love letters. He only hoped Elizabeth would agree.

Chapter 46

As soon as Sir John Montford entered the parlor, he took the same chair his daughter occupied whenever she visited the Darcy townhouse. Remembering Georgiana's comment about Miss Montford's nose pointing toward the street, Darcy looked to see if it was a family trait. It wasn't. But with such important business at hand, he had to chuckle to himself at the ridiculousness of thinking about someone's nose at such a moment, but his amusement was short-lived, as his thoughts were interrupted by Sir John's gruff voice.

"I assume you know why I am here?"

Darcy nodded, although he wasn't quite sure what he was agreeing with.

"Darcy, I know your father was a liberal man, but he would not approve. I daresay he would not approve. You have gone too far."

"You object to my politics?" Darcy asked.

"You know I do, and that is the seed that bore this rotten fruit. If it weren't for your liberal notions, all of this Whig nonsense about Catholic emancipation and expanding the franchise and God only knows what else, you would never have treated my daughter the way you did."

Darcy was not happy with his performance regarding Letitia, but he did not think he had mistreated her. And what on earth did Catholic emancipation and expanding the franchise have to do with anything? He almost wanted to laugh. He would have to make it a point to visit the House of Lords when Lord John Montford made his maiden speech. It should prove interesting.

"First, it was this Bingley fellow. Letitia told me you thought he was a gentleman. Well, let me set the record straight; he is not a gentleman. Nor are his sisters." A flustered Sir John added, "You know what I mean."

Darcy sighed in relief. At least now he understood what his transgression was: his association with his lower-class friends.

"Think of what your revolutionary ideas have done to your sister. To encourage my daughter to associate with people of such low rank, and then to learn that this Mrs. Garner would also be attending—the wife of a coffee broker—a man who earns his living by prowling the docks and negotiating prices. He is nothing more than a glorified peddler."

"Forgive me, Sir John. I have not had an opportunity to speak with my sister, so I am not sure what you are referring to."

"The tea, man. The tea. Miss Darcy came to my home yesterday for the purpose of inviting Letitia to tea. Fortunately, she mentioned the names of the guests to my daughter's companion, who immediately informed me. I find your sister blameless in all this. But I must warn you, Darcy, her association with these people will affect her pursuit of a marriage partner. She will find offers scarce if this continues."

"I appreciate your concern for Georgiana. However, I am her guardian, and I will do what I think is best for her," Darcy said through gritted teeth. "By the way, my grandmother was a Catholic."

Sir John noted the change in Darcy's voice and knew he had strayed from the matter at hand. He moderated his tone, as he had no wish to offend a Darcy, especially since it was an association with the Darcy family that he had been after in the first place.

"I want no hard feelings between us, Darcy. However, I must ask that you stop seeing my daughter. She was not brought up to…"

"I understand your concerns, Sir John," Darcy said, interrupting, "and if I have hurt your daughter in any way, it was not intentionally done. May I ask that you convey to Miss Montford my wishes for her health and happiness?" Darcy stood up to let Sir John know the conversation had come to an end.

"I thank you for taking this so agreeably. But a word of advice. Your idea of a courtship is rather unconventional. Coming and going, disappearing for weeks at a time, no letters. That will not win you the affection of any lady. I tell you this since your father was a friend of mine, and I am sure he would have given you the same advice."

Darcy nodded his head but said nothing, and rang for Rogers to see his visitor to the door. After watching a hackney take the odious man away, Darcy poured himself a brandy and took a chair in front of the fire, and with the first taste of liquor, he felt every muscle in his body relax. It was over. It was finally over. The peril had passed, and he was a free man. Now nothing stood between Elizabeth and him.

Ordinarily, Georgiana would have come downstairs to find out what had happened, but she was nowhere to be seen. But there was no mystery there, and her brother rang the bell for Rogers.

"Ask my sister to join me. Immediately."

From the way Will was sitting in front of the fireplace, with all of his attention being directed toward the fire, Georgiana could not tell how things had gone with Sir John, but she suspected that her meddling in the Montford affair had been revealed.

Darcy let her stew for a few more minutes before beginning. "You have been busy, Georgiana."

Georgie shook her head, pretending that she did not know what he was talking about. She was not prepared to admit to anything as she might make an unnecessary confession.

"Do not shake your head at me. The friend you visited yesterday was Letitia Montford. How very clever of you to arrange for a tea and share the guest list with Mrs. Redford. Of course, all of those invited to this imaginary get-together were ladies with whom Miss Montford would not associate. As a result, Sir John wants me to keep as far away from his daughter as possible, lest I contaminate her by insisting she mingle with people not of her class."

"Oh, Will!" Georgiana ran to her brother and kissed him, and then she did a bit of a dance to show him how happy she was. "It worked. I did not know if it would, but once I realized I had an ally in Mrs. Redford, I thought it might. And it did. It did work."

"You interfered in my personal affairs. Again."

"But you cannot complain of something that turned out so well."

"I most certainly can. What you did, young lady, was very

wrong, beginning with your part in arranging to have Elizabeth go to Pemberley."

"But if it had not been for our conspiracy, you would have gone to Kent to visit Anne and not Pemberley, where you waltzed with Elizabeth. It turned out perfectly. Better than any of us had reason to hope."

"Lucky for you that it did. However, I insist you stay out of my affairs. I believe you have benefited from beginner's luck, but you could end up doing more harm than good. Sir John has a temper, and this might have turned out quite differently."

"I thought about that. But Sir John would not risk alienating you with a display of temper, and our concern that this whole affair might damage your reputation or cause you to lose friends was never a real threat. You *do* have a reputation, and it is spotless. Besides, you have more and better friends than Sir John could ever hope to, including people such as the Bingleys and the Gardiners."

"Well, apparently Letitia was very much in favor of ending our unorthodox courtship. Richard informed me that he has learned from gossip at his club that she prefers Jasper Wiggins to me in any event."

"Jasper Wiggins? Really? I know his sister, Adele."

"Georgie, leave it alone. The young Wiggins will hear of Miss Montford's freedom soon enough from Sir John." Looking at her with a stern eye, he repeated, "Leave it alone."

But Darcy could see the wheels spinning and suspected there was little he could do to stop his sister from plotting and planning. She should be a novelist. But then he smiled, and Georgie knew exactly what he was going to say: "Tomorrow, we go to Hertfordshire."

Chapter 47

Knowing that Mr. Bennet and Lydia would soon arrive at Longbourn, there was a tension at the breakfast table that was palpable. Each of the sisters had their own reasons for being upset. Mary thought that to sneak off with a man in the dead of night was immoral. Kitty was upset because she knew she would have behaved better than Lydia if she had been allowed to go to Brighton, while Jane thought of the unhappiness Lydia had caused her parents. But because of Mr. Darcy, it was Lizzy who had something to lose, and for that reason, she was unsympathetic to anything her mother had to say on her youngest sister's behalf.

Because Lydia was Mrs. Bennet's favorite, her mother was prepared to forgive and forget and to chalk up all her actions to youthful indiscretion. However, there was still an underlying anger because she had been made to suffer unnecessarily, and Lizzy, not Lydia, was to bear the brunt of it.

"Lizzy, I do not like your tone of voice when speaking of Lydia. I would think that you, of all people, would be more sympathetic to your sister. With Wickham being so very bad, her heart will be broken because there is no one to love her."

"No one to love her!" Lizzy answered in an exasperated voice, and she thought about how everyone had sprung into action in order to keep their sister from ruining her life. But Jane cautioned Lizzy with a look. Although most of their mother's episodes of nerves were theater, Jane knew that this event had greatly upset her.

"But why *me* in particular, Mama?" Lizzy asked in confusion.

"Because you have no one to love you either. It did not have to be that way. You could have had Mr. Collins, but you lost him to Charlotte Lucas. And now Mr. Peterson won't have you. According to his letter, he has made an offer of marriage to his cousin, Miss Gayle. I knew something like this would happen. With you running around on holiday in Derbyshire, I knew Mr. Peterson would not wait. But, Lizzy, you must do your part in finding a husband. You cannot rely on Jane to carry you through."

Lizzy stood up. If she remained in the breakfast room a moment longer, she might say something to her mother that she would come to regret, and Jane followed her upstairs.

"Obviously, Mama opened a personal letter addressed to me and learned that Mr. Peterson 'will not have me,'" Lizzy said, throwing herself back onto the bed pillows. "Jane, I am so tired of all this drama. First it was Mr. Darcy and Miss Montford and now Lydia and Wickham. It really is getting to be too much."

"Well, you might have to put up with all this drama a little longer because Uncle Gardiner's carriage has just turned into the drive."

As expected, Lydia's entrance was as dramatic as a Shakespearean tragedy. She had not cried during the long journey to Longbourn, but now that she was at home and had a friendlier audience than her father and uncle, she renewed her copious weeping even before the front door had closed behind her. The emotionally spent sixteen-year-old girl had to be assisted to her room by her mother, Aunt Gardiner, and Kitty, and while Mr. Gardiner went to the kitchen in search of a meal, Mr. Bennet summoned Jane and Lizzy into the library. He quickly summarized for his daughters the events that had taken place in Brighton.

"There is no doubt Wickham intended to lure Lydia away from the Forsters. By his own admission, he had no intention of marrying her, so his sole purpose was her seduction. I do not understand it," their father said, shaking his head. "The streets of Brighton were teeming with handsome young women. He could have approached any of them, but instead, he picked Lydia. It does not make any sense to me.

"The other thing that has puzzled me greatly is Mr. Darcy's involvement in this whole affair. Colonel Forster told me that Mr. Darcy's presence was invaluable as Lydia was in a near constant state of hysteria, and no one, not even his wife, could get her to calm down until Mr. Darcy offered to speak to her. Ten minutes later, he came downstairs and not another peep was to be heard from her until she saw your uncle and me."

"Did he give a reason for his actions?" Lizzy asked.

"Yes, he said that he has known Wickham since he was a boy on the Pemberley estate and knew him to be capable of the most immoral behavior. He felt that if he had made known Wickham's character, this could never have happened. Although it would have been a relief to take the weight of all that guilt off my shoulders and to have put it on his, I could not do it. It was my dereliction of duty as a father that was the true cause of all this unhappiness.

"Mr. Darcy remained in town for another two days and offered the services of his solicitor, but when I tried to thank him, he was embarrassed and said I owed him nothing. The man is an absolute cipher—as stoic a fellow as I have ever met."

"What will happen to Wickham?" Jane asked.

"According to Colonel Forster, because of Mr. Darcy's intervention, from a military point of view, Wickham has not actually done anything wrong, so he will not be brought up on charges. Other than withholding his last month's pay and being forced out of the militia, the only thing Colonel Forster can do is leave him to his fellow officers. Because Wickham owes debts of honor to so many of them, he will be lucky to get out of Brighton alive. Additionally, the colonel sent an aide around to the shops and public houses to find out how much Wickham owed them. His debts are significant, and the colonel is confident he will end up spending some time in debtors' prison unless some benefactor comes forward, an unlikely scenario."

Turning his full attention to Lizzy, Mr. Bennet continued, "I believe the family owes you a debt of gratitude, my dear." Lizzy's heart started racing at the thought of what Mr. Darcy might have shared. "Mr. Darcy said that because you have been such a good friend to his sister, he felt obligated to do all he could to prevent Wickham from succeeding."

"Is that the only reason he gave?"

"Yes, what other reason could there be?"

"I can't think of any," and Lizzy felt her eyes filling up with tears.

Her father came over and hugged her. "I know why you are crying. But no harm has been done, and in a week or two, I will have forgiven Lydia, as well as myself. And all will be as it was."

Lizzy nodded, "Yes, all will be as it was."

Despite her grief, Lydia's appetite remained unaffected, and Mrs. Hill received word that a tray should be prepared for her and brought up to her room. When Lizzy saw how her sister's inexcusable actions were being rewarded, instead of punished, she went to her room and shut the door. She did not want to speak to anyone—not even Jane.

When Jane checked on her an hour later, she found Lizzy sitting in the window seat reading a novel. Jane knew that her sister could be brought low by events, but she always got up, dusted herself off, and moved forward.

"While you were sleeping, an express rider came from London with a letter for you." Because the expensive stationery had a D stamped into the seal, there was no doubt that the letter was from Mr. Darcy.

After taking the post from Jane, Lizzy sat with it on her lap unopened. "If this is another letter from F. Darcy, I think I shall scream," and she broke through the seal.

When Lizzy had finished the letter, she started crying in big heartfelt sobs, and tears poured down her face. Jane had to think that Mr. Darcy had changed his mind, and his courtship with Miss Montford would go forward. But when Jane read the contents of the letter, she realized that Lizzy was crying as a means of releasing all the emotions she had kept in check for so long. Mr. Darcy had declared in simple, but elegant, language that he loved her, and because of that, everything that lay hidden had burst out into the open. Her tears flowed in happiness and relief.

When she had composed herself, Lizzy read aloud the closing lines of Mr. Darcy's letter:

> *The hours go slowly, but soon I shall be in Hertfordshire. Once we are together, it will require an act of God to separate us.*
>
> *Love, Will*

"Jane, he loves me, and there is nothing to keep him from me." After wiping her tears, she continued, "We are not antici-pating any volcanic eruptions or earthquakes, are we?"

Jane smiled at her sister. "No, Lizzy, there will be no acts of God to keep Mr. Darcy from you, and since Gaius and Lucius are in Scotland, there will be no local calamities, either."

Chapter 48

JOHN LUCAS CAME BY early in the afternoon to say that the wedding of Charlotte and Mr. Collins would take place in the village church on Friday at 10:00.

"I hope Charlotte knows what she is doing," he said in a voice that showed how unhappy he was with his sister's choice of husband. "Mr. Collins is driving everyone at Lucas Lodge to distraction. He is always going on about something that is of no interest to anyone but himself. At least I can get up and leave, but Charlotte can't. And once she gets to Kent, she will not have any place to hide to get away from him."

"Charlotte will be fine," Jane reassured him. "Since Mr. Collins rarely requires a response, she may choose to ignore him if she is so inclined."

"I hope you are right because, excuse me for being so blunt, he is a pompous arse," and he took his leave.

John Lucas's departure was quickly followed by the arrival of Tom Smart, one of Mr. Bingley's servants at Netherfield. "Miss Bennet, I've come to tell you that Mr. Bingley's back, so I expect we'll be seeing a lot more of you at Netherfield."

"Most definitely," she said, and she could not suppress a smile. "How do things go with Mr. Collins and Mrs. Crenshaw?"

"I never seen anything like it. Mr. Collins will say something about Lady Catherine, which will cause Mrs. Crenshaw to remember something what Lady So and So said, and so it goes. And when Mr. Collins ain't talking, he's humming. It is irritating, but it does give us fair warning that he's coming, and we make ourselves scarce."

Before leaving, Tom asked if he might say hello to Mrs. Hill in the kitchen, and the sisters exchanged glances, knowing that the person he really wanted to say hello to was Betsy, their kitchen maid.

After he left, Lizzy said, "Love is in the air. Tom and Betsy, Mr. Collins and Charlotte, Mr. Bingley and you."

"And Lizzy and Mr. Darcy," Jane said, completing the list. After reading Mr. Bingley's note and tucking it in her pocket, she told Lizzy that they had been invited to dine at Netherfield Park. "Mr. Bingley is to send his carriage at 3:00. I think I shall put on one of my better frocks. Will you do the same?"

"There is no need for that. Once Mr. Bingley sets eyes on you, he will not see anyone else. It will be as if I am not there at all."

"Well, let us dress up anyway."

"Whatever you say, as I am in a most agreeable mood."

As soon as Bingley and the Darcys entered the foyer of Netherfield Park, the now voluminous Mrs. Crenshaw attempted to embrace her brother. Also there to greet the party from London was Athena. Although the little imp made a perfect curtsey and welcomed Miss Darcy to Netherfield Park, Georgiana would trust her only as far as she could throw her.

When Charles informed his sister that Jane and Elizabeth would be dining with them, Mrs. Crenshaw could barely contain her enthusiasm.

"Oh, that is such good news, brother. Mr. Collins has gone to Lucas Lodge to visit Miss Lucas, who has completely recovered from her illness. I must confess I am glad that he will not be at table with us. He talks a good deal and rarely gives the other party a chance to say anything, but he is a pleasant man and, for the most part, has been good company."

Georgiana and Will looked at each other. This was a complication they did not need. Once Mr. Collins realized he was under the same roof as the nephew and niece of Lady Catherine de Bourgh, they would become a captive audience. *That* was not going to happen if Georgiana had anything to say about it.

As soon as the carriage conveying Jane and Lizzy pulled up in front of the manor house, Mr. Bingley was out the door and whispered in Jane's ear. It was obviously something very special as Jane nodded her head in approval. After greeting Mrs. Crenshaw, Charles suggested they go into the drawing room, but told Lizzy that a friend of hers from town had asked that he deliver a letter to her and that he had placed it on the desk in the library.

When Lizzy went into the library, it was very dark, with only the glow of embers in the fireplace providing any light, so she was startled when a man stepped out of the shadows.

"Hello, Elizabeth."

"Mr. Darcy!" and she placed her hand over her chest to calm her heart. "You are not in London?" And she could hear the quaver in her voice.

"No, I am not in London. Do you not know why I am here?"

"I would rather not guess. Can't you just tell me?"

Darcy stepped forward and traced the outline of Elizabeth's face with his fingers. "I am here so that I might tell you how much I love you—unconditionally, with no restraints, and with all my heart." And then he kissed her, and all the passion of their first kiss at Pemberley returned, and she felt drawn into his very being, that is, until she heard someone coming down the hall, and that someone was humming.

"Mr. Darcy, quickly," and she took him by the hand and led him to a space between two bookshelves, and she put her finger to her lips and whispered, "It is Mr. Collins."

As the reverend went in search of a book, the lovers remained stranded. For fear that she would break out laughing at the absurdity of their situation, Lizzy buried her head in Mr. Darcy's chest.

Mr. Darcy reacted differently. He gathered Lizzy in a tight embrace and ran his hands down her back until they rested on her waist, and then he pulled her hips toward him. Without hesitation, she moved against him, and she felt a warmth in every part of her body. After pulling her sleeve down her arm, he kissed her shoulder with his lips and tongue, and she thought that there was nothing as wonderful as this. When they finally heard the door close behind the humming parson, Lizzy pulled up the sleeve of her dress and stepped away from Mr. Darcy. As he moved toward her, she placed her hands upon his chest and said, "Please, sir. We are not married, and I fear if we continue, we will be acting as if we were."

"You are right," he said, half laughing and half in agony. "Why is Mr. Collins at Netherfield?" he asked and shifted his weight to deal with his discomfort. After Lizzy explained about the postponed wedding, he inquired, "Do you think he will come back to the library?"

"It is possible. When he stayed at Longbourn, to my father's great distress, he was in and out of his library all day long."

"Then we must go elsewhere." After thinking about the rooms that were available, he finally decided on the billiards room. "No one will go in there at this time of day."

"But it is across the foyer. We might be seen."

"Well, then we will have to risk it. I have much to say to you, and I will not be kept from it. Once Mr. Collins finds out I am here, he will seek me out and talk and talk and talk. At Rosings Park, I was sequestered with that gentleman on a rainy afternoon and had the privilege of listening to him expound on the pollination of cantaloupe."

Now Lizzy started to laugh. "Are you suggesting that we tippy-toe across the foyer to the billiards room?"

"No, I am suggesting that we run," he said with a smile, and taking Lizzy by the hand, that was what they did.

Chapter 49

THE REASON MR. COLLINS had been able to make a selection from the many volumes stacked on the shelves of the library in such a dimly lit room was because he only read two books: *Fordyce's Sermons* and Thomas Secker's *Four Discourses on Self-examination, Lying, Patience, and Contentment*. With its title concealed in the fold of his arm, he walked around the house with one or the other of those books merely as an affectation. He had successfully fooled all of Charlotte's family, as well as Mrs. Crenshaw, into thinking of him as a voracious reader. However, the reason for his success in doing so would have disturbed him. No one cared what he read.

When Mr. Collins went into the drawing room, he was happy to see Miss Bennet and Mr. Bingley. As gracious a hostess as Mrs. Crenshaw had been, he was getting tired of her constant interruptions. Unlike Charlotte, who sat quietly doing her needlework while he talked, Mr. Bingley's sister was not a good listener.

Mr. Collins was pleased to report that his darling Charlotte had fully recovered. "To think Charlotte's loving presence as the companion of my life might have been denied me," Mr. Collins continued. "Fortunately, there was an intervention, and I believe it very likely divine, that saved me from a life lived in loneliness and alone."

While her cousin rambled on, Jane wondered how Darcy and Lizzy were doing in the library, and she decided that if it was taking them this long, then they must be getting on quite well. Mrs. Crenshaw was so happy to have company other than Mr. Collins that she had not yet noticed Lizzy was missing.

"May I speak, Mama?" Athena asked, with an angelic expression. Because Athena was the oldest child remaining at home, she was allowed to sit with her mother and the other adults so that she might fetch whatever her dear Mama required.

"Yes, my sweet."

"I have heard Mr. Collins say that Miss Darcy and Mr. Darcy are relations of Lady Catherine de Bourgh. Does Mr. Collins know that they are here?"

"Mr. Darcy! Miss Darcy! Here at Netherfield?" Mr. Collins said in a voice indicating his astonishment. "I am deeply moved that the niece and nephew of my esteemed patroness should have come so far to be witnesses to my wedding."

"Yes, they are here, but Miss Darcy is resting, and Mr. Darcy is writing business letters. However, they will join us shortly," Jane said in an attempt to silence Athena.

"But I saw Mr. Darcy go into the billiards room with Miss Elizabeth," Athena responded, now with a sharper edge in her voice.

After Mrs. Crenshaw stopped laughing at the absurdity of a lady being in the billiards room, she told her daughter, "That was very funny, Athena, but please let the adults speak."

"But I wasn't being funny, Mama. I saw Mr. Darcy holding Miss Elizabeth's hand as they ran across the foyer to the billiards room."

No one was laughing now, not even Miss Bennet, whom Athena did not like at all. She was the reason Gaius and Lucius were in Scotland, and if it weren't for her interference, the bossy Mr. Campbell would not be coming to Netherfield. As soon as he arrived, Athena and Darius would be subjected to endless recitations of sums, spelling vocabulary words, and reading poetry and stories with morals.

"Surely not," Mr. Collins said, rising. "Miss Elizabeth is an unmarried woman. I can assure you my cousin would never be alone in a room with a man who is not her relation."

"I can show you," Athena said, looking straight at Jane.

Charles did his best to alert the couple of their approach. He walked slowly, but loudly, and pretended to have a fit of coughing. Jane hoped it would be enough. As the door creaked open, she was reminded of the time Mr. Carter's wagon had overturned on High Street in Meryton and how everyone had gathered around to see how many of his chickens had been killed. She took a deep breath and closed her eyes.

After successfully crossing the foyer, Darcy had shut the door to the billiards room and started laughing. "Now I understand Antony a little better. There is something to be said for clandestine meetings. Do you know he once had to climb down a trellis, for reasons I won't mention, and he had to jump the last few feet and landed in a hedge? I never thought the story was funny until now." And then he put his arms around Lizzy's waist and picked her up and spun her around.

Although Lizzy would have gladly stayed in Mr. Darcy's embrace, she realized that one of them had to keep a cool head, and it was not going to be Mr. Darcy.

"Why are you stepping away from me? Do you not trust me?" Darcy asked.

"Of course I don't trust you. You are a man."

"I have waited all these many months for you, and now I am to be denied a few kisses?"

"You have waited for me! It was not I who was running back and forth to London. It was I who waited for you."

"Let us agree that we were both waiting, but what is the harm in a few kisses now that we are together?"

"Because we cannot stay here. The servants will be coming in to stoke the fires and…"

"The servants will not come in here until we are called in to supper. They have enough to do without tending fires in empty rooms."

"All right. I shall concede that point. However, Mrs. Crenshaw knows I am here. Surely, she is wondering what has happened to one of her guests."

"She thinks you are with Georgiana."

"Why would she think that?"

"Because that is what Georgiana told Bingley to say."

"My goodness, what a clever girl."

"You don't know the half of it," he said, laughing at the thought of all of his sister's maneuvering. "Now, may I kiss you?"

"You said we were going to talk."

"I did not say that was all we were going to do." He briefly kissed her before putting his arms around her again. He could hardly believe that after all this time and all the hurdles, he was finally free to hold the woman he loved. But then he suddenly stepped back and asked, "Was Athena in the foyer when you came in?"

"Yes. Why?"

"Elizabeth, you have to leave immediately," he said, taking her by the hand and walking with her to a door that was hidden by the wood paneling. "There is a door just like this one on the other side that will exit into a hallway leading to the foyer. Please go quickly. I do not trust Athena."

Darcy had barely thrown off his jacket, chalked his cue, and tossed a few balls in the pockets before he heard Bingley knocking on the door, and he was not surprised to see Athena among the group.

"Hello, Bingley. I hope you don't mind that I did not immediately join your party. I have been in carriages too often of late, and I was not quite ready to sit down again. Please forgive me, Mrs. Crenshaw," he said, bowing, "if I caused you any inconvenience."

"None at all, sir," she replied.

"Mr. Darcy, this little girl was having some fun at our expense," Mr. Collins stated. "She thought Miss Elizabeth was in here with you."

But Athena knew what she had seen, and the little schemer dropped to her knees, looking under the table to see if Elizabeth was hiding there.

"A lady in a billiards room? Well, that would be very odd," Darcy answered. "But no harm done," he said, looking down at the kneeling Athena.

"That is very generous of you, Mr. Darcy," Mrs. Crenshaw said, but she was not amused by her daughter fabricating a story about one of her guests, and she sent for Tom Smart and asked him to escort Athena to the nursery. Shortly thereafter, Lizzy and Georgiana came into the billiards room, walking arm in arm, and both smiled as they passed Athena on her way out.

"Lizzy, whatever possessed you to leave the library and go into the billiards room?" Jane asked on the ride to Longbourn. "My heart was in my mouth at the thought of everyone finding Mr. Darcy and you alone."

"It wasn't but a minute or two after Mr. Darcy and I had started talking that we heard Mr. Collins approaching. We hid between two bookshelves for what seemed like an eternity," a very pleasant eternity, Lizzy thought. "We were afraid he might come back, so we hurried across the foyer. We were talking when Mr. Darcy practically pushed me out of the room, and it was a good thing he did. I had barely circled around to the foyer when I could hear Mr. Bingley knocking on the door."

"From Mr. Darcy's sour look all through supper, I suspect you did not have ample opportunity to talk. He is not very good at hiding his feelings."

"That is because he does not try. He is a man who is used to having his own way and scowls or pouts when he does not get it. It did not help that Mrs. Crenshaw never stopped talking, and of course, there is Mr. Collins, who requires no further comment. But the reason Mr. Darcy excused himself after our meal is in my pocket." Lizzy showed Jane a note Mr. Darcy had written to her.

Dearest Elizabeth,

When, where, and how are we to meet? I have much to discuss with you, but no place in which to discuss it. Please advise.

Love, Will

"Poor Mr. Darcy," Jane said, laughing. "He is very unhappy that he cannot be with you. I am sure Mr. Bingley could empathize with him as he has the same complaint."

"I understand Mr. Darcy's frustrations, but there are good reasons why unmarried ladies should not be left alone with their suitors," Lizzy said, while thinking of the passion of Mr. Darcy's kisses and his reaction to them. "When he leaned against me in the study at Netherfield, it was impossible not to notice that there seemed to be a third party present, and I had to be very careful, because it would be two against one."

Jane nearly doubled over laughing. Lizzy had always been more comfortable in discussing the relationship between a man and a woman, but now that she was experiencing love for the first time, Lizzy had thrown off all restraints. It gave Jane hope that a week from Saturday, her wedding night would be pleasurable—something she had not anticipated.

Mr. Darcy was neither smiling nor laughing. Because all of his efforts had been directed toward disentangling himself from Miss Montford so that he might be with Elizabeth, he had not given any thought to what would happen once he got to Hertfordshire. Since the weather had turned cold, there were to be no strolls along woodland paths or walks to the gazebo or riding in the park. It seemed as if their brief respite in the library and billiards room might be the only time they would be alone together until they were married. He would have to wait until Charlotte's wedding and hope that he could have a few minutes to speak to Elizabeth alone.

As for their engagement, it could not be publicly announced for several weeks, at a minimum, or it might prove embarrassing to Miss Montford and risk Sir John's ire, and it would not make him look very good either—courting one woman while romancing another. Good grief, what a mess!

And there was no guarantee he would even have time to talk to Lizzy at the wedding breakfast. Since his efforts to ingratiate himself with Bingley's neighbors had succeeded, he would have all the local gents wanting to speak to him, and he would have to be personable to their wives or risk offending anew. What he needed was something to draw people's attention, so they would not notice if Elizabeth and he managed to slip away. Yes, some kind of diversion was required, but what? Fireworks? A bonfire? And then an idea came to him, and he knew just what to do. He went to his desk and began writing,

Dear Antony…

Chapter 50

FINALLY, THE DAY OF Charlotte's wedding arrived, and the house hummed with activity as everyone made ready for the wedding. Mr. Darcy had made his carriage available to the Bennets, and Lydia and Kitty had climbed in ahead of their mother and older sisters. Because of their lack of seniority, the two youngest Bennets had to give way, but not before Lydia had commented, "Mr. Darcy did not send the carriage for you, Lizzy. Everyone knows that he does not like you, but we became friends when we were together in Brighton. Mr. Wickham..." Jane shooed Lydia away from the carriage. Even the patient Jane had tired of Lydia and her stories of Brighton and her dear Wickham.

While Bingley stood by the church door so that he might assist the Bennet ladies, Darcy, along with Georgiana, waited inside the vestibule for Lizzy to arrive. Because no one knew of their relationship, the couple had to be satisfied with furtive glances, of which there were to be many. Even though Darcy realized the necessity for circumspection, this endless waiting was having a deleterious effect on him and the only possible explanation for his sending Mercer to London with a note asking Antony to come to Netherfield. He hoped that was not a mistake.

When the bride walked down the aisle, Lizzy was elated. Charlotte Lucas, who did not like any fuss, had chosen a pale yellow dress that showed off her complexion and dark hair beautifully, and the effect was more than satisfactory. In contrast, Mr. Collins wore his parson's suit with black hose that accentuated his spindly legs, but because he was so happy that his wedding day had finally arrived, his whole demeanor was one of pure joy. Even Lizzy had to smile when she saw the beaming parson.

The wedding breakfast was attended by intimate friends and family, all wishing Mr. and Mrs. Collins joy. In short order, the musicians began playing, and couples flocked to the dance floor. Darcy dearly wanted to ask Elizabeth to dance, but his presence in any venue always drew scrutiny. He did not want anyone gossiping about him until he was prepared to make an announcement, but surely one dance could do no harm? He had been making his way toward Elizabeth when there was a commotion in the foyer. The source of the excitement was quickly revealed: Antony, Lord Fitzwilliam, had arrived.

Darcy and Georgiana looked at each other in alarm. Antony wasn't supposed to be here. The note had specifically told him to go to Netherfield Park. To add to the confusion, the earl was not alone. With him were his daughters, Amelia and Sophia, and a Madame Konig, who was being introduced to the guests as the girls' "traveling" governess.

Sir William and Lady Lucas's joy at having an earl in their home could barely be contained. When Lady Lucas was excited, she always spoke too loudly and in a shrill voice, and while his wife was nearly shouting, Sir William was almost speechless, hemming and hawing and harrumphing his way through his introductions of Lord Fitzwilliam.

After acknowledging everyone's bows, Antony asked to be directed to the bride and groom. Using his prerogative as a member of the nobility to always get his way, as soon as Lord Fitzwilliam made eye contact with Mr. Collins, he let him know that he must wait his turn as the earl would first speak to his wife.

"Mrs. Collins, my heartfelt congratulations, and may I add that you are absolutely glowing, bringing much-needed sunshine to a drab autumn day? I hope you do not mind me joining you on this the happiest of occasions. I was supposed to go to Netherfield, but when I learned there was a wedding in the village, I could not resist. My only regret is that I arrived too late to attend the ceremony and thereby serve as a witness to the exchange of vows."

"It was a simple ceremony, milord," Charlotte said, trying to hide a smile. The sight of this aristocratic dandy, in his green brocade jacket standing next to her husband in his parson's attire, was too funny for words.

"When it comes to church services, Mrs. Collins, simple is good; short is even better. May I ask, did you cry? I did at my wedding. In fact, my brother had to keep handing me one handkerchief after another, and it did not stop with the ceremony. I cried all through the wedding breakfast and for a good many days after that.

"And this gentleman is now your husband," he said, turning to Mr. Collins, who bowed so low that his hand brushed the tops of his shoes. "Mr. Collins, your reputation has preceded you. Lady Catherine de Bourgh has remarked on how diligently you tend to your flock. I know that same sense of obligation will have you spending all of your time talking with your guests, so I shall not detain you a moment longer. But, first, please allow me to introduce my daughters, Amelia and Sophia, and their traveling governess, Madame Konig."

After overcoming the surprise of finding Lord Fitzwilliam attending the wedding festivities of her friend, Lizzy had to make a real effort not to laugh. The earl was as colorful as any of the ladies at the breakfast. His footwear, with their gold-thread stitching, jeweled buckles, and high heels, was as out of date as his attire, making him look like a courtier in the court of a newly crowned George III. But then Lizzy realized that this show had a purpose, and the gaudiness of his apparel was deliberate. She was convinced he had come to Lucas Lodge as a diversion, and when she looked at Mr. Darcy and he would not return her look, she knew she was right.

It was his little cousins, Emmy and Sophie, who saved Mr. Darcy from a stern rebuke. After bending down so that both girls could kiss him on his cheeks, Lizzy had heard him say: "When I last saw you, I thought it was not possible for you two to get any prettier. But I was wrong. Here stand before me two of the loveliest young ladies in the kingdom," and the pair squealed with delight. The girls then introduced Madame Konig to Mr. Darcy, and Lizzy looked for his reaction to the woman he knew to be his cousin's mistress.

"Madame Konig, I am pleased to meet you," Darcy said,

bowing, and he gently took her hand. Although Madame said nothing, her gratitude to Mr. Darcy of Pemberley for his recognition was evident on her face.

"Lizzy, the governess…" Jane said.

"Traveling governess," Lizzy answered, correcting her sister.

Jane had to look away for fear of laughing out loud. "Is the traveling governess who I think she is?" After Lizzy nodded, she continued, "My goodness, even in her staid governess clothes, she is absolutely stunning. I think her eyes are actually violet."

"Yes, I think so as well. But what I find so appealing about her is the way Lord Fitzwilliam's daughters keep looking at her. They obviously are comfortable in her company, and, I suspect, quite fond of her as well."

After mingling among the guests for several minutes, Lord Fitzwilliam finally made his way over to Lizzy, and after inquiring about Mrs. Gardiner and expressing regret for her absence, he asked to be introduced to her family.

"Milord, this is my eldest sister, Jane," and after Jane had curtseyed, he took her hand and briefly kissed it. "Miss Bennet, while at Pemberley, I told Miss Elizabeth that if her sisters were half as lovely as she was, then your home must be aglow with all the beauty contained therein. Mr. Bingley is very fortunate indeed."

Jane acknowledged the compliment in full blush. She had never met an earl before, and here he was holding her hand, with his mistress standing but a few feet away.

"And you are…?" he asked, looking at Kitty.

"Catherine Bennet, milord."

"Catherine? Hmm? I think not. Catherine is too serious a name for someone with such an engaging smile. I would suspect you are known as Kate or Kitty to your friends."

This compliment practically caused Kitty to swoon, and Mary nearly did when Lord Fitzwilliam took her hand in his and held it all the while he was addressing her. "Another beautiful Bennet sister. But you are different from your sisters. I see a look of intelligence in your eyes. You must own to it, Miss Mary. You cannot hide it from me. Beauty and intelligence in one lovely lady. How blest you are."

Upon hearing the compliment, Lydia snorted, causing the earl to turn his attention to her. "The youngest Bennet sister, Miss Lydia, I presume? Have you come out into society, my dear?"

"Yes, milord, this past year."

"You are very young to be out, only four or five years older than my Amelia, and because of your youth, I am sure you are eager to find that perfect gentleman, fall in love, and get married. Please allow me to caution you that such decisions should be delayed for a number of years until you are more mature. Marriage is forever, so be cautious. Forever is a very long time."

Why was Lord Fitzwilliam talking to her like this, Lydia asked herself? He had said only nice things to everyone else. And what did he know anyway? He was hopelessly out of fashion, and his shoes were particularly ugly. As soon as the earl turned his attention to her mother, Lydia walked away.

"Ah, here we have yet another sister," he said, taking Mrs. Bennet's hand. Mrs. Bennet started giggling as if she were a young girl at her first dance, and when she informed the earl that she was the girls' mother, he went on and on about Mr. Bennet taking a child bride. All the while Lord Fitzwilliam was complimenting his wife, Mr. Bennet was watching, and he saw, for the first time in years, the young woman he had married a quarter of a century ago. Because of Lydia's unfortunate adventure, he had promised himself that he would take greater care of his daughters. He now broadened that promise to include his wife.

While Antony continued to enchant all the female guests, Lizzy went over to speak to Charlotte. "I cannot account for the earl's presence, Charlotte, and I am very sorry he has come as he has drawn off all of the attention that should rightly be yours."

"I am happy he has come. You know I do not like being the center of attention, so I can assure you that Lord Fitzwilliam's arrival is welcome. Speaking of the devil," Charlotte said, stepping away from Lizzy to make way for His Lordship.

"Miss Elizabeth, may I introduce you to my two little jewels, Sophie and Emmy."

Lizzy was in complete agreement with Lord Fitzwilliam's description of his daughters. Their dark hair, hanging in ringlets and tied with ribbons and bows, contrasted beautifully with their cornflower blue eyes. Both were wearing gorgeous dresses with frills aplenty.

"I am so pleased to meet you, Miss Amelia and Miss Sophia," Lizzy said. "When your father and I were guests at Pemberley, he mentioned you at every opportunity, and you are as pretty as he claimed. But who is your friend?" Lizzy asked while looking at Madame Konig.

"This is our traveling governess, Madame Konig. Our real governess, Mrs. Hall, is on holiday, and Papa's friend came with us. She tells us stories about living in Vienna," Amelia, the elder of the two, said.

"My English is imperfect, Miss Bennet," Madame Konig said with a slight lisp. "I am better in French, but I am happy to meets you."

"Madame Konig, I am pleased to meet you as well," but before Lizzy could engage her in conversation, Lord Fitzwilliam asked her what she thought of his entrance.

"With the exception of a royal procession, it was second to none, milord."

"Then I have succeeded, as my purpose was to create a diversion, and the reason for the diversion is waiting for you in the study. From what I have heard of your past experience, I suggest you lock the door." After bowing and smiling, he took his leave.

Looking around the room, Lizzy realized that Mr. Darcy was no longer present, and with all eyes on the earl, she backed her way out of the room and went in search of the master of Pemberley.

Chapter 51

WHILE LIZZY WAITED FOR her eyes to adjust to the dim light of the study, Mr. Darcy came up from behind her and put his two arms around her waist and pulled her tightly against him.

"I shall not let you go until you say that you are not angry with me for Lord Fitzwilliam's appearance, and before you say anything, you must know that he was supposed to go to Netherfield. I certainly did not know he would be traveling with an entourage."

"But why did you ask him to come at all?"

After releasing her, he took her hand and walked with her to the sofa, but before he sat down Lizzy suggested that they lock the door.

"That sounds promising."

"It is nothing of the kind. We do not want a repeat of what happened in the library at Netherfield. That is *all* I meant by my request."

Darcy let out an exaggerated sigh because he would not have minded a repeat of what had happened in the Netherfield library, but he went and locked the door as requested.

"Mr. Darcy, please tell me why you invited Lord Fitzwilliam to Netherfield? Is it because Mrs. Crenshaw talks too much, and you wanted someone equally loquacious to entertain her?"

"It is not just that she talks too much. Forgive me for discussing such things with you, but she is so heavy with child that I live in fear that she will stand up and from under her skirts an infant will appear."

Lizzy started to laugh at the picture he had drawn. "From that comment, I gather that your wife will be spending a good deal of time in her apartment when she is with child."

Darcy looked at Lizzy with that quizzical expression she found so endearing. "Why are you speaking of 'my wife' as if she is unknown to you?"

Lizzy said nothing. Did he really think she could talk as if they were betrothed when he had not made her an offer?

"Oh, of course, I see. Well, that is a good opening for me. Shall I stand or kneel?"

"It does not matter," Lizzy said, and she could barely hear her voice over the sound of her heart beating. "Please proceed."

"Elizabeth, as you know, I am not good with words, so I shall simply state that I love you from the depths of my heart, and I am now asking that you become my wife."

Lizzy fell into his arms and clung to him and nodded her assent, and he kissed her with a passion that was even greater than their previous rendezvous, and she felt her reserve crumbling as he kissed her neck and shoulders and moved his body against hers. But even though she was enjoying it immensely, she knew that she had to stop him, and she pushed back.

"Mr. Darcy, please. We cannot continue in this manner. We *must* rejoin the others." With his face flushed with passion, he asked in an elevated voice why they must leave when things were going so nicely. "Because of Ellie Timlin, the butcher's daughter, who married Joe Egger five months ago…"

"When you see Mrs. Egger, please extend my best wishes for her health and happiness, but would you enlighten me as to why she is being discussed at this particular moment?"

"You need not be sarcastic, Mr. Darcy. The Eggers are the parents of a little boy born earlier this month," and when he shook his head, indicating he still did not understand, she continued, "Let me repeat. The Eggers married five months ago."

When the information finally sunk in, Darcy released Elizabeth.

"Mr. Darcy, I am a lady, and, therefore, until we are married, we must appear together only in public or with a chaperone."

"Of course, you are a lady, but a few kisses do not make you less so." After looking at her expression, he added, "All right. More than a few. But, Elizabeth, do you realize that once we announce our engagement, all eyes will be upon us?"

"Of course, I do. Perhaps you can condole with Mr. Bingley," she said, teasing him.

"Very well. In that case," he said, "it would be best if I returned to London."

"Oh, I see how it is. Because I will not meet with you in secret, the next time I see you will be at the church door on the day of our wedding?" she asked as she moved away from him.

"No, you misunderstand me," he said, taking her hand and gently coaxing her to his side. "What I meant to say was that I would not see you until Jane's wedding. After that, I shall speak to your father, and then we shall make the announcement of our engagement."

"But what about our courtship, Mr. Darcy?"

"A courtship? Have I not been courting you?"

"No, you have not. One letter and two secret meetings is hardly a courtship. And speaking of letters, you must promise me that when you write in the future that all your letters will be like the second one, and none like the first."

"That is unfair, Elizabeth," he said in high dudgeon. "I was in a crowded room with Mrs. Forster, the colonel, and his aides, and with Gregg waiting for me to finish the letter, and I felt as if everyone in the room was watching me."

"I understand, but was it necessary to sign the letter, 'Yours, F. Darcy'?"

Seeing that he had hurt her, he said, "You are right. I should have signed it, 'Yours, Fitzwilliam Darcy.'"

Lizzy laughed. "You are lucky you wrote that second letter before I saw you again, or you would have received the cold shoulder from me."

"I will take your shoulders however I can get them," and he moved to kiss her, but she held up her hands and gently pushed him away.

"As I was saying, as part of our courtship, you must visit me at Longbourn and call on my parents, and when you cannot, you must write me letters. Now that I have had a letter from you, I know you are capable of it."

"But I am out of stationery," he said with a smile, which Lizzy did not return. "Was not my letter self-explanatory with no need for elaboration?"

"Self-explanatory. No need for elaboration. Such words of love, Mr. Darcy. I think I shall faint. You put me in mind of Benedick's failed attempts to write poetry for Beatrice."

"But the play ends with Beatrice and Benedick marrying, so all's well that ends well."

"Clever response, Mr. Darcy, but you have the wrong play."

Chapter 52

WHEN LIZZY RETURNED TO the drawing room, she quickly made her way through the crowd to stand next to Jane and Mr. Bingley. With a knowing smile, Charles took his leave, and Lizzy found herself blushing at the idea of someone knowing that she had met Mr. Darcy in secret.

"Was I missed?" Lizzy asked, scanning the crowd.

"Not at all. Lord Fitzwilliam claimed everyone's attention by asking Charlotte to dance and suggesting that Mr. Collins ask Mrs. Konig to do the same. Have you ever known of an instance where a governess, even a traveling one, danced with her master's guests? I cannot wait to hear what Mrs. Draper and Lady Lucas have to say about all this.

"I was able to speak with Mrs. Konig," Jane continued. "Her English is not the best, and she cannot pronounce *th*. But the effect is absolutely delightful, and she is charming everyone. Despite her relationship with the flamboyant lord, she is very reserved. But enough about Madame. Do you have news to share?"

And Lizzy whispered to her sister that Mr. Darcy had proposed, and looking around to see if anyone was listening, she told Jane that she was insisting on a courtship. "We do not know each well enough, and I do not want him to have any regrets. I shall tell you more later; Charlotte is coming."

"Charlotte, you appear winded," Lizzy said after having watched her dance a jig with Lord Fitzwilliam.

"I am. His Lordship is a vigorous dancer."

"Are you enjoying your day, Charlotte?" Jane asked. Like Lizzy, she was concerned that the uninvited guests were stealing the show.

"I truly am, so please stop worrying. In another hour, it will all be over as we are running out of food and punch. I know that you both have had reservations about this marriage, so I wish to reassure you. When everyone's attention was focused on His Lordship, Mr. Collins came over, and after taking my hand, he said that he only wanted three things in life. The first was to be a good husband, the second was to be a good pastor, and the third was to be a good neighbor to Lady Catherine and her daughter—in that order. It touched my heart in such a way that I am no longer worried about other things."

"Oh, Charlotte, that was so sweet."

"Yes, Jane, it was. Despite his peculiar behavior and his propensity to talk too much, he is a good man, and I am fortunate to have him. And what about you, Lizzy? Are we soon to have another wedding? Oh, please do not look at me like that. Granted, you are better at concealing your feelings than the gentleman, but it is obvious to a friend of so many years that you are in love. When are we to wish you joy?"

"Not until after Jane's wedding. The gentleman must first

speak to Papa, and we must have a courtship. His life is so different from mine. I cannot imagine having a duke as neighbor. His sister was named after Georgiana, the Duchess of Devonshire. I try not to think about it because, if I do, I shall get cold feet."

"You must forget about all those other things and enjoy your courtship," Charlotte told her friend. "He is much changed since he first came into Hertfordshire, and you are the reason."

While Darcy waited in the study for sufficient time to pass following Elizabeth's departure, he decided that she was right. There were good reasons why young ladies were not left alone with their suitors. If she even suspected the content of his dreams, she would not have sat next to him on the sofa.

Darcy was pouring himself a brandy when the door creaked open, and Antony, Lord Fitzwilliam, the hero of the day, stepped in.

"There you are, Darcy. I see you have helped yourself to the brandy. If you would pour me half of what you have, I would appreciate it," and he sank into the leather sofa recently vacated by Elizabeth and started to rub his toes through his shoes. "Did you know that as you get older, your feet flatten out, and you can no longer fit in your old shoes? As a result, my feet are killing me, but I dare not take them off as I will not get them back on. I look ridiculous enough without walking around unshod."

"Those shoes must be ten years old if they are a day," Darcy said, laughing.

"They are older than that. They are from my days as a bachelor. I have kept almost everything from the time before I was dragged off in chains to serve my sentence with Eleanor."

"Madame Konig is charming," Darcy quickly said. He wanted to distract Antony from his wife, a subject that often brought him low. "I did not have a chance to talk to her myself; the line was too long. But from what I overheard, I would imagine that she is very pleasant company."

"She is more than pleasant. She is kind, and my girls adore her. And if you have any worries as to where she will be sleeping while at Netherfield, Antonia will be with the girls in a room on the second floor, while I will lay my head on a pillow in a room on the first floor. No romantic interludes are planned."

"I didn't think there would be. You are always at your best when you are with your children."

"Thank you for that and for your kind words about Antonia. She always puts a smile on my face. How can you not love someone who says zis, zat, and zee other zing? It is adorable. And speaking of adorable, if I may judge from the smile on Miss Elizabeth Bennet's face, you have some good news to share."

"I do. We are unofficially engaged, but…" and Darcy stood up and started to pace. "Antony, this is a whole new experience for me. The only women with whom I may claim a relation-ship were both widows and five years older than I was. I met Christina Caxton in France when I was twenty years old, and I was the one who knew nothing. But that is not the case with Elizabeth. I think I may have frightened her by my advances. It is not that I mean to overpower her, but it is bloody difficult to go backward. I am a man of the world, and I cannot pretend to not want things that I do want. I have to tell you that I am on the point of exploding, and holding her hand while dancing does not satisfy."

"Move up the wedding date," Antony said, stating the

obvious. "You have the wherewithal and connections to buy a special license, so you may marry her the same day Bingley marries Miss Bennet."

"Elizabeth wants a courtship."

"Oh, that is too bad. Because if your courtship of Miss Montford is any indicator of your talent in that area, Elizabeth will be disappointed."

Darcy rolled his eyes, but then he had to laugh. Had there ever been a worse suitor than he had been with Letitia Montford?

"But it was so different with Letitia. In all the time I was calling on her, I never once pictured myself actually kissing her."

"I had the same thing with Eleanor, except we were married."

"So what do you suggest I do to satisfy Elizabeth's need for a courtship?"

"Flowers always work. Jewelry is nice, but in Miss Elizabeth's case, simple is better, and you must resign yourself to authoring love letters. It is the most personal thing you can do for a lady before you are married, and although you may write about how much you desire her, in most cases, less is more. You do not want to frighten her. It is a bad start to a marriage when you have to pry your spouse's fingers, one at a time, from the bedpost on your wedding night. Ask Eleanor. Although I very nearly succeeded in holding her off."

"I still intend to go to London," Darcy said, shaking his head in amusement at Antony's comment. "I need to find out if it is known that I am no longer courting Miss Montford. That may determine the length of the engagement."

"Not necessary. I think it was the day after you left London that Sir John was making the rounds in the dining room at White's telling everyone that he had practically pushed you out the door because of your ideas regarding the mingling of the classes."

"Montford is a typical bully," an annoyed Darcy said. "He was lecturing me on my willingness to befriend people such as Bingley, but as soon as I responded, he backed down. Once he is given his barony, he will be even more obnoxious than he is now. But while Sir John was busy belittling me, was anyone paying attention to what he was saying?"

"One person in particular showed quite a bit of interest. Mr. Jasper Wiggins nearly spit out his steak when he heard Miss Montford was available."

Darcy broke out into a broad smile. "God bless Jasper Wiggins," he uttered under his breath. "Antony, how does one go about getting a special license?"

When Darcy returned to the drawing room, he immediately asked Lizzy to dance. He decided that if people had seen them together, it would be less of a surprise to her Meryton neighbors when they became betrothed. As the music began playing, Darcy stated that he would very much like to send her a few gifts as tokens of his affection. Antony was correct as to her preferences: flowers, jewelry, but in moderation as to their size, and love letters.

"I shall write from London, and you can judge for yourself as to whether or not I am successful as a writer of *billet doux*."

"I look forward to it, Mr. Darcy," Lizzy said with a smile, knowing that she had won.

Chapter 53

THE DAY AFTER CHARLOTTE'S wedding, Mr. Bingley sent his carriage for Jane and Lizzy so that they might come to Netherfield Park. As expected, as soon as the carriage pulled up, Charles was out the door, while Mr. Darcy waited inside. This was the perfect sketch of the two men's characters: One wore his heart on his sleeve, while the other kept it tucked away in his coat pocket.

"Everyone is outside," Charles explained. "Apparently, Mrs. Konig loves the cold weather. She bundled up Amelia, Sophia, and His Lordship, and Mr. Campbell did the same with Darius and Athena. Even little Minerva is out there. She has so many layers of clothes on that she can barely walk, but Georgiana is assisting her."

"Are you enjoying your guests, Mr. Bingley?" Lizzy asked.

"Mrs. Konig is a delight. I only wish her English was a little better because it is a bit of a challenge to converse with her. As for Lord Fitzwilliam, he could liven up a funeral."

"I do not think Mrs. Konig has been in the country very long, and her English is better than my French. But that is my own fault because I would not give myself the trouble of practicing."

After the two couples chatted briefly, Jane and Bingley went to one end of the drawing room, while Elizabeth and Mr. Darcy walked to the other.

"Well, Mr. Darcy, it seems that we are alone again—at least for a while," and they sat down next to each other on the sofa. Lizzy, who had been expecting a quick kiss, was disappointed when Mr. Darcy did nothing. "Why do you not kiss me, Mr. Darcy? Or is that something you do only in secret in darkened rooms?"

"You want me to kiss you? After saying that you did not want to be alone with me because of my kisses, now you are asking for one? Well, I am not going to kiss you. I want you to know how it feels to want something that you cannot have." This remark was clearly in retaliation for her demand that they have a courtship.

"I am well acquainted with the feeling of not having what one wants, but it is your choice," she said, straightening her dress, embarrassed that she had asked a man for a kiss and had been denied, and so she brought up a topic she knew would make him equally uncomfortable—love letters.

"I have not forgotten, but instead of a correspondence, I was going to suggest that you visit your aunt and uncle, and since we will be together in town, letters will be unnecessary."

"A correspondence? You do not correspond with the woman you love. You write her love letters. Well, actually, others do; you don't. Oh how you do wiggle out of things you do not want to do," Lizzy said, pretending to pout.

"All right then, I shall promise to write you letters so passionate that the paper will burn your fingers. However, you must do something as well. You must work on improving your French to the point where you can converse with Mrs. Konig."

"But I have not studied French in years."

"And I have written only one love letter."

"Very well," Lizzy said, but this time she really was pouting. "You do not have to write me letters."

Darcy burst out laughing. "If your French really is that bad, Georgie can tutor you."

"*Non, merci. Je suis content de vivre ma vie sans parler d'avoir à parler français.*"

"Oh, dear. I see the problem."

"That was unkind. Accurate. But unkind," she said, and she gently pushed her shoulder into his. "In all seriousness, it is not just my poor French. We come from such vastly different backgrounds, and you move in a society that is a world apart from my own."

Darcy went quiet for several minutes. This reminded him of the time he had come to Longbourn to apologize for his unfortunate remarks made at the assembly. It had taken him a long time to find the right words because he was doing something new: apologizing to someone not of his rank.

"Actually, I have given the matter a lot of thought. Falling in love with you has made me rethink everything. All my concerns regarding my Norman heritage or being the grandson of an earl, once scrutinized, seemed unimportant. You asked if the marriage of a Devereaux to a Fitzwilliam caused a hullabaloo. It did. But they married anyway, and the earth continued to spin on its axis.

"I did not realize that by befriending Bingley, I had stepped into a different world—a much more expansive and inclusive world. Two generations ago, Bingley's grandfather was a blacksmith in the North of England, and now his grandson has more money than most earls. To live as my father did is to look backward. I want to go forward.

"As to the matter of London society, that too will change, albeit at a much slower pace. But if your concern is rubbing elbows with the ladies of the *ton*, it will not happen because I do not associate with the Prince of Wales and his followers. Even so, there are enough Caroline Bingleys in society who would enjoy making your life unpleasant. But I do not care about what other people say. Let them throw their best punch. I can take it because I will be with you."

While waiting in the foyer for the carriage to be brought 'round, Darcy told Elizabeth that he would be leaving for London in the morning.

"You and Jane will be busy making preparations for the wedding and breakfast, and I must go to London as I have business with George Bingley. He has written a second letter asking that I return to town as I am venturer in several of his schemes, and it will also serve another purpose. You will miss me so much that you will move up our wedding date and forego a courtship."

"You are very sure of yourself, Mr. Darcy," she said, smiling.

"Yes, I am, because I am sure of your love for me and mine for you."

Lizzy thought she would melt. "Mr. Darcy, since you have addressed all of my concerns, we shall talk about a wedding date when you return."

Darcy took Lizzy's hand and led her to the area under the

staircase and kissed her good night. "Elizabeth, I promise that you will not be sorry as I shall make you the happiest woman in England."

"Yes, I know."

Chapter 54

Longbourn was in a state of upheaval. Corsets, chemises, stockings, and dresses were all thrown about, and Lydia and Kitty were elbowing each other for room in front of the mirror. While Mama and Mrs. Hill were helping Jane to get dressed, Aunt Gardiner and Betsy assisted Lizzy. Even Mary, who professed to have no interest in baubles and beads, was wearing earrings and a cross necklace.

With a house full of ladies running hither and yon, and with orders being shouted or praises being bestowed, the volume had risen to such a level that Mr. Bennet and Mr. Gardiner had removed to Mr. Philips's house until such time as they were summoned to the church.

Mrs. Bennet was all aflutter, and since she had no intention of relaxing until the vicar had pronounced Jane and Mr. Bingley to be man and wife, she would take brief rests before going back into the fray. She thought about how congratulations would pour in and smiled at the thought of Jane being the talk of the county for months, if not years, because no one could possibly make a more advantageous marriage than her dear Jane. Every time she said, "five thousand a year," Mrs. Bennet started giggling. With such a son-in-law, she would never again have to worry about the entail.

Lizzy was possibly as nervous as Jane. She had not seen Mr. Darcy in a week, but he had surprised her by writing a love letter to her, and as promised, it had burnt her fingers with its passionate prose, and she kept it in a chest under her bed under lock and key.

When Jane walked down the aisle in her beautiful ivory dress and diaphanous veil, many whispered that the village had never seen a more beautiful bride nor such a handsome groom, and because she had endeared herself to all, everyone, including Mr. Bingley's sisters, wished her joy.

The day was sunny, but cold, and so the guests quickly got into their carriages and wagons and made their way to Netherfield Park for the breakfast. Every Bingley brother and sister and all of their children were in attendance, and Lizzy found this gathering of Bingleys to be most agreeable, including Caroline Bingley. Lizzy had learned that Miss Bingley, and possibly her twenty-thousand-pound inheritance, had drawn the attention of Lord David Upton, and it appeared that her future might include having everyone address her as "milady."

Darcy made the rounds as if he were the groom, visiting with Charles's neighbors and joining in a conversation with George and James Bingley, both of whom were discussing new investment schemes, eventually making his way over to Mrs. Crenshaw. But after she had informed him that she may have misjudged how far along she was, he bowed and made his way to the other side of the room where an amused Lizzy waited.

"Mr. Darcy, you look ill at ease," Lizzy said. She had noted how short his conversation with Mrs. Crenshaw had been.

"Do not be surprised if, between the toasts for the bride and groom, you hear a baby's cry."

"You need not worry. Dr. Paterson is here."

"You find my discomfort funny; I do not. So let us change the subject. You have said nothing of my letter."

"Well, let me say something now. Shame on you!" she said, laughing, and soon left his side, but not before rewarding him with her brilliant smile.

As soon as Lizzy departed, a merry Mr. Bennet joined Mr. Darcy. "What a display of finery and array of food we have, Mr. Darcy! But such a joyous occasion merits all this folderol, does it not?" Darcy nodded his head in agreement.

"It gladdens a father's heart to see a daughter well married to someone she loves, as that is not always the case, and now that Jane is married, it will be Lizzy's turn. I hope she is as fortunate as her sister because she is equally deserving of a fine man. I do not think I could part with her if that were not the case."

"Naturally, a father would wish for such things," Darcy said, and he shifted uneasily.

"Mr. Darcy, I am giving you an opening, and you are not taking it."

Darcy looked at Mr. Bennet, smiled, and laughed. "Is it that obvious?"

"Not as obvious as Mrs. Crenshaw being with child, but close."

"I am embarrassed to be found out so easily."

"Don't be. It was in this very ballroom where I fell in love with Mrs. Bennet. By the end of that long-ago evening, there wasn't a soul in the room who doubted that we would marry because I could not hide my feelings for her. In addition to being the most beautiful lady in the county, I was attracted to Mrs. Bennet because she had the ability to make me laugh, which is a necessity if a marriage is to survive the storms that will rise up every now and then. I think you require the same thing."

"I do, sir. But I suspect Elizabeth's wit has a bit more bite to it than Mrs. Bennet's does."

"No doubt. My daughter has a satirical eye, and I must congratulate you on winning her affection. It is my understanding that the first time you met Elizabeth you insulted her. Something about her being rather plain and not wanting to dance with her?"

"I plead guilty," Darcy answered, "but Elizabeth has forgiven me."

Mr. Bennet started to laugh. "A word of advice from an old married man. Although she may have forgiven you, she will never forget, so be prepared to hear about it for the rest of your life."

"Fortunately, we make a joke of it now."

"Yes, at the beginning of your marriage, you may joke about it, but wait until your first argument when it will once again rear its ugly head. Hopefully, that is far into the future. So when are you to call on me, Mr. Darcy?"

"As soon as possible."

"Ah, that quickly then," he said with a hint of sadness. "I know that a father should not favor one daughter over another, but I am a man of many faults. I enjoy Lizzy's company so much that it will be difficult for me not to have her about, but I am comforted in knowing that she will marry a man with a generous heart. You see, I am convinced that if you had learned of Wickham's designs on any other vulnerable young lady, you would not have acted any differently. And so, Mr. Darcy, I am placing Elizabeth in your care, and I look forward to seeing you tomorrow, after church, for tea."

From across the room, Lizzy looked to Mr. Darcy for some indication of what the two men had been discussing, but noting her interest, he gave nothing away by his expression. But Lizzy gave him such a look that he smiled and nodded his head, and she placed her hand over her heart in acknowledgment. It was exactly as she had hoped it would be.

Chapter 55

MR. AND MRS. CHARLES Bingley joined the Bennet family for tea. They had left behind a house near to bursting with relations and wanted something less hectic for their first full day together as husband and wife. With Mr. Darcy, Mr. Bingley, and their father engaged in conversation, Lizzy motioned for Jane to go upstairs, and they both quietly disappeared from the parlor.

"Well?" Lizzy said as soon as she had closed the door.

Jane knew exactly what Lizzy wanted to hear. "Everything is fine, but I cannot begin to tell you how odd it is to have a man lying on top of you," and she started laughing. "It did hurt, but for such a brief time, and the whole thing was over sooner than I thought it would be."

"I am glad to hear it."

"Are you glad to hear that it did not hurt or the length of the experience?"

"My dear sister, what a change one night can make. You are a married woman and may speak of such things."

"But there was a surprise—other than the obvious one. I had in my mind an idea of what would happen, and it was very close to what I had imagined. However, during the night, Charles rolled over, and we began again. I had not expected that."

From Lizzy's expression, nor had she. "Twice in one night?"

"Three times if you count this morning," Jane said. "Apparently, Charles finds it quite enjoyable, and each time, it *was* a little easier. I think it is something I could come to enjoy, that is, when it becomes less awkward."

Although Lizzy nodded her head, indicating that she was happy to hear that it had gone reasonably well, nothing in her expression showed that it had put her mind at ease.

When the ladies returned to the drawing room, they found that Mr. Bennet had invited Mr. Darcy into his *sanctum sanctorum* for a glass of port. Mrs. Bennet found nothing unusual in this because she knew how indebted the family was to Mr. Darcy and assumed that Mr. Bennet wished to thank the gentleman in private. Charles, who was in on the plan, was left behind to entertain all the ladies while the men went about the business of discussing the marriage contract. While in London, Mr. Darcy had had his solicitor draft the document, and after perusing it, Mr. Bennet set it aside.

"You are very generous, Mr. Darcy. But then I had no worries on that account. However, what does concern me is that you and Lizzy come from very different worlds, and there will be struggles because of it. You shake your head, but I can assure you there will be occasions when Lizzy will say the wrong thing or not curtsey properly or not acknowledge someone's rank. But you must be patient with her.

"My second concern is Lizzy's habit of always speaking

the truth. So be prepared for people, who are not used to such honesty, talking about her or cutting her or some other such nonsense. It is only your rank that will protect her."

"And my love. That too will protect her. Because if anyone injures her, they injure me. I am not a vengeful man, Mr. Bennet, but I take care of my loved ones, and any unkindness toward Elizabeth is unacceptable."

Mr. Bennet was pleased with his answer and patted his future son-in-law on the back and marveled at how life held so many surprises. Mr. Darcy of Pemberley was to marry his daughter. Who would have thought it!

It was Kitty who first noticed how long her father and Mr. Darcy had been gone. "I wonder what they can be talking about?"

"They *have* been gone a long time," Mrs. Bennet said. "Mr. Bingley, do you think anything is wrong?"

"No, absolutely not. No reason to think that at all," and he looked at Jane, who looked at Lizzy, and now Mrs. Bennet turned her gaze on Elizabeth.

"Lizzy, do you know what is keeping Mr. Darcy?"

"Yes, Mama. He is asking Papa for permission to marry me."

"What!" She jumped out of her chair, and the quick movement caused her to become dizzy, and she fainted. Jane, who was used to her mother's spells, quickly went for the smelling salts. When Mama had recovered, she asked her daughter, "Lizzy, did I understand you correctly? You are to marry Mr. Darcy?" Mrs. Bennet said in a voice that was more croak than speech.

"I am, Mama. I know that he did not make a very good first impression…"

"Oh, who cares about that?" she said, sitting up. "I never gave it another thought," a statement that everyone knew to be completely untrue. "Oh, Lizzy, how rich and how great you will be! What pin money, what jewels, what carriages you will have! Ten thousand a year!" The exclamations continued for several more minutes until Mrs. Bennet became uneasy at the length of Mr. Darcy's visit with Mr. Bennet. She was taking no chances.

"Elizabeth, go knock on your father's door and tell him we have heard the good news, and they should come out so that all might share in their joy. Go quickly, now."

Lizzy was saved from embarrassment when the two gentlemen emerged from Mr. Bennet's library. Mrs. Bennet looked to her husband, and when he nodded his head and smiled, she immediately went to Mr. Darcy and showered him with praise. Embarrassed, he asked if a bottle of wine might be opened to celebrate the occasion. Mr. and Mrs. Hill were immediately summoned, the Hill sons and Betsy were sent for, and the wine was opened and flowed freely.

Kitty and Mary offered their congratulations, and a chastened Lydia, who had learned of Mr. Wickham's true nature from her father, whispered hers as well.

Not given to displays of emotion, Darcy stood silent. Seeing his discomfort, Lizzy went to him, and when she slipped her hand into his, Darcy gave his bride-to-be a smile that would have melted even the coldest heart, causing her mother to exclaim, "What a match you have made, Lizzy! I think I shall go distracted!"

Jane and Charles wished the couple joy and asked when they would marry.

"We have not as yet decided," Lizzy said, looking at her future life's partner.

"Perhaps we have," Darcy said, correcting her. "With your father's permission, I would like to speak to you alone." Mr. Bennet motioned for the couple to go into the library.

"Close the door, Lizzy," her father warned her. "Little pitchers have ears and big ones as well."

As soon as they were in the room, Darcy swept Lizzy up in his arms and kissed her in such a way that Lizzy decided that she would agree to any date he suggested. Sitting down on the sofa, and with her hands firmly clasped in his, he began. "I have a plan, and I would ask that you not say anything until I have said all." After giving him a quizzical look, she agreed.

"I am suggesting that we marry immediately."

"What do you mean by immediately?"

"You have already interrupted me, and I have uttered only one sentence." After clearing his throat, he continued. "As I was saying, I think we should marry immediately, and after a reception at Longbourn for just a few friends and family, we shall leave for Pemberley with Georgiana."

"Just a few friends? Not a wedding breakfast?

"You do not follow directions very well, do you? Please allow me to continue. Because of the rain this past autumn, Georgie and I were unable to host the harvest dance for our neighbors and tenants. I promised all that I would have the dance in the spring. So what I am proposing is that we marry now, go to Pemberley, and in the spring have the wedding breakfast at my estate. Your family will stay with us, and our friends will stay at the inn at Lambton, at my expense. We shall have marquees and tables out on the lawn, filled to overflowing with food and drink. I will hire musicians from London, and we shall all dance until dawn." Lizzy sat quietly mulling over the details of his plan. "You may speak now. It is your turn."

"I still do not know what you mean by immediately."

"This week."

Lizzy started laughing. "This week. But I am not prepared. I have no dress."

"Did you not tell me yesterday that you had trimmed your favorite dress but chose not to wear it to Jane's wedding because it was too fancy? And I know of a recently married lady who can lend you her veil."

"But we must announce our banns. The only way we could marry now is if you were to buy a special license." Darcy reached into his inside pocket and pulled out a special license. "As I have said before, you are used to having your way in all things."

"Will I get my way this time?"

"What of my wedding ring?"

Darcy took a jewel box out of his pocket, and in it were two rings. "The emerald ring belonged to my mother, which my father chose for her because she had green eyes." Lizzy had to hold back her tears as she looked at a beautiful, delicate, perfectly proportioned emerald set in a gold filigree setting that had once adorned the hand of Lady Anne Darcy. Beside it was a wedding band of woven gold to match the emerald setting that Darcy had commissioned weeks earlier. As he did on those occasions when he was anxious, concerned, or unsure of himself, he placed his hand upon his chin and went back and forth across it with his index finger as he waited for her answer.

"I agree to your plan," Lizzy finally said. "Do you have anything else in your coat pockets?"

"As a matter of fact, I do," and he took out a thin piece of paper and placed it in her hands. "That is another love letter. I suggest you read it in private and then burn it. I would not have given it to you if you were not to be my wife in such a short time."

Lizzy blushed. If it was anything like the last one, it very might well self-ignite.

"I love you, Mr. Darcy."

"And I love you, Elizabeth. But considering that we are to be married this week, don't you think 'Mr. Darcy' is a little formal?"

"Then what shall I call you, Mr. Darcy?"

"Those who love me call me Will."

"I love you, Will," and she kissed him and then placed her head on his chest, and they remained in each other's embrace until propriety moved them to join the others.

Chapter 56

MRS. BENNET COULD HARDLY believe her good fortune in having two daughters so well married. It was true that Jane had made a fine match. But Lizzy! Oh, my! She was to be married to a man who had ten thousand a year and very likely more. What a wedding they would have. She would go with Lizzy to London to have her gown made by a *modiste*, who would address them in French. She was sure Mr. Darcy would order a new carriage, most likely white, whose interior would be lined with the finest pearl white satin. Mrs. Bennet was sure that dukes and earls would attend, and because of that, it would be best if the wedding breakfast was held at Netherfield. She was planning the menu when the lovers returned to the parlor.

Unwilling to let Mr. Darcy out of her sight, Mrs. Bennet insisted that he stay for supper, and Jane and Charles were welcome to stay as well. During the meal, it was her intention to learn every last detail about the upcoming wedding, and thus the inquisition began. Would they marry in the spring or summer? Summer, she suggested, since there was so much to do, and because there would be so many guests, it would be necessary to use the gardens at Netherfield, and for that, they needed fine weather. Mr. Bennet finally interrupted his wife and asked that she allow Lizzy and Mr. Darcy to speak before making any additional decisions on their behalf.

"Mama, Mr. Darcy and I have decided to marry in the village church later in the week," Lizzy responded, ignoring her mother's open mouth and stare. "Of course, we will need to consult the vicar, but we were thinking possibly Friday. The ceremony will be followed by a reception here, after which time, Mr. Darcy and I shall leave for Pemberley."

"Oh, Lizzy!" a disappointed Mrs. Bennet exclaimed. "Even Jane had more than what you are proposing."

Bingley, who was already immune to insults from his mother-in-law, laughed to himself at Mrs. Bennet's suggestion that a Darcy wedding must be bigger and better than a Bingley wedding. Money was good; money and a pedigree were even better.

Lizzy looked to Mr. Darcy, who then explained his plan, and after Mrs. Bennet realized that she would be a guest at Pemberley and that her friends and neighbors would be invited to the manor house of which her daughter was now mistress, she set aside all objections and gave her approval. Before going into supper, Jane pulled her sister aside and suggested that she wear her wedding dress.

"Lizzy, the gown is so beautiful. With a few alterations by Mrs. Lyle, the gown will look as if it was made for you. I would be honored if you would wear it."

Lizzy did not see any reason why she should not. The two sisters had been wearing each other's frocks since they were children, and Lizzy readily agreed.

Now that everyone knew that Lizzy and the gentleman from Derbyshire were engaged, as anticipated, Mr. Darcy became the focus of their attention. Although he escaped further inquiries with his departure, Lizzy was peppered with questions from her mother and sisters until she begged to be excused so that she might retire. She had a letter to read.

> *Dearest Elizabeth,*
>
> *You told me that I should have been ashamed of myself for writing you such a torrid love letter. Well, shame on you for reading another one. Although I think that bodes well for me. I will see you in my dreams and for tea tomorrow. I love you.*
>
> *Will*

Lizzy felt as if her face was on fire as she was blushing from head to toe. After complaining of the contents of his first letter, she had rushed upstairs to read the second, and he had anticipated it. Well, he would never know she had read it as she would never own to it. Although she had committed the first letter to memory, she retrieved it from the chest under the bed, and after reading it twice more, she placed it under her pillow, hoping that she would dream of Mr. Darcy.

As soon as Lizzy saw Mr. Bingley's carriage coming down the drive, she went out to meet Jane because she would have the bridal dress with her. After placing it in Betsy's capable hands, the two sisters followed their maid upstairs to their bedroom.

"Where are Mr. Darcy and Mr. Bingley?" Lizzy asked.

"With every member of the family and Mr. Darcy at Netherfield, George Bingley called a business meeting this morning. I swear that man is all work and no play. But after the meeting, everyone will go home, and to that I say, 'Amen!'" Jane let out a puff of air to show her relief at their departure.

"Did something happen?" Lizzy asked.

"I found an acorn in my coffee cup this morning, and when I looked at Athena, she had a look of victory written all over her face. But enough about the Bingleys and Crenshaws. You are to marry on Friday. What happened to your courtship? How did all of this come about?"

"It was because of what happened in London that I shall have no courtship. Mr. Darcy went there for the purpose of talking to his solicitor about the marriage contract, but while dining at his club, he said that he felt as if everyone was staring at him. Finally, his good friend, Andrew Baring, the banker's son, came over and said, 'Sorry, Darcy. Better luck next time,' explaining that he had heard from Sir John that morning that Miss Montford was to marry Jasper Wiggins."

"My goodness! That was fast!"

"Indeed! While Mr. Darcy was doing everything he could to ensure that Miss Montford might be spared any embarrassment, her father was making arrangements for her to become engaged to Mr. Wiggins. It seems that Mr. Wiggins Sr. is very rich and very ill, and when he dies, Jasper will get it all. With so much money at stake, Sir John thought he needed to move quickly. Once Mr. Darcy heard about the engagement, he thought, if she is not waiting, then I am not waiting. After purchasing a special license, he rushed back here to ask me to agree to move up the wedding date and to speak to Papa."

"Well, this cannot come as a total surprise to you. You have often said that Mr. Darcy is a man who likes to have his way."

"Yes, he does. But this time, I am in complete agreement," and Lizzy smiled at the memory of Mr. Darcy's proposal. "You would think that with the wedding on Friday that I would be in a tizzy—running around like a chicken with its head cut off. But there is little for me to do. You have provided the dress. Mama is to arrange for the food. News of the wedding is being relayed in town and on the farms by John and Adam. I have written to Aunt and Uncle Gardiner and Charlotte, although I doubt she will be able to come on such short notice. All that is left for me to do is to pack up everything I will be taking to Pemberley. So here I sit, waiting for Mrs. Lyle," she said, folding her hands and twiddling her thumbs.

"So tell me," Lizzy said, changing the subject, "what have you been doing at Netherfield Park, other than trying to get out of the way of an abundance of Bingleys?"

"If you are asking about last night, it was the wedding night *redux*," and Lizzy raised her eyebrows. Jane had been married two days, and she and Charles had made love six times. "Apparently, this activity has now become Charles's favorite thing," Jane said, laughing. "However, tonight, I am going to ask if I may sleep through the night. He falls back to sleep right away, while I lie there awake. But he will agree to anything I ask."

"I know this is a very personal question, but does Charles undress you?"

"Good grief, Lizzy! Certainly not. I am in bed and under the covers when he comes in. What made you ask such a question?"

"Because I do not know what to expect. I have been thinking about the man I was to marry since I was thirteen, but I never went past the wedding."

"Well, you certainly have a vivid imagination. Such a thing would never have occurred to me."

But it *would* have occurred to you, Lizzy thought, if you had read Mr. Darcy's letter.

"For me, the best part is afterward when I lie in Charles's arms, and we speak of our future together. And, Lizzy, you will have the same thing. Mr. Darcy is so in love with you that he will want to make you happy in all things."

She just wished she knew what "all things" included.

Chapter 57

ON THE EVE OF their wedding, Mr. Darcy sent his carriage to Longbourn for Lizzy with a note saying that all of the Bingleys had departed, including Mrs. Crenshaw, and it was safe to come to Netherfield. Lizzy thought it an excellent idea as her mother was driving her to distraction. All during her fitting, Mama had been buzzing around Mrs. Lyle making suggestions regarding the lace trim and rosettes that were being added to the hem and sleeves of the gown. After that, she went downstairs to check on Mrs. Hill's progress with the preparations for the next day's reception. From there she visited her three young-est daughters to make sure they had chosen their best frocks. Although Mr. Bennet had informed her several times that he was not in need of such information, Mrs. Bennet stopped by to give her husband an update on all that was going on.

"Mrs. Bennet, I am only interested in what is required of me. I am to give Lizzy away, and then I am to get out of the way."

Georgiana greeted Lizzy as soon as she stepped into the foyer. Taking Lizzy by the hand, she led her to the drawing room and to a lady unknown to her. The visitor was sitting in the chair closest to the fire, her legs covered by a quilt, and with an exquisite black shawl decorated with red roses draping her shoulders. She had a complexion so fair that it was almost translucent, and her finely carved features and sky-blue eyes were framed by coal-black hair. Although she looked as frail as a China doll and kept a handkerchief in her lap to hide her coughs, she gave the impression of being someone who was made of sterner stuff.

"Elizabeth, I want you to meet my dear cousin, Miss Anne de Bourgh."

"Miss Elizabeth, I am so pleased to meet you in person. I have heard so much about you from Colonel Fitzwilliam and Lord Fitzwilliam and from letters sent to me by Georgiana. Even Will, who is a terrible correspondent, wrote extensively of your attributes, and I can see that his praise of your beauty was not exaggerated."

Lizzy was deeply touched. Miss de Bourgh loved her cousin so much that she had left her warm hearth at Rosings Park to travel in very cold weather to see him married.

"Elizabeth, you see we have another guest," Darcy said as he entered the room. "Once I realized that there was a possibility that we might marry sooner than expected, I wrote to Colonel Fitzwilliam, asking that he bring Anne to London. In this way, the people dearest to me will be witnesses to the happiest day of my life."

Lizzy did not know if it was a combination of the strain of waiting for each other for all those months or the fact that this man of few words had said such a beautiful thing, but tears came to her eyes.

"Miss Elizabeth, it is not too late to change your mind," the colonel said. "It seems every time you and Darcy are together, he reduces you to tears."

"It is a small price to pay for such company," Lizzy said, dabbing her eyes with Mr. Darcy's handkerchief.

"Richard, have you thought that it might be you who distresses Miss Elizabeth?" Darcy asked, and everyone laughed.

Anne motioned for Lizzy to come and sit beside her on the sofa. "Lord Fitzwilliam sends his love and regrets, but he has decided to stay at Rosings Park to amuse my mother, and his presence makes my absence possible. My mother does not yet know of your marriage, and when she does, she will shout and carry on and threaten. But someone in every generation needs to shake things up, and this time, it will be Will. In my mother's generation, it was a Fitzwilliam marrying a de Bourgh. Mama will tell you that the first Lord de Bourgh made his money in the importation of fine wines and spirits. Not so delicately put, he was a smuggler. But she chooses to forget that part of our history."

"Miss Elizabeth, when you go to Rosings Park," Richard said, "and eventually you *will* go to Rosings Park because my aunt requires an audience for her orations and she will miss Darcy, Anne will sit quietly next to Mrs. Jenkinson, her companion, and say nothing. But appearances can be deceiving. On more than one occasion Anne has gotten the better of her mother."

"No more about my mother," Anne said, interrupting. "I have come to Hertfordshire to visit with old friends and to make new ones. And before I forget, Miss Elizabeth, I visited with Mrs. Collins before leaving for London, and she sends her congratulations. She was not at all surprised to learn of your engagement. It seems my cousin was unable to hide his feelings for you. However, Mr. Collins does not know of the happy event, and Mrs. Collins said that it is best that she tell him at a time of her choosing."

It was a most engaging evening because it was apparent that the Fitzwilliam clan enjoyed each other's company immensely. They told funny stories about their childhood, including running through Pemberley's maze or staging plays at Rosings or fishing in Briarwood's streams. It was nearly 9:00 when Lizzy reluctantly announced that she needed to go home.

Darcy rode with Lizzy to Longbourn and told her that they would break their journey at Wick Manor near Northampton. "It is a handsome manor house owned by the Haydon family, but since they are all in town for Christmas, Rupert Haydon said that I should make myself at home, but we will stay only the one night." As the carriage turned into the drive, he asked her if she had read his second letter.

"No. I told you that I would not."

After looking at her with a suspicious eye, he asked again, "Elizabeth, did you read my second letter?"

"No," she said, laughing. "You may ask as many times as you wish; my answer will remain the same."

"Well, then it is pointless to ask again. But it was not a fruitless exercise because now I know that if you ever tell me an untruth, I shall know it. You are terrible at deception." He took her hand and kissed it, but made no attempt to do more. "Tonight, I am on my best behavior, but it is the last night that I shall be."

After visiting with her mother to learn the present state of affairs regarding the reception, Lizzy hurried to her room and got the chest from under her bed, and after climbing back under the covers, she read the now familiar words:

My dearest Elizabeth,

Even the thankfully few days that remain before our wedding are too many. I do not sleep for thinking of you, imagining you in my arms and in our bed. If you knew my deepest wishes, indeed, if my actions at Netherfield dismayed you, my thoughts would alarm you. But, Elizabeth, how can I stop? Until I met you, I prided myself in having control over the baser instincts that govern most men. Now I find that I cannot control where my imagination roams, and it roams over the delights of your body. The night we wed I will sweep you off your feet and carry you to our bedroom. You will stand before me, and I will undress you. And as my lips find yours, our passion will rise together. A month ago, I wanted you. A week ago, I yearned. Now my only thought is to know you, all of you. Can I make it any clearer? I want you immediately, entirely, completely, irrevocably, so that you will be mine forever.

All my love, Will

After folding the letter and putting it back in the chest, she recalled what Jane had said. "Mr. Darcy will want you to be happy in all things," and now she had pretty a good idea of what "all things" might include.

Chapter 58

MRS. LYLE HAD PERFORMED miracles in altering Jane's wedding dress for Elizabeth. She had worked tirelessly, adding rosettes to the new lace hem, tucking lace into the bodice, shortening the sleeves, and trimming them with tiny rosettes. When Lizzy saw the finished product, it looked like a completely new dress, and she loved it.

What Mrs. Lyle had done for the dress, Mrs. Hill was doing for Lizzy's hair. "There won't be a curl out of place today, Miss Lizzy, because I put a pearl pin in each one of your curls. But I left it long in the back," and she held up a mirror so that Lizzy might see the results.

"It is perfect, Mrs. Hill. Thank you so much."

When the bride came downstairs, there were oohs and aahs from all the ladies of the house, but from Mr. Bennet, there was silence. He was doing everything he could to keep from crying. He had not shed a tear when Jane had married Bingley because she would be nearby at Netherfield Park, but Lizzy, when she was not in town, would be in faraway Derbyshire. There would be no dropping by to visit the Darcys.

Because the day was so cold, no one was standing outside the church in the hopes of catching a peek at the bride. All were huddled inside trying to keep warm while keeping an eye on the church door.

Lizzy and her father stepped into the vestibule, quickly closing the door behind them. After removing her pelisse, Lizzy took her father's arm and whispered, "I love you. Nothing has changed." Oh, but it had, Mr. Bennet knew.

With the exception of Kitty and Lydia, who had not stopped staring at Colonel Fitzwilliam, who was dressed in his regimentals, all eyes were on the bride, and when Elizabeth walked down the aisle, she could hear whispers about how lovely she looked. But it was the look on Mr. Darcy's face that she wanted to hold forever in her memory. He had gazed at her with such love that she felt as if her heart was growing, and when the time came for him to place the wedding band on her finger, he experienced the same feeling.

After the vicar had pronounced Mr. and Mrs. Darcy to be husband and wife, the newlyweds walked down the aisle, and after greeting everyone in the vestibule, they encouraged the shivering group to go to Netherfield immediately, especially Anne de Bourgh, who was dressed from head to toe in a fur coat. It could not possibly have been good for her to be out in such weather.

At Netherfield, everyone was waiting for the bride and groom to come into the drawing room, and when they entered holding hands, they were greeted with a rousing tune by the fiddlers, and Colonel Fitzwilliam led the guests in a round of huzzahs. The same musicians who had played at Jane's wedding breakfast had been brought back for Lizzy's celebration because the dancing would go on well into the evening.

The happy couple circulated around the room receiving the congratulations of all, and everything the couple said was met with nods of approval by their guests.

After many toasts, the fiddle player plucked on his strings, a signal that the dancing was to begin. Mr. and Mrs. Darcy led the first dance, a lively jig, but after two more sets, Darcy indicated to Elizabeth and Georgiana that they would need to leave within the hour if they were to arrive at Wick Manor before dark. Both ladies went upstairs to change into their traveling clothes. When Lizzy said good-bye to her sisters and mother, there were tears in her eyes, but when she said good-bye to her father, the tears flowed.

"Be happy, my dear. That is all I ever wanted for all of you," Mr. Bennet said, patting her hand.

Mr. and Mrs. Darcy got into the carriage, followed by Georgiana, and Mrs. Brotherton, who was carrying Pepper. All burrowed under the fur blankets, and because she was now Mrs. Darcy, Lizzy scooted over to be closer to her husband, but he moved closer still.

Because the driver needed to go slowly in case there were any patches of ice, the journey took much longer than expected. When the party finally turned into the courtyard at Wick Manor, they were met by four men holding lanterns. Once in the house, Mrs. Cower, who had served the family for decades, and Mr. Bendlow, their butler, who had been with the Haydons since he was a boy, were there to greet them.

"Mr. and Mrs. Darcy, on behalf of the Haydon family, may I congratulate you on your marriage and welcome you to Wick Manor. We are delighted to have you visit with us on your wedding day," Mrs. Cower said. And she then turned her attention to Georgiana. "Is it possible that this young lady is Miss Darcy? I have not seen you in at least two years and how you have grown. Have you come out? Belle of the ball, I am sure.

"Because of the cold, we have lit fires only in your bedrooms as we have found it difficult to keep the public rooms warm. I have arranged for supper to be served upstairs. I have kept it simple, not knowing when you would be here."

"Mrs. Cower, I believe I can speak for my wife and sister when I say we are more tired than hungry," Mr. Darcy answered, and they were led to their rooms. As soon as they had eaten, Georgiana and Mrs. Brotherton retired. Mrs. Cower came in immediately after and asked Elizabeth if she should have the maid come in.

"That will not be necessary, Mrs. Cower," Mr. Darcy answered. "However, we shall have an early start tomorrow, so perhaps some bread and cheese for breakfast."

"I will see to it. Good night to you both. If you need additional blankets, they can be found in that chest there. I can't remember when it has been this cold."

With the housekeeper gone, Mr. and Mrs. Fitzwilliam Darcy were alone. When Mr. Darcy had told Mrs. Cower that she did not require the assistance of the maid, Lizzy had swallowed hard. Her husband really *was* going to undress her, and she was so embarrassed by the thought that she did not know where to look.

"It is freezing in here, so let us get ready for bed," Will said. "Shall we begin by taking down your hair, Mrs. Darcy?" And he led Lizzy to the dressing table. "I have never done this before, but I daresay I can remove pins as well as anyone else." After pulling out more than a dozen pins, he asked, "How many do you have in there? Just when I think I am done, there is another group hidden in your curls."

"Let me do it. There are only a few left," and after Lizzy had found the last one, she picked up the brush and started to brush her hair.

"May I do that?" he asked, taking the brush from her hand. "You *do* know that whenever you wore your hair down, you were tormenting me."

"I had no idea of doing any such thing."

"I doubt that."

"It is true that I was aware of your preference, but I just wanted you to be as unhappy as I was at our dismal prospects, but certainly not tormented."

"Ah, I see the difference."

"Besides, with all my curls, I have difficulty keeping them from popping out, and sometimes, especially in rainy weather, it is easier to wear my hair down, tied with a ribbon."

"Then let us hope for rain."

Darcy took Lizzy by the hand and led her to the bed. He turned her around and undid the buttons of her dress, and she felt her corset loosen as he undid the stays. But then he stopped, and Lizzy turned to look at him.

"I think you will be able to manage the rest on your own."

"But in your letter, you wrote…"

"I know what I wrote. But one thing at a time. Now, my clothes are in the next room, which has no heat at all. So if you would get ready for bed as quickly as possible, I would appreciate it."

With the room so chilly, there would be no dawdling, no time to think about what was about to happen, and she quickly went about her toilette. After one final look in the mirror, she knocked on the door to let Mr. Darcy know that she was ready. Will entered the room to find her perched on the edge of the bed.

"I did not know which side of the bed you wanted to sleep on," she explained.

"I always sleep in the middle," and then he smiled, pulled back the cover, and gestured for her to get in. As soon as they had settled in, Will pulled her to him, and she rested her head on his shoulder and placed her hand over his heart.

"It beats for you, Elizabeth."

"And mine for you."

"Was everything to your satisfaction today?" Darcy asked.

"I can't say. The day is not over yet," and Darcy burst out laughing, and Lizzy placed her fingers upon his lips. "Your sister will hear us. And, yes, it was a perfectly lovely day. You looked very handsome."

"And you were positively radiant," Darcy said as he pulled his wife to him.

"Just think, if you had not insulted me, there would have been no need for an apology. You might just as well have gone back to London, and nothing would have come of it."

"And so let me say it again, Mrs. Darcy, you are more than tolerable and definitely handsome enough to tempt me," and he kissed her deeply and ran his hands along her body. After lifting her gown and helping her out of it, she felt his warm hands caressing every part of her, and she yielded to his every movement. He shifted his weight so that his leg was between hers, and he moved against her, listening to her soft moans as she lay beneath him. After hesitating for a brief moment to tell her that he loved her, he entered her, and she wrapped her legs around his, pulling him deeper into her. She continued to move with his rhythm, and when she felt his final thrust, she ran her hands up and down his back until his breathing grew quiet.

"Are you all right, Elizabeth? I have heard that sometimes..."

"You did not hurt me," she said, kissing him. "What you did was to make us one, inseparable and complete," and she lay in his arms until he fell off to sleep.

While Will slept soundly beside her, Lizzy could not sleep at all. His lips and hands had given her more pleasure than she could have ever imagined. Eventually, with this sweet memory, she too fell off to sleep, but sometime during the night, she rolled over and put her arm around his waist. Although barely awake, Will began again, and when first light came, Will could think of no better way to start their day than by making love, and in this, Elizabeth was in complete agreement.

Chapter 59

As SOON AS THE carriage entered the long drive to Pemberley, Lizzy pressed her nose against the window, and with a hard frost covering the lawn and with the sun sitting low on the horizon, everything had a silver glow to it.

"This is now your home, Elizabeth," Georgiana said. "Welcome to Pemberley."

When Mr. Jackson opened the double doors, Lizzy saw that the foyer and double wrought-iron staircase were all hung with Christmas greens and red ribbons. Assembled in the entrance hall, in two lines, was the entire staff of Pemberley in their spotless uniforms, shined shoes, and freshly pressed caps. Mrs. Darcy smiled at every servant and tried to commit their names to memory, but there were so many, and there would be more in the summer. At the end of the line were Mrs. Bradshaw, Mrs. Reynolds, and Lizzy's lady's maid, Ellie.

After quickly squeezing Ellie's hand, she addressed the housekeeper. "Mrs. Reynolds, how good it is to see you again."

"And you, ma'am. Welcome to your new home. May I

remind you of the time when I took you on the tour of the house? I said that I did not know who was good enough to be the wife of my master, but now I know."

Mr. Jackson then introduced Mrs. Bradshaw, Pemberley's iron-willed cook. By her very posture, Lizzy could see that she was a woman who was used to being obeyed, and so Lizzy would follow Will's suggestion and agree to everything she said.

Elizabeth thanked the staff for their warm welcome and told them she was grateful for their service. In his role as lord of the manor, Mr. Darcy stated that Pemberley was very much like a family and that all must work together so that everything ran smoothly. The thought occurred to her that some members of the family worked a lot harder than others.

After Georgiana dismissed the servants, Lizzy realized that Christmas was in two days, and she had done nothing for them.

"I have seen to it," Georgiana reassured her, "my last duty as mistress of Pemberley, and I gladly turn the keys over to you."

Lizzy had butterflies in her stomach just thinking about all these people looking to her for direction. She only hoped that her husband was right when he said that the servants ran Pemberley.

Will directed Lizzy to the staircase leading to the first floor and told his wife that unless there were guests in the house, the public rooms were used infrequently in the winter. "We have a sitting room upstairs, and that is where we spend most of our time, especially on a day like today."

Georgiana led Lizzy to her apartment. "This was our mother's room. I think it will give you an idea of what she was like, and of course, she had the best view of the gardens."

The canopy over the bed, the draperies, bed covers, and upholstery were decorated with fabric with soft green colors with tiny white flowers and gave the room a warm feeling, and the picture frame paneling, embellished with Classical Greek designs in each panel, created an aura of elegance. Will, who was standing by the door, looked to her for her approval, and she nodded enthusiastically.

"In the morning, after breakfast, we shall bring in the Yule log because it will be Christmas Eve," Georgiana said, "and I shall acquaint you with our traditional holiday supper with our servants. It is held below stairs in the servants' quarters, and it is great fun. But you have had a long journey, and so I shall say good night and sleep well."

When Georgiana left, Lizzy put her arms around Will's neck, and standing on her toes, she kissed him and thanked him for loving her and for bringing her to Pemberley. He picked her up and carried her to the bed and lay beside her.

"Will, you have your boots on."

"They are not on the bed."

"But still…"

"Very well. How quickly you have taken to being a wife, but if you insist that I remove my boots, I am going to remove everything else and get ready for bed. Pemberley is warmer than Wick Manor, but it is chilly enough."

"Shall I send for Ellie?" Lizzy asked.

"I will be happy to perform the same duties that I did last night."

"Then I shall not ask her to come in. It will be easier tonight. Fewer pins."

"Don't move. I will be right back," and Darcy went to his room, realizing that when provided with the proper motivation, preparing for bed could go very quickly, and he hurried Mercer along.

Darcy had been pleased with their first night together. Although there was some evidence of nervousness, Elizabeth seemed to respond to his every kiss and caress, and he wondered if she would be completely at ease tonight now that she had known him. But he did not have to wonder long as he watched her remove her nightgown and climb into bed. As they lay together, Elizabeth believed herself to be the happiest creature in the world. Perhaps other people had said so before, but no one with such justice.

THE DARCYS HOSTED THE promised harvest dance to coincide with the May Day celebrations, and the day was as perfect as they had hoped. Every bedroom at Pemberley was filled with visiting relatives, and every room at the inn at Lambton was occupied by friends of the families.

Children danced around the Maypole, and there were jugglers and acrobats entertaining the guests. The white marquees, with their colored streamers, held every sort of game, and the largest of them was filled with tables practically bowing under the weight of so much food. Roaming minstrels played their tunes, and a magician retrieved coins from Mrs. Draper's hat and Mrs. Long's ear. When he asked Mrs. Bennet to pull a handkerchief out of his pocket, the cloth went on for yards, and she broke out into a fit of laughter and her husband joined her in her merriment. Lizzy waved to Charles and Jane, who was no longer able to conceal her pregnancy, as well as Kitty and Lydia, who had spent a good part of their day following Colonel Fitzwilliam around, but there were other handsome men to catch their eye as well.

Over a period of a month, Anne de Bourgh had been ferried from one manor house to another, so that she could be at Pemberley for the fete. As predicted, upon hearing of the marriage, Lady Catherine had been all storm and thunder for a week, threatening to sever all ties with her nephew, but as Antony pointed out, she did not have all that many visitors coming to Rosings Park to begin with. Did she really want to cut ties to the few who still came to Kent? As a peace offering, her nephew suggested that she send Elizabeth something as a token of her regard, and a surprised Elizabeth opened a gift box that contained a pearl necklace given to Lady Catherine by her sister, Lady Anne Darcy.

Lady Margaret, dowager Countess Fitzwilliam, arrived at Pemberley in a carriage with her son, Lord Fitzwilliam, and Mrs. Konig. Her Ladyship had traveled to Pemberley with her son's mistress? Lizzy looked to Will for an explanation. "Later," he whispered.

The countess, with all her haughtiness, reminded Lizzy of Lady Catherine, but that was where the similarities stopped. She liked to talk, but she also listened. She was excessively fond of her granddaughters and tolerant of Antony. She walked the grounds of Pemberley like a queen on the arms of her sons, and it was she who decided who would dine with her. After being notified that he was one of the chosen few, Antony demurred. "My dearest Mama, I am truly blest as I am able to see you so often in town, and it would be selfish of me not to share you with others."

"Sit down, Antony, and say as little as possible."

"I have no wish to annoy you, Mama, but you know better than anyone that it is beyond my capabilities to remain silent."

"Try."

This was obviously a scene that had played out many times before as neither could keep a straight face.

Earlier in the day, Antony had shared with Elizabeth that he had successfully rid himself of Briarwood. With the money from the sale of the Fitzwilliam manor house, he had been able to greatly reduce his debts, and in the House of Lords, he was gaining a reputation as someone to be reckoned with regarding entitlements for the Prince Regent.

"Mrs. Darcy, I understand I give you congratulation," Mrs. Konig said. If the lady from Vienna had been gorgeous in her governess attire, she was absolutely stunning in one of the new dresses that had been made for her in London, courtesy of the countess. "I vish every joy. Childrens makes our lives full."

"The Darcys are to have an addition to their family, and I know nothing of it?" Antony asked, pretending to be hurt. "Why wasn't I told about this?"

"Why weren't you told?" his mother asked. "Other than the fact that you cannot keep a secret? Oh, don't pout, Antony. I have just learned of it myself from Georgiana."

After everyone had eaten their full, the servants lit the torches, the musicians tuned their instruments, the dancers gathered, and Mr. and Mrs. Darcy led the first dance. Lizzy would have danced well into the night, but all the preparations required for such an event had tired her out and Will wanted her to rest. Now that she was assured that the combined efforts of those above stairs and those below had resulted in a good time for all, she wanted to get off her feet. Will took her by the hand and led her up the stairs to the terrace, so that she might watch the dancing while sitting down on a bench.

Georgiana followed them up the stairs to let them know

that Mary and she were perfectly capable of seeing to the guests. There was genuine excitement in her voice because she loved a country dance, and tomorrow, she would turn her attention to the start of her second season, which would begin in three weeks' time. She was eager to be in town to see the latest fashions, and while Lizzy and Georgie shopped, Darcy would see to his business affairs. George Bingley was greatly increasing his wealth, for which he was grateful, but the man had more meetings than Parliament.

"Will, I was very surprised to see Lady Margaret and Mrs. Konig in the same carriage. I am happy for Mrs. Konig, but I confess that I do not understand."

"That was much more than a carriage ride. It is the dowager countess's way of acknowledging Mrs. Konig and the relationship she has with her son. Simply put, Mrs. Konig may now move in society with Antony, and it is no longer necessary for her to pretend to be the girls' governess. The countess has a lot of influence among the ladies of the *ton*, and all will understand what has been done. I know you would wish that they could be married, but under the circumstances, this is the best one can hope for. You only have to look at Antony to know that he is happy with the arrangement."

"Yes, I must accept what cannot be changed, and on such a night, I shall think only happy thoughts."

"Well, Elizabeth, now that you have had your wedding breakfast, are you happy?"

"As you well know, I was happy before this day, but our wedding breakfast is a little different from others, is it not? I do not imagine that many brides are with child on such a day."

"Oh, I don't know. Just think about Ellie Timlin, a name I

shall never forget. I was in the study at Netherfield Park, greatly enjoying myself while kissing you, when you mentioned her name, and that was the end of that."

"Yes, I remember, and we were very fortunate that we were not discovered," she said, rising. "Please stay as long as you like, but I am for bed," and she kissed him good night.

"Shall I send for Ellie?"

"No. I promised the servants that once the torches were lit that they could have the rest of the evening to themselves. They have all been working since before dawn."

"Then may *I* assist you? I still know how to pull pins out of your hair."

"You used to take my pins out twice a day."

"Yes, but I am a considerate husband, and as noted, you are with child."

Lizzy knew that Will would come to bed with her and would offer to rub her back or legs or whatever was asked for, and then the touches would become gentler and go in other directions, and the night would end exactly as he had hoped.

As they climbed the stairs, Will promised never to be parted from her even when she was old, gray, and toothless.

"Thank you for that, kind sir," she said. "But, truly, it is the days between the beginning and the end of our shared lives that will determine our legacy, but we have had made a good beginning."

"It is much more than a good beginning. I believe we have something very special—like Romeo and Juliet, Guinevere and Lancelot, Troilus and Cressida."

"None of those turned out very well," she said, laughing.

"But our love is different, and some talented author…"

"Authoress."

"Some talented authoress will write a novel about the world's greatest love story, that of Fitzwilliam Darcy of Pemberley and Elizabeth Bennet of Longbourn."

"I like that idea, Mr. Darcy, a love story for the ages."

Taking her husband by the hand, she brought him into her bedchamber and, after kissing him, whispered to him that she was in need of his assistance.

"For pin removal?" he asked hopefully.

"Yes, Mr. Darcy, for pin removal."

Mary Lydon Simonsen, the author of *Searching for Pemberley*, *The Perfect Bride for Mr. Darcy*, *Anne Elliot, A New Beginning*, and *The Second Date, Love Italian-American Style*, has combined her love of history and the novels of Jane Austen in her third story inspired by *Pride and Prejudice*. The author lives in Arizona.

The PERFECT BRIDE *for* MR. DARCY

by MARY LYDON SIMONSEN

If the two of them weren't so stubborn…

It's obvious to Georgiana Darcy that the lovely Elizabeth Bennet is her brother's perfect match, but Darcy's pigheadedness and Elizabeth's wounded pride are going to keep them both from the loves of their lives.

Georgiana can't let that happen, so she readily agrees to help her accommodating cousin, Anne de Bourgh, do everything within their power to assure her beloved brother's happiness.

But the path of matchmaking never runs smoothly…

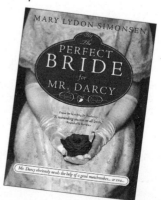

978-1-4022-4025-6 ◆ $14.99 U.S./£9.99 UK